W9-CKP-807

The Life Manager and Other Stories

OTHER BOOKS BY MIRELA ROZNOVEANU
(Published in Bucharest, Romania—Titles in Translation)

CRITICISM:
Modern Readings. Essays, 1978

D. R. Popescu. A Critical Monograph, 1983

The Civilization of the Novel: from Ramayana to Don Quixote,
Vol. I—1983, Vol. II—1991

FICTION:
Always in Autumn, 1988

Life on the Run, 1997

Platonia, 1999

Time of the Chosen, 1999

POETRY:
Apprehending the World, 1998

BOOKS PUBLISHED IN THE U.S.:

ESSAY: *Toward a Cyberlegal Culture*, 2001, 2002

POETRY: *Born Again—In Exile*, 2004

FOR MORE DATA ABOUT THE AUTHOR SEE ONLINE

Dicționarul Scriitorilor Români (*The Dictionary of Romanian Writers*)

http://biblioteca.euroweb.ro/dictionar/

and

http://pages.nyu.edu/~mr24/

THE LIFE MANAGER AND OTHER STORIES

Mirela Roznoveanu

Eastern Shore Editions

iUniverse, Inc.
New York Lincoln Shanghai

The Life Manager and Other Stories

All Rights Reserved © 2004 by Mirela Roznoveanu

No part of this book may be reproduced or transmitted in any form or by any means, graphic, electronic, or mechanical, including photocopying, recording, taping, or by any information storage retrieval system, without the written permission of the publisher.

iUniverse, Inc.

For information address:
iUniverse, Inc.
2021 Pine Lake Road, Suite 100
Lincoln, NE 68512
www.iuniverse.com

ISBN: 0-595-31861-4

Printed in the United States of America

Contents

Acknowledgments

Grateful thanks are due to the following: essayist and translator **Stefan Stoenescu** for having strongly urged me to adopt English as a vehicle for my literary writings, poet **Margareta Horiba** for her sensitive reading and sound editorial advice regarding parts of the manuscript, and last but not least poet **Terence Hegarty** for reading parts of this manuscript in its early stages and for the final pre-publication review of the whole text.

Mirela Roznoveanu

His Berthas

It was a very annoying winter. Snow storms, icy cold, a sad sky, and a lot of flu around. At the beginning of March I was so sick and tired and depressed that one afternoon I couldn't go straight home. I got off the Number Six train on Third Avenue to do some shopping around Bloomingdale's. There was a deli nearby, on the corner of 59th Street, where the food was eatable. Good for a frugal dinner. Lately I've been off my diet but still I didn't enjoy the food.

It was both snowing and raining in Manhattan but I was sensing something new in the air. Old fancy samples displayed in Bloomingdale's windows made me think of the crisis of art. Bloomingdale's flags tried to hide the former big store Alexander's that looked like a skinless elephant going into bankruptcy. Fall and winter had passed away so quickly! I realized my favorite seasons (summer and spring) did not exist in New York any more. Time ran too fast in this city. Maybe this is true for every heart, not only for the human heart, but also for the heart of the world.

In Pax Deli, as it was called, I ordered a cappuccino with cinnamon and chocolate, a frozen yogurt, and strawberry cheesecake. My shopping had been satisfactory. I felt the delicious taste of life. *C'est la vie*!

"Would you like a turkey sandwich before dessert, Miss?" I heard a voice behind me. "Your dinner doesn't have the main course." I did not want a main course.

The deli was empty except for a man sipping coffee at one of the tables. He was smiling friendlily.

"I've just bought one," he said. "I don't feel like eating it and I have too much food home." He raised his hand.

"Oh, yes, Mr. Lawrence, right now," said the waiter, or was it the owner? lifting two big pots with regular coffee and decaf and filling the man's cup. After that, as in a known ritual, he added a few drops of half and half.

"Would you mind if I kept you company?" said the gentleman, bringing the sandwich to my table.

Did I have a choice? I don't know why I said yes. Mr. Lawrence moved to my table. I usually don't talk with unknown people and, besides, I prefer to eat alone because this is the time when my imagination roams free giving me exciting thoughts.

Mr. Lawrence wore gold-rimmed glasses. His face, free of stress, seemed to be that of a retired, polite, and detached businessman. He was about sixty, of medium height, and chubby, with short chestnut hair almost white at the temples. He had a delicate nose and a strong neck. He wore a designer blue shirt with a white collar and golden buttons, and a soft brown leather jacket with an open zipper. When he spoke, a few gold teeth sparkled in his mouth. A gold bracelet and a golden Cartier at his wrist gave him a wealthy, well-balanced look.

"This sandwich is absolutely fantastic," my interlocutor said. "My friend, the owner, is a maestro."

"Thank you, thank you." I heard the owner's voice. And to me: "We have known each other since the inauguration day."

"Are you sure?"

"Of course. Don't you remember I gave you a big cake at a 50% discount?"

"Oh, you are right," Mr. Lawrence said quickly. "But you never offered me a discount like that again."

The sandwich was really good. I thought I should pay Mr. Lawrence for it.

A few teenagers walked into the place. They brought in the clamor of the street.

"They come from the movie," said Mr. Lawrence. "The show is over." He pointed to the nearby movie theater.

I didn't have time to respond because something unusual happened. A beautiful and elegant woman broke the teenagers' line. She ordered calmly a few things in a sad voice. After that, just as in a dream, she paid, tasted the coffee, cookies, and pastries one by one, and, gliding on the floor like a ballerina, left everything on the cashier's desk and went back out on the street.

"My God, she is so beautiful," I said in a low voice. I lost my breath.

"Do you think so?" Mr. Lawrence wanted to know my opinion.

"Absolutely," I answered. "Angelic and monstrous at the same time, the New York woman high style…"

"Well, she reminds me of a few things in my life," he said. He seemed nervous.

"A former lover?"

"Two, both having the same name."

"That's a lot," I said.

"I agree. But think what I felt."

"Did you love them?" It was as if he had invited me to ask for a confession.

Affirmative.

"Why didn't you keep at least one of them?"

"Well, it's complicated," he said, taking a sip of his coffee.

"Did you love them both?"

"It's difficult to say, he confessed, shaking his head. "According to my numerology reading, I loved each of them, and they both loved me."

He wiped away a nonexistent coffee drip from his cup.

"Did they have tempers?"

"Not only have I never seen my Berthas lose their tempers with me, I've never seen them lose their tempers with anyone."

"But you broke off with both of them!"

"I wouldn't have done that if…"

I had eaten more than half of the sandwich. I started on the cake and the yogurt. I like this combination very much.

"May I have a teaspoon of your yogurt and cake?" Mr. L asked me. "I am on a diet. But I can taste."

"If what?" I pursued the interrupted thread of the conversation. I put a piece of cake with yogurt on it on his plate.

"Well, in life it's sometimes easy to win a woman, but it's a performance to keep her. This is true also for women regarding men." Voluptuously he was tasting my cake with strawberry yogurt.

"I've never thought about it."

"You see, this is my case. All the women in my life—I don't know, God is my witness how many there were—were special. Smart, intelligent, bright, beautiful, successful. Each one was a unique creature.

"The first Bertha gave me the best vacation of my life. I met her in Florida. It was immediately after my divorce. I felt so lonely and so depressed in those days! When I saw her gorgeous body near my deck chair, I thought that God had sent an angel to comfort me. I fell in love with her and she fell in love with me during our first wonderful night.

"Our apartments were located in a brand new expensive and elegant hotel in Miami Beach. From the beginning Bertha impressed me with her dresses, her fine taste, her elegance, her right instinct of love. As if that wasn't enough, she had a strong brain made for business too. Her father was in the aircraft industry. This is big money.

"Back in New York, I continued to see Bertha every weekend. She lived in Connecticut with her very wealthy family."

"What was wrong then?" It sounded perfect: love, beauty, money! Mr. L let me wait for the answer. His face changed.

"Bertha lived in a wonderful house."

"And?"

"She liked to stay in the best hotels, to eat the best food, to drive the best cars…"

"And?"

"I had a good job on Wall Street, but, you know, I couldn't afford to spend as much as she did…and her mother sensed my situation. I spoke with Bertha about that, but she didn't want to lower her standard of living…Then her mother forbade Bertha to see me and she put pressure on her to break with me. I was aware of everything, but it was impossible for me to stop seeing her."

"Why didn't she leave her parents?"

"Are you kidding? There were hundreds of millions involved. I was crazy about her…I only woke up when she deeply hurt me…"

Mr. L stopped. After a few seconds he continued with his warm voice, bringing back a dark and buried past. "She got pregnant. And she had an abortion without telling me. I was a man who did not deserve a child. You see, at that time I had only one million dollars in my bank account."

I had at that time only one thousand dollars in my bank account. I could not quite grasp the difference between one million and one hundred million. Mr. L lit a cigarette and the owner pretended not to see him. Mr. L used my empty yogurt cup as an ashtray.

I was curious about the second Bertha. Two failures having the same name.

"My second Bertha lived right here, across Third Avenue, near my apartment on 61st Street. I had with her the most wonderful sex I ever had in my life. She liked me too."

Mr. L wiped his gold-rimmed glasses and looked at me. He looked very proud of himself.

"You are very beautiful," he said out of the blue. "I don't like your face with no makeup on it. And your earrings are quite old-fashioned. You also need to get your hair done. You will get a lot of money if you listen to me…" He smiled and begged to be forgiven. He did not want to make me feel bad; only to make me look terrific.

At that time I was desperately trying to make a living. I was an immigrant in my third year. No time for manicure, makeup, or hair-dresser. And no money either. I explained this to Mr. L. He disagreed. Forget about learning and struggling. It was time to get a rich man. Only stupid people and ugly women have to fight for existence. An intelligent and beautiful girl would go, for example, for a rich lover or for the adult industry. You can become rich overnight, Mr. L stressed. Your figure looks great, your body seems outstanding, and you only have to sell yourself at the right price.

I was a shy and innocent intellectual coming from a country where such things were unthinkable. I did not expect ever in my life to be told such things. I wanted people to praise my books, my wit, and my articles, not refer me to the adult industry. My first impulse was to leave. But the writer in me prompted me to stay. It was uncanny. And the uncanny is appealing for writers.

I assured Mr. L I would think the matter over. Meantime, I wanted to know about his second Bertha.

"She was a whore," he said with admiration. "She knew how to get me. She nailed me so close that I asked her to move in to my place. I was even considering getting married to her. Why not? Sex and good company are what we are looking for in life."

I was in shock. A man accepting happily to marry a woman who charged him for sex.

"I was a fool." Mr. L shifted his cigar from one hand to the other. He leaned his elbows on the table as if trying to get more sympathy. "She got more money charging for sex than from becoming a wife. She had three men like me by that time. She had a thriving business. She did not want to spoil it. She left with a lot of jewels from my apartment."

"Did you find her?" I was thinking of calling the police, and of Bertha returning the stolen things. Mr. L ordered a yogurt for himself.

"No, I did not do that." He wanted to preserve that relationship. In fact, they had met many times in the past year. He paid her good money. He put her in his last will. They were getting along nicely. The problem was that they could not stand each other for too long at a time. That is why he was lonely. He slept during the day, and went to restaurants by night. That day was an exception. He had forgotten to take his sleeping medication for daytime.

I did not quite understand the situation. Mr. L explained that he hated daylight. He liked nighttime. He also liked a very low temperature in his apartment. To his delight, outside was like inside his apartment right then. Yet he would consent to five degrees higher.

"Bertha was perfect for me," he stressed. "She kept me company during the night, slept during the day, liked coolness in the apartment, watched porn movies, ate fat food and sweets and smoked."

"She is perfect for me," he said again and again with sorrow. "Too bad she is now in Arizona. Today would suit us nicely."

"Why don't you go there?"

"It is too hot." And after a moment of hesitation: "Something happened to her. The same as with the first Bertha." He explained that actually this was what had separated him from the first Bertha too.

"Lately she no longer likes cold weather and cold surroundings. She refuses to get naked at sixty degrees Fahrenheit. But she did that before. For I cannot perform in a warm environment."

Mr. L was fat. No wonder he did not like to be warm.

The owner of the coffee shop brought ice water to the table. And an actual ashtray. I noticed that Mr. L had no coat, gloves or hat on. He was dressed in a leisurely fashion, as if it were a sunny day.

"I lose customers because you smoke," the owner said. In fact, he was blackmailing Mr. L. The tip was supposed to be commensurate with the offense.

"I am sure she is in love with me," Mr. L continued. "After twenty years she is finally in love with me. But we cannot live together."

They had been speaking on the phone. They were carefully planning for a day with a balanced temperature to suit them both. He was paying her for her constancy and love. He was planning to go to Arizona although he could not stand the weather. And Bertha disliked New York on account of its cold climate. There were a few days in the spring and a few in the fall enjoyable to both.

He stopped talking. He watched the time, counting the hours until Bertha would arrive, or he would go there, or they would see each other in another place. But what place? How expensive? And how to get there? And what to tell her? This year or the next? Money was not a concern, but he had a habit of telling people he would not be tricked by hungry sharks.

"Could you keep me company?" He said at last. "It would be so nice to meet during weekends. Do you have a boyfriend?"

I didn't. And I wasn't a Bertha. And I truly hated cold weather. He was telling stories about his loneliness and my future in the adult industry. He had connections. He could be of help.

I ran.

Pity is a bad thing to live by.

To accept other people's pity would be sinning against you.

I saw Mr. L again a few months later, in the fall. He was at the same table at the same Pax Deli, with a lady in his company. After they left the shop, they exchanged a few loud words on the sidewalk. He handed her something which I supposed was money. She took it and vanished through Third Avenue Bloomingdale's doors without looking back.

It was a warm day. A day when Berthas hate going to a cold apartment.

Doña Juana

They had not been ashamed to make love in front of her. They had left the curtains open and the sunlight swept every corner of the room. From the bed, a mirrored wall gave them a sensation of lounging on a balcony high above the city, the drone of Manhattan streets reaching them from afar. The sunlight played over the paintings of the knights and ladies on the walls and rested on a life-size portrait of a girl dressed in white. She appeared to be from the end of the eighteenth century. A pink rose nestled in her golden hair and in her hand she held a white flower. At the edge of her skirt nuzzled a white puppy. It was said about her that she had died young, before becoming a bride. She was a picture of innocence except for her large eyes that betrayed a certain melancholy and at the same time a knowing curiosity, as if she was making a mental record of what she had witnessed that afternoon.

Positioned directly opposite the girl in white was a twentieth century painting of a woman in the flower of life. It was a portrait of a dark haired lady in a low-cut garnet dress that enhanced her breasts and shoulders. She had fair, almost transparent skin, green eyes full of mirth, and a mocking smile. She tilted her head, giving her a girlish and flirtatious look. Her lips spoke of sensuality, independence, power, and the lavish curly hair against a green velvet curtain covered almost the entire background of the painting. In the sunlight her eyes moved as if alive.

From the corner of her eye Mary perceived an alliance of some kind between those two, the girl and the woman. It was as if they disliked any other female presence in the room. They took a proprietary attitude, laying claim to everything including Guillermo. Mary felt strangely unwelcome. Or was it merely her uneasiness with the situation that had given life in her imagination to all those walled witnesses?

In the two weeks that had passed since they met at a wedding of a mutual friend, Mary Jones and Guillermo Sanchez had lunched together on more than a couple of occasions. Mary, dark-haired and gracious with a charming smile, talked readily about her work with a major charitable Catholic organization dedicated to helping displaced and homeless children around the world. Guillermo pretended to be interested while he took in her sensuous charm. Mary was flattered by the attention of this cultured, aristocratic Latin American high-powered lawyer with roots in Mexican history, who spoke both French and Spanish, although she was sure that such a suave and seductive bachelor was not really interested in having an affair with someone like her. She was conscious of her background in the American heartland.

Guillermo's life was already busy with more than a few women, she knew. Some talk of a scandal in Mexico involving an underage girl of a wealthy family had reached her ears. There was even a darker hint of a homosexual liaison, but she refused to listen to any of this and pushed it all out of her mind. She was absorbed in a project that was supposed to begin soon in the Sudan, and at first she had not taken Guillermo's overtures too seriously. But she wondered if in his heart he desired something special from her, a romance even. At first he was merely attractive, blue-eyed, blond, slim and with thinning hair, a few years older than her forty, she guessed, and stimulating company. But one day, suddenly overwhelmed by her feelings, Mary was conscious of her fear of losing him.

She had succumbed to his persuasive lovemaking and it was now as if they had all the time in the world. They explored each other with tenderness, advancing toward a point of complete understanding. Voluptuousness was coupled with the fear of loss of liberty through love. Mary felt they both knew that belonging to the other was linked with a certain amount of distress.

"Let's have a bath." He spoke softly, caressing the arms she had wrapped around him. "But without the cross around your neck," he added. "I don't want your God with me in the bathtub."

Was he serious? Mary took off her cross and chain and placed them on the coffee table. She explained to Guillermo that her faith was part of her life, despite her skeptically trained mind, in an age demanding scientific proof. She held a deep desire to believe against all odds.

"Do you believe your God could be around here now?" he asked, but without waiting for an answer he talked about his own agnosticism in his self-assured way. To him the freedom to dispense with religion was paramount. Mary felt as so many times before like a stray sheep asking for answers and guidance in her life.

Stepping into the hot water, a strong light awoke her sense of shame. But she did not withdraw her body from Guillermo's touch, although she felt as if on a stage. She closed her eyes, lowered herself and drifted away, hiding from the uncertainty of the moment. They were silent for a while. Under the bright, unforgiving light Guillermo suddenly appeared impersonal, as if detached from her in body and spirit. With his arms across his chest, once in a while scooping water over his face and keeping his eyes half closed, he looked at her from the other end of the tub as if he had never seen her before. It was he who broke the silence.

"Why is a woman like you single?"

He spoke softly, relaxing more deeply into the hot water. Had he forgotten that they had already been through this? Mary thought it was an inopportune moment, but answered his question anyway.

"I told you my fiancé died in a plane crash on his way to our wedding. From Kenya, where he was working for the United Nations."

She grew tense, recalling events that had happened ten long years before. There had been no other man in her life. Her fiancé had been an ambitious man from England always reaching for the stars. He would soon have been appointed his country's ambassador to the United Nations. Guillermo was interested now. She suspected that the tragic chastity of the situation appealed to him.

"Life is a hard-headed battle sprinkled with a few moments of pleasure," he said as if commiserating with her that she had lost her fiancé and was stuck with him, Guillermo, instead. But from the way he was looking at her, Mary could hear the cynical undertone.

Suddenly, like in a bad dream, Mary could visualize Guillermo's former mistresses, how he had abandoned each one of them after fulfilling his urge to possess her—women he had made love to on the same bed, and bathed with in the same tub. She was merely his latest acquisition. So this was the way it would end. She sensed a warning from someone close by but there was nobody, and then fear. She would not give in to it. Not now, not here. She was too vulnerable.

As if to reinforce her thoughts, Guillermo remarked: "An individually perfect life need not be a moral life."

Mary found it in herself to laugh. "Am I to understand you are a Don Juan?" Quickly and under her breath she said the Lord's Prayer, making the sign of the cross with her tongue. Out loud she said "Don Guillermo?"

"What about you? Why are you not married?" She tried to shift the focus of the conversation by putting to him the same rude question.

It was then she caught sight of a figure through the half open door. The woman in red from the painting was staring at her. With her hands she was holding up her long red gown. It had only been a fraction of a second but from the shifting of the air Mary could tell that someone was there behind the door.

Mary called out from the bathtub, ready to jump from the water. "Did you see her? The lady in red?" Breathlessly she tried to get out but Guillermo stopped her.

"What lady? What's the matter with you?" Guillermo was amused by her fear. He kissed her in order to reassure her there was nothing the matter.

"I saw the woman in red from the painting behind the door."

"You have too vivid an imagination," Guillermo tried to calm her down while fixing her with his stare.

"She is glaring at me all the time, following me with her eyes," Mary added, not caring that she might seem hysterical. "Who is she?" She returned his stare.

Guillermo did not answer right away. He crossed his fingers and looked innocently at his broad chest. Then, after a while he explained that she was a distant member of his family. She had died many years before in Mexico in an accident. Her name was Doña Juana. And pretending that he wanted to answer the lapsed question, he went back to the thread of their conversation and explained why he had remained single.

"South American women are sensual, but unfortunately in daily life childish and irresponsible. Do you like the painting over there?" Guillermo pointed to another oil painting hanging next to the bathroom door. It was the portrait of a fine-featured and attractive woman.

"*Regardez-moi bien*, she tried to stab me once."

"Without motive?"

"That's right." He shook his head. Looking at him, Mary was distracted by his deep olive complexion, and unconsciously she began caressing his leg, as it stretched there next to her hip. Guillermo's eyes clouded over. He was a sweet "baby-man", if such a thing could be imagined, a mixture of innocent cruelty and enchanting sensuality.

"So, why haven't you ever been married?" Mary tried again.

"For me, Latin American women are objects of pleasure. European women are attractive, but too formal, while American women are impossible! And they all want commitment, marriage, and family. Marriage is nothing but trouble. I do not want trouble. I am not ready to commit." He was altogether charming and untroubled by the fact that he had had sex with an "impossible" American woman only moments before.

Mary shifted a little, making small waves in the water. It was as if the woman she had seen behind the door was still there in front of her eyes. Her own long brown hair clung wetly down her neck. Her pupils had opened so wide that one might have thought she was drugged. She lay immersed in the water, hiding her skin and also trying not to notice his touch. She wondered if Guillermo saw in her face the immaturity she felt so keenly herself. Her cheeks were on fire. To hide her insecurity she played with her hair, wrapping it into a knot.

"American women think only of money and expensive dinners. In bed they are impersonal. I believe they are missing something, though I can't tell you precisely what. But this is not your case," he added politely, turning the tap handle to add some hot water.

Mary was quiet for a moment but could not keep from asking if he had any children from his liaisons.

"I don't really know, but I think that I may have two. Let's see: a long time ago, I lived with two women at the same time, and I have the feeling that I got both of them pregnant. That was when I was living in La Paz in Bolivia. One of them used to visit me almost every week, from Bogotá. But after a time, she disappeared and I never saw her again."

"And you didn't try to find her?"

"Why?" Guillermo seemed surprised.

"Did she just run off?"

"I think she was afraid I might take the child away from her."

"Sex without love?" Mary said, with a tone of sadness.

"I have a saying," laughed Guillermo, "sex with love is wonderful, but it is not too bad without it either." And he added: "A man is attracted to the spirit of one woman only, but to the bodies of many." He began comparing experiences with women of different ages, the attraction for young women whose bodies were supple and exquisite while he had to make an effort to overlook their childishness. The whole situation was absurd. Had he forgotten she was there?

"What about the other child?" she said, really concerned.

"I cannot even be sure I do have another child." Guillermo looked at an imaginary object on the ceiling. "In any case, the woman I truly loved and wanted to marry was unable to have children."

"Why didn't you marry her?" Mary had difficulty controlling her voice.

"Because she couldn't have children. That's why we broke up. But I really loved her."

The water began to have a soothing effect on Mary. Guillermo's sentences lost their sting. His revelations were like a narcosis playing on the scene, perverse in their disclosure. It was as though she was hearing through his voice a philosophical explanation of the logic of seduction.

"She married someone in Paris. Her marriage turned out to be conventional and utterly boring."

Guillermo encircled her ankles with his arms. Tenderly, he kissed her toes one by one, and then pressed them against his chest. Mary saw that Guillermo was so relaxed, so absolutely himself and so uninhibited, that she could have asked him anything and been sure to get an honest answer back.

She was afraid to continue. She needed to protect herself. But between curiosity and pleasure, and with a keen desire, the body of Guillermo fascinated her more that any truth. His skin had silvered nuances and an unusual savor. She had never before felt such a powerful attraction, even though she feared at the same time it might be trickery born of her own hunger for love.

"I love the taste of your body," she said. "Have I found my prince? And why didn't I years ago?"

"You have to kiss a lot of frogs before you find a prince," laughed Guillermo, kissing her breasts. "Let's go to bed."

He seemed to accept that the woman with him in the bathtub had a curious propensity for transformation. He must have seen her expression change at every turn in their relationship. At that moment she must have looked like a girl with fiery cheeks under the effect of first love. They kissed hungrily, in front of that mirrored wall. The sun had vanished beyond the skyscrapers, and turning her head Mary sensed again a kind of illusory life taking hold of the paintings on the walls. While rocking on his chest in the large bed she transformed herself into an entirely erotic persona capable of all possible expressions of love.

"Why haven't I met you before?" Mary heard him speak as if in a dream. She didn't know if it was his question or an echo of hers. The girl in white and the lady in the garnet dress were staring at her from the wall. Soon Mary felt again the cruelty of those smiles and the presence of those men and women from centuries gone by. One of them, a nobleman, looked so much like Guillermo that it could well have been him in an earlier life.

"Come with me." Guillermo said. What did he mean?

The phone rang. He ignored it. The answering machine started. Mary heard some banal words, and one of Guillermo's old flames ended the message with "I love you." Guillermo kissed Mary hard on her lips. "I love you." Before she could make any remark he said once again: "Come with me," this time adding: "The more I have you, the more I need you." This was about spending a full week together in Huatulco, where he had always gone alone. But now, he said, he was unable to spend a single night without her.

Mary closed her eyes and snuggled next to his shoulder. She could hear his breath and feel the beat of his heart. But she also felt watched, as if Doña Juana was there propping up her head on her hand and witnessing their lovemaking. She was aware of a strange perfume and a faint and incomprehensible presence. Did this Doña Juana want to tell her something? Had she been in communication with the girl in white?

As if under a spell Mary was overcome by a feeling of abandonment. The only thing that drove her forward was her desire to be with Guillermo. Out of the window went all her previous plans, such as spending the Christmas holidays with her parents in Des Moines.

The sound of emergency vehicles reached them, the sound of reality with no effect. So Mary decided to go with Guillermo to Huatulco, despite the warning that lingered in the air.

It was early afternoon when their plane landed in Bahias de Huatulco on Mexico's Pacific Coast. It had been just a leap from the dark and freezing morning in New York to a blazing tropical afternoon. A luxurious car drove Mary and Guillermo to Hotel la Marina and was later to take them to the place where Guillermo's friends were expecting them. Mary wondered who these friends might be. It was clear she would not have Guillermo entirely to herself. Already the distant warning repeated itself but in this paradise it was easy to ignore. They were allowed a brief rest, and then they should be ready for the unimaginable.

La Bougainvillea estate was located on a bluff above the sapphire waters of the ocean gently hugged by the Sierra Madre Mountains. Along a path of lush vegetation and cascades of magenta flowers draped over adobe walls, Mary and Guillermo advanced toward a huge open terrace partly covered by a canvas roof. The lounge in the open-air portico shimmered with silk tablecloths fluttering in the breeze. A telescope faced an island in the shape of an elephant, and a pool built on different levels gave the impression of dropping down into the ocean, though beyond it was a plunge of eighty feet. Mary, who had never seen such a luxurious place, thought she could spend her life here gazing at the ocean during the day and at the canopy of stars during the night.

La Bougainvillea with its *haut monde* from all corners of the globe had brought fame to Huatulco. A well-known English architect who came every year said it was the only place in the world to relax. He was right, but there is more, murmured Guillermo in Mary's ear; things nobody could know without living there. His close friend Luciano de las Ventanas, a successful architect now in his late fifties, had built this house for the love of his life. His own strengths and weaknesses could be seen in the palace he had built. It was a hide-and-seek place, an invitation to intimacy and love, filled with unexpected nooks, vertiginous stairs, mysterious rooms, open-to-the-sky hallways. Everything was exposed, erotic, and daring.

Unlike the opulent houses in Mexico City, La Bougainvillea had no guards at the entrance. In answer to Mary's concerns, Luciano de las Ventanas explained how difficult the approach was. "This place is impossible for *secuestradores* to get to. You have to take a plane to get to Huatulco. The road is impassable even for the *guerillas*, hundreds of miles through the tropical forest. If I were to hire guards, or install electronic devices to monitor the entrances, I would probably end up attracting burglars. And don't forget, the President of Mexico has a mansion next door. You are safe here."

Luciano looked at Mary boldly with his dark blue eyes, casually and knowingly. Tall and athletic, with a wide chest and shapely waist, his hair almost white, Luciano looked like a legendary Hollywood actor. His wife Viviana, although very polite, was strangely vague when speaking. She was a good deal older than her husband, extremely vital, but with piercing eyes and hard lines around her mouth. They were so poorly matched one could not help but wonder at the secrets of their marriage. Viviana's eyebrows shaded her eyes and gave her the look of a woman who had seen and done it all but kept to herself.

Luciano and Viviana told Mary that from the terrace they could scan the horizon for dolphins and whales. They were the host couple for the party that would take place later that night. Luciano suggested that perhaps they would like to take an aromatic mineral bath. And he told them that in the secluded garden, two levels below, there was a white tent with comfortable couches where they could nap. Viviana, less practical, took Mary aside and told her of the power invested in this place by the mountains and the sea to relieve worries and stress and of making human beings aware of the vibrating energy of the universe. Enthralled, Mary wanted to believe and give herself up to such powers.

It was New Year's Eve. All night long the Chinese lanterns, hidden under steps and in bushes, or hanging from the trees, lit up the terraces and the intricate stairways dropping dangerously down toward the ocean.

Five levels down in the rift valley along the seashore, more than fifty people dressed in white gathered to celebrate the advent of the New Year. A path of stones and concrete blocks led across the deep water to an artificial island made of steel and cement blocks. Built out there by Luciano at Viviana's request, it was a tiny man-made outpost embraced by the forested island in the shape of an elephant, which closed off the gulf. In the moonlight it looked like a white plate on the lagoon. Refreshments were served by torchlight on this white island while a mariachi band played love songs.

Mary lost Guillermo to his friends who hadn't seen him for a year. Everybody was asking him about their relationship. Was she his girlfriend? His fiancée? A nonchalant Guillermo kept answering "friend". It made her feel unprotected and it hurt, but to her surprise it seemed to relieve everyone else. In Mexico, as a "friend" she had no power over him. She was a visitor and nothing more. Soon, Mary found herself conversing with the rich and gorgeous. Her familiarity with New York provided her with the necessary capital. The work of charitable organizations in Africa was off the radar screen for this crowd.

Diamond necklaces and extravagant evening gowns materialized out of the night on the verge of the torchlight. These women, Mary saw, were troubled by their denial of their own womanhood. They would do anything to look younger and be noticed. Yet they were unwilling to give up any part of what they had already appropriated through their carefully prearranged marriages.

The not very fashionable knot-fronted chiffon-hanky dress, bought a few years before from a store in the Village, the white stripy heels and inexpensive freshwater pearls made Mary self-conscious. She blamed Guillermo for not preparing her for this. She felt those women's eyes scrutinizing her with smug superiority. Yes, she was merely a bagatelle, and they would know how to deal with her.

Lilia, Pepa, Leonore, Elvira, and Suzy were married to the princes of Latin American banking, beer, tortillas, chain hotels, tobacco, and political corruption. They were in the middle of conversations about familiar topics and events, partaking in their annual ritual. Like a flock of migratory birds having traveled thousand of miles to meet here, still tired, they seemed to keep the same formation as in flight. Viviana, in a V-necked double layered silk-over-satin dress, the V reaching almost to her waist, was clearly their leader. She wore her brown hair cut very short and looked a bit like an aggressive child. Her painted lips and nervous fingers were hypnotic.

Pepa, from Bogotá, middle-aged and outrageous, with black hair and dark complexion, gloried in a skimpy silk-tulle dress. Unfortunately her sleep-deprived features made her look more her own age than was intended. It was clear she was bored with her companion, Diodoro, a quiet man faithfully at her side. Suzy, an English lady in her early sixties, skinny and affecting aristocratic manners, had married rich Humberto, owner of a chain of hotels on Mexico's Pacific coast. She always said with unflappable sincerity that what made her leave London was Humberto's unconditional love for her as well as his wealth.

"Did you really leave London for Humberto?" Lilia asked, and from her tone one could guess that she asked the same question whenever she heard the story. "I love London, but Roberto hates it. Perhaps because of the rain?"

Long-limbed and slim, Lilia transmitted an erotic alertness, accented by her black eyes and black braided hair looped low on the back of her neck. Her clinging and virtually transparent white dress drew attention to her curved hips and protruding nipples. Despite the fact that Lilia's muscle tone showed the strain of three child-births, her husband Roberto, well connected with the business world through his winning beer trademark, worshipped her to the extent that he wanted to see the outlines of her body wherever they went.

"Your dress is thrilling." Viviana's compliment deliberately hinted at Lilia's provocative appearance.

"Roberto's taste." Lilia pretended scorn. "You know he wants to see my body all the time." It was a tired excuse.

"Can you believe another year is gone?" Elvira broke in. "I have missed this glorious place and all of you girls. God, I had a terrible time with my older son." This referred to the young man's failure to live up to the expectations of his family. Almost twenty, he had no plans for the future. They had bought him an apartment in Mexico City where he was studying classical music. Her complaint was not about money, but about his reclusive temperament.

Elvira, a glamorous Mexican woman approaching her forties, caught Mary's attention because of a skeptical expression in her eyes. She was the only one who ignored Viviana's rule of white and wore a flaming red evening gown with a deep plunge front and back showing her passion for color. Mary was instantly reminded of Doña Juana. Elvira's only adornment was a purple bougainvillea floating in her long dark hair. Her husband Miguel, an influential man in the

Mexican government, and also connected with the cocaine Mafia, was Luciano's cousin.

"I didn't know marriage was so boring," muttered Leonore, the youngest in the group. "My life is worse than before. You pushed me into it. I hate Cuernavaca."

Leonore blamed all these experienced women for her marriage to Julio, Suzy's and Humberto's son. She had imagined that as a married woman she would enjoy greater freedom. And it was not true at all. After the wedding she moved to Cuernavaca with Julio. She deeply missed Mexico City and the company of her friends. Now, her comments provoked laughter and jokes. She was a skinny girl in her twenties, with red-gold hair and snow-white limbs, wearing glittering pants and a flamboyant top that left her waist partly uncovered. Julio owned a hotel in nearby La Crucecita, so she had to stay there and not at La Bougainvillea. Leonore's lavender eyes showed no personality, but everyone was fascinated by her youth and competed in giving her advice.

"Wait, my dear," Pepa laughed, "this is just beginning. The excitement will start soon." There was a telling smile on her face, as though she would soon disclose a big secret to the innocent and petulant Leonore. Suzy pretended she did not hear. Diodoro, holding Pepa's hand, never listened to what the women around him talked about.

Guillermo drew close to Elvira and urged her to have a sip from his glass of wine. Elvira took the glass and sipped from the spot where Guillermo had drunk. Elvira shook her dark hair softly at Guillermo's bold caress. And then, as if awakening from a sleep, Pepa pulled Guillermo to her side, without letting go of Diodoro's hand.

She began to speak of her successful business in Colombia, and especially of the day when she had received a few envelopes with flower seeds she had ordered from New Zealand. She noticed that one envelope had no name on it. She took special care of those seeds; she was curious to see what would grow from them. To her astonishment, magnificent white flowers came out in the spring. She tried without success to find the name of the flower in catalogs. Little did she know at the time that botanists would be unable to identify the species. She was the only one in the world to own these flowers whose unheard-of beauty, sent to her by God, made her filthy rich. She brought baskets of them to Huatulco for Viviana. Fresh specimens were arriving every day by plane from Bogotá. They pervaded La Bougainvillea. It was Pepa's special gift to all of them.

"People are saying that the flowers are so sensual that they emanate the odor of sperm. I haven't noticed anything like that," giggled Pepa. "Anyway, this minor detail does not seem to bother my customers," she added in high spirits.

Inhaling every one of Pepa's words, Guillermo was transformed before Mary's eyes. Symmetry deserted his features, making him look much older. He was swallowing, his lips moist. His nostrils flared. His blue eyes grew languid. He seemed to be drawn towards Pepa against his will, ready to make love to her then and there. As Mary watched transfixed, an odor of sperm invaded the little island. Confused, she moved away thinking she was imagining things. Was Guillermo's sudden desire for Pepa really noticeable to the senses or was it those flowers? However beautiful, Mary could hardly imagine they were a gift from heaven.

Mary lost sight of Guillermo as she was removed by Lilia, Viviana, Suzy, and Elvira to the other side of the artificial island. She felt utterly humiliated, and the memory of Guillermo's complacent remarks about his erotic conquests came back to her, intensifying the feeling that she was not welcome there. She tried to adopt an air of calm composure while moving slowly off toward the southern end of the island. She wandered among them all, confined to this glittering outpost, trying to imagine how she was seen by these people. She felt as if all their eyes were glued on her. Tormented by loneliness, she was forced to play her part in a drama that was just unfolding.

As the old year passed into the new, and huge balloons carrying candles were launched into the sky, Guillermo was there holding her in his arms. Her bitter smile had no effect on him. He chose not to notice. That night Guillermo wanted her again and again, with a violence she had not felt in him before. And there came a moment when, to his displeasure, Mary, exhausted, could no longer submit to his desire.

After lunch the next day she went off to sleep alone. And he came back with the same hunger. But later, when dinner was served on the open terrace at the top of the five levels of the cliff, Mary was keenly aware of being unwanted. Viviana tried to be polite, while Suzy looked through Mary as if she were a transparent screen. Lilia's eyes smoldered with erotic tension as, once again, Guillermo stood glued to her hip to hip. They were engaged in a private conversation that Mary felt had a secret meaning for the others. Lilia's hair fell wildly down on her bare shoulders and on to Guillermo's face as he sank his white teeth into the last slice of mango.

"That was mine," said Lilia, smacking her lips.

Guillermo handed her the piece with the imprint of his teeth in it. Murmuring something, she placed the slice of mango in her mouth.

That night, Mary and Guillermo moved from Hotel la Marina to La Bougainvillea. Mary was disconcerted to discover that one of the main paths going down to the beach passed through their bedroom. There were no locks on the doors. Guillermo was used to it. There was no danger. If anything, the unsecured door whetted his persistent hunger for her body. Fear began to creep into her consciousness. The fact that no privacy was possible in La Bougainvillea sharpened her senses.

All night long Mary smelled the odor of sperm. She kept drinking water from a large crystal carafe placed on the night table. In the morning, she found blood on the sheet and a small cut near her shoulder. She searched the bed and found a quartz crystal just under her pillow. Guillermo, uncharacteristically alarmed, took the object and flushed it down the toilet, telling her not to say anything about it. Then casually, he said that it had probably mistakenly been put there by a maid.

After a breakfast of fresh tortillas and avocado soup, Viviana invited Mary to come and sit by the swimming pool where they reclined on deck chairs for a couple of hours, making small talk.

Viviana confided in Mary that Huatulco provided her with friends she never had before. She talked about the troubles of managing such a huge house as La Bougainvillea with its large number of servants. She didn't trust any kind of local food. Everything was flown in by plane, even bread and water. Mary expressed dutiful concern at the number of people to be fed, and Viviana launched into an account of her day-to-day food planning. Then she told Mary that she looked happier and more at ease than when she had arrived. She confessed that it was not at all easy to live with a genius such as Luciano, a very demanding and tyrannical man obsessed with his work. Her great pleasure, Viviana said, was to obey him.

Mary also learned something disturbing from Viviana. It was about Guillermo and his love affair with Doña Juana, the woman from his bedroom painting. She had been his mistress. Viviana described Doña Juana as a beautiful and cynical woman who liked to play with men, destroying marriages, hearts and lives. She was rich and independent and nobody could penetrate to her heart, except Guillermo, but soon after she fell in love with him she died in an accident. Guillermo was grief-stricken and the memory of Juana was likely to haunt him all his life.

That evening Mary was in agony. Sitting by the pool, the tropical sun had burned her fair skin and she could hardly tolerate the touch of bed sheets. She came down with fever and Viviana gave her lotions and a sleeping pill. She was a Midwestern girl, with a fair complexion, too innocent and unprepared for the tropical Mexican wilderness. How careless of her not to know how to take care of her skin.

During the night Mary was vaguely aware of movements in the room, but all she remembered were her dreams. Once she was awoken by thirst and saw that Guillermo was gone. She thought that he had perhaps stayed on the terrace with Luciano and Viviana. In the morning, while Guillermo was still sleeping deeply, she took the gold cross and chain from her purse and put it around her neck. Devils had appeared throughout the night in her dreams, taunting and interrogating her. She had struggled with one of them on a beach. She killed him with some heavy chains and dragged his body out into the sea.

It seemed to her that morning that her brown hair with its reddish highlights had become thicker, wilder, fuller. Her irises were so large and green that they almost effaced the pupils. According to Guillermo, these effects were due to humidity and sex.

Then, while walking along the rocky shore with Lilia and Elvira, the chain was chaffing her sunburned skin and she fumbled to take it off. Lilia tried to help her but lost her balance and the chain slipped away and was instantly lost in the foamy surf among the rocks.

Afterwards came a deep thirst for margaritas. Lying down in the cool shadow of the white tent near the swimming pool, Mary no longer cared about Guillermo's ongoing flirtation with Pepa. When Mary sniffed at Pepa's magnificent white flowers, which were present everywhere, she discovered they really did smell of sperm.

When she told Guillermo about it he was amused. He also had explained to her soon after the lunch served under the tent by the pool that flirtation was not only acceptable but expected in this society. It was an innocent game that added spice and enjoyment to their vacation. He claimed she was too moral, too serious, too full of stereotypes; she would have to let go in order to enjoy life. Mary had challenged his insensitive behavior with Pepa and Lilia and Elvira. He had humiliated her before all those women. But Guillermo dismissed her anxiety, assuring her that nothing could interfere with his deep obsession for her.

"You of infinite beauty and intelligence," he uttered, "you are matchless. No other woman can compare with you."

"Even Doña Juana?"

Guillermo reflected silently while looking out over the ocean. "We loved each other," he confessed. "Her influence over me changed me a lot. It is as if she passed on to me her cold heart and thirst for sex when she died, something she would call 'donjuanity'. I feel that being in love with you I am gradually being cured of her poison."

He was a sweet talker. There was no escaping the hypnotic sound of his words. Flattery was but one small maneuver in a boundless strategy of persuasion. And he was perfectly aware of the seductive powers he held over women. By alternating indifference and affection, cruelty and kindness, cynicism and passion, he attracted, held, and dismissed the objects of his attention.

Diodoro sat on the white couch and drank margaritas with Mary while Guillermo stretched his tall body on a lounge chair outside the tent. It was quite pleasant under the canvas roof. Diodoro seemed devoted to Pepa, but it was obvious that devotion was not the feature she ranked highest in a man. Charming as Diodoro was as a companion, Pepa obviously preferred Guillermo. Mary wanted to ascribe the situation to the boredom of married life but she saw clearly that Guillermo's powers were at work, his lovely teasing, his mixture of immaturity and sexuality, his blue eyes and steady look.

Relaxing in the shade, Mary felt her mind go numb and her soul blinded by desire for Guillermo. At that moment she wanted nothing else in life but his arms around her, his warmth enveloping her in his sweet embrace. It was Don Juan she had met, she knew it now, the man who awakened a woman's deep sexuality. Before, it had seemed shameful to her to think of herself as a passionate lover. Now she was ready to pay anything to be with him. She found herself thinking of him as "the spermatic man," Don Juan himself, in front of her, loving her but also surrounded by other women, heedless of the feelings of them or anyone else. He was a mortal free to please and be pleased, with the natural grace of an innocent creature beyond morals or commitment. And also beyond the reach of punishment.

Diodoro looked pained and avoided Mary's eyes. Soon Humberto, Julio and Miguel joined them while Viviana, Pepa, Suzy, Leonore, Lilia and Elvira, in all their gorgeous semi-nudity, descended on Guillermo, birds of prey masquerading as laughing, chattering girls. Mary felt Humberto grasp her bare feet.

"I do this for Suzy every night," he said, starting to massage her toes with strong fingers.

Over his gleaming bronze shoulder Mary saw Guillermo sink into the maw of female sexuality. Suddenly blazing with desperate passion she started up, panicked, only to find her body snared by Humberto's grip, now seconded by the fluid motions of both Julio and Miguel as they adjusted her back pillow and delivered her more inescapably into Humberto's expert hands. Through hovering waves of scorching sun it was as if Guillermo and Leonore were flagrantly coupling in the pool while the other women kissed and caressed them. Before Mary's eyes it was a scene writhing like a knot of snakes.

A rapid darkness descended on her. She stopped struggling and in anguish fell back into the overpowering maleness enclosing her, and instantly the mirage vanished. There was no Dionysian initiation ceremony, just playful women flirting with a good-looking man on a hot afternoon in a swimming pool. Leonore's husband was on the couch beside her. She remembered a book Guillermo had shown her in New York, a book of lavish reproductions of erotic Indian harem scenes; they had made her aware of how mistaken she had been about what went on in harems. The Maharajah or the Prince or the King did not take a desired body from the harem to a private chamber, but summoned as many as he wanted to attend to his sensual pleasures all at once.

As Mary recovered, drained, from her hallucination, the edges of her sensations blurred and she began to wonder what had brought her such shock and horror. The first thought that came to her was that she had been fighting her own sexuality for years. While she was blaming the scorching sun and her jealousy, she heard Julio complaining that Leonore had been an unwilling sex partner lately. Diodoro, expressionless, suggested that he give her a potion of a product discovered by Viviana at La Crucecita market. Viviana was a great believer in local witchcraft.

"Do you know, Mary," Miguel said, considerately and with an insinuating glint in his eye, "that the breeze on the terrace next to the room where you sleep cools you wonderfully during the hottest hours of love in the night?"

Then he confided that he liked to have sex with Elvira in a huge glass tub at their place suspended over the steep drop, which made them feel as if floating in outer space. They did not care if anyone could see them from the valley below. Their mansion, he said, was actually one immense bedroom; even the bathroom had no door, because he couldn't bear the idea that Elvira might keep any secrets from him.

Mary expressed curiosity at such an unusual architectural extravagance, and Miguel invited her to visit their place for breakfast the next morning.

Surrounded as she was by courteous and attentive men Mary looked happy. She was happy. Men, she now realized, had always meant so much to her, even in the years of loneliness after her fiancé's death. Suddenly everything had another meaning. It was as though she was emerging from a long hibernation. Had it been her destiny, she wondered, to come with Guillermo to Huatulco? She liked to flirt and see them salivating while talking to her, devouring her body with ravenous eyes. In the midst of this excitement Mary noticed in herself a sorrow, a sweet continuous pain concentrated in her womb, the presence of an inexplicable lovesickness. It was the pain of desire, which had been there all the time, now impossible to ignore. Growing, and intensifying.

"Has anybody noticed my sickness?" she asked herself, gazing, concerned, into the faces of those men she had lured into her presence.

In the middle of the night, Mary wanted to have sex under the stars. Her burning skin did not diminish her desire for Guillermo. Her emotional range had deepened wildly. Guillermo opened the glass doors of the bedroom so that from the bed they could see the horizon of the ocean, the moon and the stars. Afterwards they moved outside on the grass, under the oleanders and palm trees. She now experienced Guillermo's thirst for love as something that did not distress her any more. Despite his scouring of her tender sunburned skin, she turned to sleep still strongly desiring him. But after a moment she sensed someone pass by on tiptoe. She got up and went out through the opened sliding doors to the terrace. A few steps brought her to the bedroom of Viviana and Luciano. Cautiously walking in the shadow of palm trees and bushes she got closer to the other side of the terrace.

On a bed lit by side lamps decorated with crystals, Viviana had taken off her dress and was holding her nakedness out to Luciano. He leaned to kiss her breasts, caressing her nipples. Mary saw how gentleness and violent possession met as their bodies united. For a long time she stood still, until a great desire growing in her forced her to leave. Thirsty, she finished her water when she returned to her room, and then also emptied Guillermo's carafe. She had already noticed that it tasted better than hers.

When Mary woke up late the following morning Miguel was waiting for her. He told her that Guillermo had gone with Luciano to inspect some tracts of land where the architect wanted to start a new development. Embarrassed, Mary saw she had to go by herself with Miguel, trusting that Guillermo would join them later.

The house of Miguel and Elvira, a few miles from La Bougainvillea, occupied three levels of a cliff rising steeply from the ocean. From an overhanging balcony Mary had a stunning view of the sapphire waters of Bahia Santa Cruz and Bahia Tangolunda, and of the three islands like pearls shaken off the promontory where the mansion was built. Pelicans and seagulls floated lazily in the air. The rocks, like the soil, had a whitish color. Flowers of pink, yellow, and red glowed on gigantic cactus plants and oleander trees. Far away across the glittering water other opulent cliffside dwellings shimmered white above the sea.

Miguel was alone. Elvira had left the night before for Oaxaca to deal with some troubles having to do with their son. Mothers, Miguel said, always know best how to handle sons. It was only a forty-minute flight, and she was supposed to come back later in the day.

During breakfast, served on the terrace, they spoke about the extraordinary beauty of the place, their lives, Mexican politics, even Mary's relationship with Guillermo. She liked Miguel's intelligent remarks, surprised at the easy intimacy they created. She did not dare to ask if the rumors of his Mafia connections were true, but she would have liked to. She felt they were having a lovers' conversation, although she did not care to define what it was she was sharing with him. And even though she had promised Guillermo she would say nothing, she wanted to tell Miguel about the quartz crystal. But instead of telling him what had really happened, she made up a story about a crystal she had found on the stairs going down to the beach. Miguel wanted to know more about the shape of the stone and what she had done with it.

"I threw it in the sea," Mary lied, wide-eyed.

Miguel gave her a reproachful glance and shook his head as if the situation was hopeless. He looked deeply into her face from the other side of the table and it was clear that she was there not for a friendly neighborly visit but for something else.

"You know," he began, trying to find the right words, "in Mexico this stone is a weapon used in sorcery. It is said that the stone penetrates the enemy's body, kills, and then returns to its owner. So, yes, getting rid of it, you did the right thing." And then: "Never forget that there are more sorcerers in Mexico than anywhere else."

Miguel's laugh seemed to cover a concern he couldn't brush off. But the next moment he turned to Mary all smiles, inviting her to look at the startling blue of the sky.

"What a lovely place this is! I could sit here all day." Mary did not quite recognize her own voice. Unnerved by Miguel's presence, she barely heard his remarks about the stone crystal and sorcery, perhaps because she had her own beliefs about spells and sorcery. She was of the opinion that a person might be powerful enough to reverse the outcome of a spell.

"This is a healthy tea prepared especially for you," Miguel said, bringing her out of her languor. "Drink up, it will heal your sunburn in a minute. Viviana should have given it to you right away." It was an old Mexican recipe prepared from algae, flowers and tree roots, cold and spicy. She emptied the small cup out of curiosity, eager to experience whatever this enchanting place had to offer. She felt no trace of fear or repulsion.

The tea did not change her inclination to remain there contemplating the bay. But she got hold of herself and said she would have to leave. Miguel silenced her, the most important part of her visit was yet to come, the tour of the mansion. And Mary thought of the bathtub suspended atop the cliff.

She got up and followed him up a precarious staircase ending in a sort of lighthouse, with a passage leading to a secluded terrace. Beyond the terrace they finally reached a circular room with an oversized bed in the middle. From there he led her into the open bathroom and beyond the huge bathtub she saw the mountains fall steeply into the sea.

A strong smell of algae and sea mingled with the heavy scent of flowers and decaying vegetation. Instantly she felt a desire to be there, in that tub, suspended between the ocean and the mountains, and she did not reject Miguel when he touched her from behind and kissed her shoulder. She turned to him and raised her arms round his neck, craving his kiss. Then, breathless, she sank to a chair while Miguel knelt and encircled her hips so his face was level with her breasts. Aroused and oddly contented, she looked at him in wonder. She felt the pang in her womb, already more intense than yesterday, and also, as though she was in Miguel's body, the pain too of his need, like a ball of fire running from his belly down his legs.

"No," she managed to say. Her eyes grew larger, expressing pure desire. It was Guillermo she felt connected to, Guillermo that she loved. Miguel touched her neck and her pearls snapped and flew around the room.

"I'll give you real ones, *mi amor*," he murmured.

She was aware of his heart beating. "*Hagamos el amor, mi cielo*," he almost pleaded, kissing her neck, bringing his mouth down, taking her nipple into his mouth.

She drew back, but only for a moment. With controlled urgency Miguel undressed her and helped her into the bathtub as the water rushed through the pipes like a hot spring. He tore off a purple flower hanging over the tub. Slowly and gently he rubbed the flower on her arms while she tried to envision his three lovers and six children. Diodoro had told her Miguel had a violent temper, and that a jealous husband had been killed by his people. Now his powerful chest was touching hers as a familiar scent saturated the air. Again and all around her, there was the odor of sperm.

She slept the entire afternoon and did not wake up until the telephone rang. It was Viviana telling her they were all on the terrace ready to troop off to Pepa's place. Was she coming? Then Guillermo showed up and stroking her hair expressed his concern. Her blistered skin looked better, but he thought she should spend the evening in bed. He left, but Mary did not want Guillermo in Pepa's house without her. She deeply mistrusted that woman. She rushed to get ready but by the time she reached the terrace they were gone.

She scanned the horizon through the telescope and tried to sort out her thoughts and feelings. What was it that had happened that morning? She and Miguel had made love in the bathtub, and after that on the immense bed. She could not explain it to herself and she gave up trying.

The sunburn, Mary was amazed to discover, had completely disappeared. A new feeling gripped her of being totally at ease with her sexual desire. Why had it ever made her ashamed to feel this way? She could not think of Guillermo being anywhere but with her that evening. Miguel's body too was there in hers, his marvelous possession of her, his nervousness, and his demand for complete obedience. She was inhibited now by the ferocity of his lovemaking.

In the pale gold light she went down to her bedroom and stood at the glass door again looking out at the sea. Her loneliness gave way to curiosity. She went out through the opposite door and, surprised by her own boldness, entered the bedroom of Viviana and Luciano.

It was as if she was looking for something. There was nothing special there beyond what she had already seen through the terrace doors above the sea. But a luxurious animal fragrance attracted and repelled her at the same time, Viviana's and Luciano's perspiration embedded in the walls and furniture. And again the odor of sperm, from a huge vase of Pepa's rank white blossoms. An accumulated bitterness of all these days suddenly filled her. She was held hostage here by a bizarre group of people and forced to witness their rituals. Mary felt panic rising within her, but after a few deep breaths she proceeded in her undefined search.

She opened another door and, leaving it ajar, stepped into a dimly lit room. After a while she made out a console with a mirror above it. On top of an orange tablecloth three thick candles were burning.

Each candle was set in front of framed identical pictures where Mary recognized her own likeness. In the mirror shadows wavered in the candlelight and her own face showed dark and distorted. The candles held her mesmerized. Was she the object of sorcery? Was Viviana wishing her dead? Viviana, with such macabre fascination for the supernatural, was likely insane.

In an instant Mary understood the meaning of the quartz crystal under her pillow and Miguel's attempts at explanations. She put out the candles and pulled out the pictures from their frames and ran back with them to her bedroom. A determination to see this to its conclusion took hold of her. She was not afraid of sorcerers nor of *santeria*, and definitely not of Viviana. She began to see that, try as she might, Viviana could not cast a spell on her, nor bewitch Guillermo. For Guillermo and Mary were in love. But she saw, too, that inexplicably Guillermo was becoming weaker in his love and that the seducer's role was being passed on to her.

It was hot, and Mary lay on the soft white couch in a see-through peignoir. In the gathering twilight, the terrace hanging over the sea was like a soap-opera stage set for a big love scene. The servants had gone to their quarters. The half-eaten refreshments on the tables reminded her it was real. But she felt like the Queen of Sheba, a lonely queen, tormented by these new feelings of overpowering sexuality. Her skin was more elastic, softer, thirsting with desire. Her breasts were tender and heavy.

"You look tired, Mary." It was Roberto coming through the unguarded door. Lilia had left a message for him, he said, something about a visit to Las Ventanas.

Thinking she should have known she would be intruded upon, Mary was embarrassed by her provocative clothing. This was the man, she recalled, who required his wife Lilia to attire herself in sexy and revealing dress at all times for him to feast his eyes.

Self-assured, Roberto put his hands on her shoulders and kissed her cheeks with that same intimacy they all used when kissing and touching. Roberto was tall and elegant, with a dark complexion, and sensual lips. He rested his arms a bit longer than necessary on her shoulders, then let his hand brush her knees. He spoke as if he merely wanted to comfort her. He had heard about her sunburn. Then he talked about Diodoro, Pepa's husband, a man with no sense of humor, no imagination, not even manners. Pepa too, alas, he said, had grown aggressive lately. It was obvious that she was on the lookout for a new lover. Sudden wealth, Roberto said, always has this effect on her type.

Roberto laughed and mocked the others, as if to cheer her, taking her into his confidence. Mary felt good in his company. He knew the legends of Oaxaca and the Olmecs. He spoke of the cruel rituals of the Zapotecs and Mixtecs and Aztecs, practices picked up by English pirates in the sixteenth century. Buccaneers had used Huatulco as a hideout. Listening Mary sensed the cruelty that dwelt below the surface of this place inextricably linked with its beauty. Her erotic charge was part of it too.

Roberto suggested in his easygoing way that they walk down to the ocean. "It is the mating season of the crabs. You must see it."

She feebly tried to decline his invitation but he insisted. She had to gain a moment's respite but she knew the insidious forces of this place had gotten to her. She had lowered her guard already in the beginning. Now it was too late to restore it. She went in to quickly put on some clothes.

It was a long and dangerous climb down, hundreds of steps, turns and dark corners. They were both barefoot. At first Mary had a hard time keeping up with Roberto, who knew the way.

"Why the hurry?" She tried to make light of it but sounded worried.

"We have to catch the full moon on that particular part of the beach," he said, but slowed down. As they proceeded he reached out a hand here and there to keep her from stumbling on the dangerous steps. This pleased Mary. As they continued to descend in a more relaxed fashion she asked about Viviana.

"She came to Mexico from Peru. She was born into a powerful family that vanished in the political struggles there. Some believe that demonic forces played a part in the disappearance. Viviana is known to be very skilled in *santeria,* the old Indians' witchcraft. You must have heard about Doña Juana, one of Luciano's former paramours and later Guillermo's mistress. She died mysteriously here, plunged to her death from one of these steps. It seemed that falling in love with Guillermo, Juana became vulnerable somehow. She was an extraordinary woman, not easily forgotten.

"Viviana is a woman of contradictions," Roberto continued. "She is generous and friendly, but at the same time secretive about herself and her intentions. I have seen her many times walking alone along the beach in the early morning hours. She knows how to lure us, eh?" Roberto laughed gently. "She certainly has the energy or the power to gather us all here every year. We are never able to turn her down."

The story of Juana falling to her death from this very path did not concern Mary greatly. It had nothing to do with her. She was conscious of her feminine odor increasing as she walked, blending with the scent of flowers. Could Roberto tell? The steps suddenly ended and they stood on the moonlit beach. Roberto's eyes gleamed as he led her to the edge of the water.

Suddenly the ground beneath Mary's naked feet was alive with slithering, writhing movements. All along the shimmering, rippling tide, crabs were copulating in the hot sand, among broken shells and driftwood. The waves washed over them and they burrowed into the sand. It seemed the entire beach was pulsing with life, an orgy of sexual pleasure.

Mary slipped and would have fallen on top of the unheeding crabs had Roberto not helped her regain her balance. Powerful energy washed over her body and mind. It came from the moonlit aura of the water, the stones, the crabs, Roberto. In the darkness she could see patches of light like luminous spheres. Far from being frightened, she seemed to gain self-confidence and develop trust in her own senses.

Roberto guided her closer to the rocks of the cliff, and they entered a different world. As they moved away from the tide, the beach was quieter. He led her toward a cave or niche in the rocks that she discovered was another room in the wild architecture of La Bougainvillea.

It was a sort of retreat, with a bed and a table. It was dreamlike and inviting in the shadow-filled moonlight. An electric fence protected it from any incursion of the crabs. Roberto found a hidden key and opened a compartment in the stone wall. She sat down at the table, watching in amazement as he screwed up his eyes opening a bottle of champagne. He filled two glasses and, handing her one, he laid his other hand on her breast. When she took the glass, he encircled her waist and kissed her.

"You're crazy," she said, slipping out of his arms with a forced smile.

He waited to see if she would say something more, but she didn't. She stood silently, her eyes resting on the moon-streaked bay, drinking the sparkling liquid that tasted like the water from Guillermo's carafe.

"Crazy for you," said Roberto, with a kind of passionate levity. "This was Juana's favorite retreat." He closed in on her again. "I am in love with you." He drew her head to his shoulder by her long and lavish hair and kissed her neck. *"Te deseo, mi amor."*

She was thinking how thick and full her hair had become, so similar to Juana's covering the background of the painting in Guillermo's bedroom. Was it the humidity that had changed its texture? And changed her skin too? She was pleased to feel power over this man. The crabs copulating under the moon were noisy with desire and abandon. They were so tightly interlocked that they did not react to anything, even death.

Mary felt dizzy. Holding her head in his hands, Roberto helped her to lie down on the bed. He told her to relax. As he sat in front of her watching her through half-closed eyelids, she felt as if their souls fused and ignited. Unable to speak, she tried to touch the thick growth of auburn curls around his face, but couldn't. She was incapable of uttering a word or lifting a finger. She observed his strong tanned legs as if they were separate from his body, independent of his chest and hips. Suddenly her thoughts were clear, the strange sounds she heard were sharp and distinct. When he lay down alongside her, he was a string of light ready to draw her into its luminosity. She finally abandoned herself to him as if to the magic of those myriad sea creatures under the rocks on the heated sand.

Guillermo came back very late that night and Mary was not at all pleased with his advances. When thirst woke her a little before dawn, Guillermo's place next to her was empty. She opened the back door and looked up and down the stairs, unconsciously trying to salve her wounded pride, for she loved him deeply and couldn't accept his betrayal. She descended one level to the pool that had the white tent beside it, a place where Guillermo had made love to her at dawn. Frustrated and angry she could not bear the heat of the night and plunged into the pool dressed in her thin gown but the water was still warm from the sun and did little to calm her.

She was wide awake now, wondering who else might be around at this early hour. Would Viviana be taking her stroll by the beach or maybe she was out looking for Luciano?

Mary was climbing out of the water when she heard Luciano's voice from the middle of the pool.

"You cannot sleep, can you?"

She looked around and saw him floating on his back, his young blue eyes and white hair just discernible in the pinkish light announcing the sunrise.

She mumbled something, embarrassed. They were alone in a world of silence, broken only by the buzz of an insect and Luciano's words.

"Come back to the pool," he said. "This is the best place to rest."

Without a word Mary slipped back into the pool and let herself relax in the embrace of the water. She tipped her head back and with her long hair trailing in the water she closed her eyes. She floated easily this way. She felt her blood pulsing, unsure whether at that moment she wanted Guillermo or Roberto or Miguel. At the same time she thought of how she might find a church and confess her sins. As she tried to say a prayer looking up into the pink sky, her legs were encircled and she was drawn toward the bottom of the pool. It felt like a dream.

She shut her eyes as she went under, holding her breath and trying to escape Luciano's hands. But he held her tight, almost crushing her. Then he pulled her to the surface.

"Don't you feel a special energy here? Have you ever heard about the shamans of Mexico?" Luciano, intense and breathless, tried to extract the answer from her eyes. Short of breath, her heart pounding wildly, she could only nod her head. She had in fact read, years before, a book that she considered pure fiction.

"You have changed so much since you arrived. I believe it is because someone like you is receptive to the powerful forces at work here. This is one of those places where the magnetic fields responsible for mutations in the universe come together. Like your beauty and intelligence.

"You are irresistible. *Te deseo.*" And after a moment: "All the women here hate you. They wish you were dead. You have taken Guillermo away from them. *El conquistador de mujeres!*" He added the last words with a laugh, all the while caressing her with fingers used to molding objects of art.

She bore his tight embrace and kisses silently. In her mind's eye she saw him making love to Viviana. What exactly was at work here?

She could not help thinking that this was not just lovemaking but a ritual with some hidden meaning.

She leaned on the bottom in the shallow end of the pool while he embraced her, searching for her. There was no way of resisting. It was as if the ritual required her complete submission.

She woke up with Guillermo beside her and drank more water than ever from his carafe which tasted better than hers. It was unclear if what she had experienced was a dream or reality. But the turmoil was growing inside her, and she was surprised that Guillermo did not seem aware of it. At breakfast she did not notice any changes in Viviana's or Suzy's attitudes. Viviana even seemed warmer to her. Suzy was as friendly as ever. But Mary felt an increase in animosity all the same, perhaps accentuated by her dream, if it had been a dream. Luckily, they were all engrossed throughout the breakfast in talking about Pepa's party. She stayed out of their conversation, afraid of being wounded by their careless remarks.

"Let's have a masked ball! Last night it was La Crucecita. Tonight is La Bougainvillea! I have it all prepared." Viviana was aggressively exposing her legs. Luciano kissed her in front of them all.

"*Mi adoración*," said Luciano, "it will always be as you wish."

"What a great idea," exclaimed Guillermo, turning abruptly with his excitement towards Elvira, whose disgruntled face showed a perpetual displeasure and disappointment not only with Miguel but with the entire world.

The masked ball was to be held that same night. They were all sitting around a table making plans on the terrace guarded by an Inca god. Guillermo and Elvira were working on the pool lights. Mary noticed Julio wandering around keeping on eye out for something. In the deepening twilight he was everywhere. He's too young, she thought. And he's obviously frustrated by Leonore, his silly wife, whose lavender eyes are turned on Elvira, certainly not on him.

It was decided that after dinner all of them would go down to the beach by one of the three paths. Between the top terrace and the beach everybody was supposed to change clothes and come down to the beach masked. There was much laughing and joking as they set out. But the paths down were dangerous, the night was dark, the moon was not out yet. Everyone delayed, forming groups in lighted corners.

Mary was picking her steps with extreme caution, hoping to recognize Guillermo on the beach. Her impatience lured her to the steepest and most direct path. At the narrowest and most precipitous point, her muscles trembling from the tension, she sat down on a bench outside a gazebo that was overrun by vines. It stood on its own little knoll above the dark sea. And here was Julio, rapidly approaching her, leaping down the rocky path like a mountain goat.

Yes, he had been stalking her. He was disguised as El Comandante, the guerrilla chief, aristocratic and sleek, complete with sword and black hat. Mary in her long silky purple dress with the crinoline became the gorgeous enigmatic mistress in an old Spanish painting come to life. She gasped with simulated panic, her wide eyes pretending not to recognize him.

"*Señora!*" Julio took a stand above her, stentorian and rigid. "You are my precious prey tonight."

He was enticing. They laughed together, Mary doubly laughing, amused at herself and at the pitch of her laughter.

"Do you think I would oppose you?" It was so easy to say, and the smile was true. Obviously, Leonore was too young to appreciate her husband's worth. No wonder he was hungry for love.

With flirtatious obedience to his show of authority, Mary took off the crinoline that supported her long skirt and lay down on the stone wall that protected the path from a sheer drop into darkness. She was suspended, vulnerable, and daring, surrounded by huge green leaves throbbing in the gathering darkness. Spring water dripped nearby. There was a cool freshness, a rich and different breeze, setting their senses in motion—like an elegant old dance, Mary thought—and luring them into its intimate domain. Her awareness crossed a threshold to a level that was new to her. Here she knew everything about herself, about life, and about Guillermo.

Julio sat by her head. Caressing her hair, he began to sing a Mexican song, in a fine velvet voice seductively varying the rhythms. It reminded her of birdsong. Distinctly she heard the song of the riverside wren, with flute tones. It was the serenade sung by El Comandante for his *corazoncito*.

Points of light from villas around the bay gently pierced the dark as Julio's sounds unhurriedly faded into silence. He kissed her lips. His fingers fluttered over the tiny white lace bordering the purple extravagant décolletage exposing her breasts.

"*Mi corazoncito*," he was murmuring, "*pedacito de cielo!*" The moon was coming up and she could see him with perfect clarity. Her eyes encouraged him.

"Here, let's do this."

She heard the assurance in his voice that said there's no rush, there are many ways to pass this precious time. In the palm of his hand he showed her a few small flattened globes, like beans or buttons.

"Have some with me as Doña Juana did. I was almost sixteen when she made love to me." Mary chose not to listen but instead chewed her beans together with him.

"Voluptuousness." Julio was speaking softly. "You are gorgeous and voluptuous and my passion for you swells. You consume me. You must enter my mind. You must enter my body. You draw me under like the waves of the sea. I want to spend all my nights with you. I want to touch you all through the day. You bewitch me. Every fiber and nerve of my being, my whole being vibrates with you. I wish you were with me everywhere I go, so we could together grow into a new stage of our lives."

Again the warm silence. Soon it was Mary who was speaking, melodiously and at length about what she was experiencing. But in her mind she was seeing Renoir's painting *Dance à Chateau*, where as always it is the man who uses his magic powers to get the girl. But Mary in her enlightened state saw that nature had granted man his irresistible pursuit in order to make him believe in his power of seduction. Would he ever realize it is the woman who seduces?

Julio was listening, perhaps to her thoughts as well as her words.

"You look like a knowing person," he told her. Fuelled by a new understanding and unfamiliar visions their minds seemed to merge with each other and the world.

"This is a place of power," he said. "Act out what you feel."

Soon Mary got down from the stone wall and entered the gazebo. She craved his embrace, his carnal warmth. When he followed her, she allowed him to have her, guiding him through each moment of love. Somehow, she realized why she was doing this. It was more than desire. She wanted to pass on what she had learned from Guillermo. She wanted to teach Julio the art of love.

"You are thinking of Guillermo, aren't you?" he said. But he wanted to have her again. She did not stop him, although she refused to meet his eager and now uncertain eyes. Her steady gaze admired the poinsettia and bougainvillea that adorned the gazebo inside and out. Julio was on his own.

"A woman is attracted by one man's spirit only but by the bodies of many," she echoed Guillermo's words to her as if in a trance. She had more to say and continued: "The desire for a body is as violent as any desire. You see, being with you I must concentrate on your body, otherwise your youth would bore me."

"Guillermo!"

Mary shouted when she got back to the top terrace, running in her long purple dress in the darkness of the night. She found him in their bedroom, angry that she had not been with the group all evening. They flew into each other's arms. Instantly he sensed the upheaval in her and putting her at arm's length looked into her face.

"You look like them. The portraits!" It was of course, about the girl and the woman from his bedroom. He was astonished and in a state of disbelief.

"You are even dressed like them! And your face!"

He was afraid to pronounce Juana's name. Looking back at him Mary saw his recognition of her own innocence and experience, the same paradox that shone in the features of Doña Juana and that ancestor of his who had died before becoming a bride and whose ghost witnessed all his love affairs.

Like a dam breaking, his rage erupted, releasing his fear that she might have been dead—those rocks, those cliffs, that crazy unmanageable dress. He vividly cursed Viviana for burdening her with that dress and starting such a stupid game. He was glad that their journey was coming to an end. The day after tomorrow, he said, they would go back to New York and start life together in earnest. He was in love with her. And then in a trembling voice he told her of her body's metamorphoses—the glow of her skin, her shining hair, and eyes. Over and over he expressed his amazement at the number of times she had radically changed her look in the space of only a few days. It was not just her hair, it was her whole person. And all the time he spoke she was besieging him, skillfully enfolding his body in hers, even using her legs to encircle him. He was in her power.

A profound need to confess seemed to seize him then. Always, he said, after Doña Juana's death, he has come here by himself to entertain the lovely women belonging to this place, all of them so appealing it was impossible for a man to choose among them. But bringing Mary was a mistake. She must, she absolutely must, know that he loved her and she had no cause to suffer. His flow of words became a torrent. Those women had no meaning for him. But he should have foreseen that, even though they were all aware of his love for Mary, they would still want him for themselves. Now he knew, he said, that during these last days in Huatulco his journey through life had changed course. It won't be one conquest after another any more, he said, pursuit without object confining him to a sterile seesaw of obsession and boredom without end. This was the poison which Doña Juana had passed onto him. He was no longer merely preoccupied with himself. He had escaped the cycle of predator and prey. She, Mary, had shown him the way to freedom. His restlessness was over. "Seduction and malediction," he kept repeating.

Mary felt the effect of Juana's poison in herself. She knew that, along with his love for her, Guillermo had passed on to her the extraordinary and terrible legacy of Doña Juana. She searched for a way to calm his frantic talking before she could respond to him. She was far from ready to confess the details of her role in his transformation. Now that the emotional battle for Guillermo was over, her relief was overshadowed by what was happening to her, what she herself had become.

Yes, Guillermo was hers now, but it turned out not to be a gain. She was disappointed, she was afraid. She felt a kind of limitation she could not bear, a drain on her whole life, vaster and more complex than she could have imagined. She saw in a flash that Guillermo would always remain for her the man she had loved with intense passion. Her desire would always be linked with his most seductive gestures; never would she be able to separate herself from him. But after those days of struggle during which she had felt such a profound sense of impurity, she had discovered something else, something totally unexpected. From jealously and trying to guard Guillermo from all those revolting women, she had come to feel sympathy towards the women and looked at Guillermo with a strange sense of indifference. At the same time she felt guilty for her complicity with them in sharing that gorgeous specimen of maleness.

The last morning was reserved for swimming and kayak races in the bay. They all met on the beach soon after breakfast. Roberto was the first one out. He swam powerfully against the strong currents of the gulf toward the elephant-shaped island and back. Miguel was next, scoring better time, which spurred Diodoro to show the best style and even better time.

The women watched laughing, screaming and cheering their men on. Luciano and Julio took up the challenge too, but a cramp in Julio's leg turned their race into a scene of panic. Everyone knew that the whirlpool currents were violent in this channel and that any weakness could mean death. It was fortunate that the two men had gone together.

Next the plan called for the ladies to display their skills at kayaking. Leonore, who was the youngest, had been chosen to go first. There was also to be a special event for Mary, the lady guest. Leonore, in a red bathing suit that complemented her snow-white limbs and golden red hair, looked like a teenager. I would never have guessed she was a married woman, Mary thought, watching as she walked hesitantly toward the kayak. Everyone knew she was unhappy with her Julio, and did not even want to make love with him. Now, in those lavender eyes that glanced her way, Mary saw a disturbing look of anxiety.

But Mary had no time to reflect on what it might mean. Viviana, Pepa, Suzy, and Lilia all descended on her and thrust her into a life jacket, despite her lack of enthusiasm. She was to go with Leonore in the kayak, they said. It was her chance to see the spectacular view of Huatulco from the ocean, and they would also visit the magnificent beach on the other side of the island, which centuries before had been a refuge of bandits and pirates.

"Can't you see that Mary doesn't want to go?" Guillermo shouted angrily at the women as he strode across to them and grabbed the life jacket and put it on himself. Was this Mary's new Guillermo? No, his lust for Leonore was there for all to see. But he made some excuses for Mary about her fear of water and especially the sea.

Leonore pursed her lips. "It was meant to be a special treat for Mary," she said.

Pepa and Viviana tried to convince Guillermo to stay and let Mary go. But his leering eyes left no doubt that he meant to savor this unique opportunity to ravish that gorgeous young body on the island's hidden beach. His officious gesture to protect Mary from danger was merely a pretext. He pushed Lilia out of the way and with a false and ridiculous air of calm assurance slipped into the kayak.

Mary watched as Leonore leaned back and pushed the kayak off the sand and away from the rocks. With grace and beauty Leonore began to fight the waves, using a double bladed paddle and her own upper body strength. Guillermo made a visible effort to match her rhythm. The kayak turned and moved slowly out on the left side of the little harbor. They were headed for the left side of the island, and due to eventually reappear around on the right. As the kayak grew smaller they commented on the likely time of their return.

Without explaining why Viviana ordered the servants to prepare a second kayak to go after them. However, this really annoyed Luciano, and a violent argument between husband and wife ensued, with Elvira strongly endorsing Viviana's idea. This unpleasant disturbance was in contradiction to all the rules of their social life. What was happening? Mary felt panic growing in her. Viviana was acting very strangely, angry at Mary's presence, then quickly denying it with a nervous smile. She was agitated, as if ready to throw herself in the water and swim all the way out to the island.

Abruptly the wind changed and the serenity was gone as huge waves gathered and crashed on the rocks and sand, driving the anxious party up on to the rocks and back to the concrete island. It seemed to Mary that the waves would engulf the continent as they drowned the little beach, catapulting stones into the air as if trying to bury them in the soil on top of the cliff.

The dense spray was hot and bright. Glimpses of a pale full moon disoriented her and she was transported to a semi-conscious state of mind. The water that splashed into her mouth tasted of iodine, algae, and Guillermo's body.

Mary saw them in her imagination making love in the sand on the other side of the island. Miguel walked with her as she paced back and forth, and a very courteous Roberto held her hand and comforted her in her obvious distress. Luciano was shouting to all who would listen that the current that day was unusually strong, with treacherous undercurrents, and that Leonore and Guillermo must fight bigger waves on their return trip. He wanted everybody to think that they were perhaps waiting out the storm over there.

When the storm subsided, there was at first only a faraway speck noticeable in the water. It was discovered by Viviana who was looking through her binoculars. Soon a canoe was ready to go out and after a little while they saw a crying and exhausted Leonore beating her breasts and screaming Guillermo's name. Yes, the stream was too strong, the kayak had overturned, but that shouldn't have meant anything, their life jackets would have supported them as they swam to the island. But Memo's life jacket was defective and the waves took him. She could not help him. Memito drowned and his body went out to sea.

They all used these terms of endearment, which until that moment had been unknown to Mary. Initially, it was a whispering, a mad sound issuing from the mouths of women gathered on a beach, the cursing and whistling of witches casting black magic spells. Sorrow and hatred merged with the strange sounds of "Memo" and "Memito". And Mary knew the hatred was for her. The life jacket full of holes had been prepared for her. Guillermo was not to be shared. She was to have been taken by the sea and he set free from her to be theirs as he had been before.

"It is you who have killed him!" It was Lilia who screamed it first, her eyes shooting venom at Mary.

"Memo, why did you bring her here?" Elvira pleaded with the sky and the ocean. She approached Mary as if ready to jump on her and strangle her. Viviana stepped between them and restrained her. The scene was like those ancient rituals in which dead kings were mourned in a ceremony with human sacrifices.

"You!" Elvira stuck a finger in Mary's face. "You were his bad luck."

Viviana kept a tight grip on Elvira, but no expression could be seen on her face. In front of them, down on her knees, Leonore was trying to speak between wrenching sobs and tears. Suddenly Viviana called Guillermo's name out loud.

Suzy stepped forward, wringing her hands. "We were all so happy before."

The men had quickly and quietly formed a phalanx around Mary, as if protecting her from the writhing mass of women. Mary rested her head on Julio's shoulder. He kissed her lips and his face came away wet with her tears. Miguel comforted her too, kissing her and holding her tight to him, and Luciano pressed his fingers hard into her shoulders.

She felt protected from the women's violence by men's bodies melting into hers. Although she felt emptied with a senseless devastation, she was still filled with desire. She yearned for Guillermo. She longed to wrap her arms around him. But deep within her was the knowledge that all these men were hers, and many more besides, as many as she wanted to have. She knew that Guillermo had passed on to her his corrupting thirst for sex and for changing the object of desire. Falling in love with her was his misfortune. He had to die for it. But the restless drive for seduction remained alive. He had died in passing it on to her.

The day fell sharply. She rested on the bed in the niche carved into the cliff. It was she who was supposed to have died that very noon. Aware of the blood speeding into her arteries she felt its complicity with the rush of the waves, and she greedily inhaled the spermatic odor of the breeze. Her flesh sang with life, but not her silent soul. It was the cold soul of Guillermo that had taken up residence in her, a legacy she was forced to carry against her will. A conscious madness was growing within her, the full freight of her awakened consciousness. She was trapped in her monstrous sensuousness, left to herself, and she knew the endless searing pain of loneliness around the circle of desire that would be hers always. Would she ever be able to recover her self or her soul?

"Here, Marianna, don't worry."

She raised her wild eyes to see who had spoken. It was Miguel who had a new name for her. He held out a glass of wine for her to drink. She was weak, lying back, hardly moving. Servants had been called and were preparing a stretcher to carry her on their shoulders up to the house.

"I'll be waiting for you next year," murmured Luciano in her ear. "You will come back. You are one of us."

Sparrowulf

It was still before daybreak. The breeze wafted a salty sea mist into the well-lit room. Even the morning star shone brighter. With all his gear in place, Shrike paced about the apartment paying careful attention to each step in his morning routine. At one moment he dashed into his bedroom to get something out of his wardrobe, at the next stepped into the kitchen taking the boiling eggs for his breakfast off the stove. He scampered down the hallway or looked in a storage place to reclaim some other necessary item, which he then crammed into his already bursting knapsack. Finally, composed and calm, he concentrated on his gear, which took up a whole wall of his modest apartment.

Shrike seemed to have stopped breathing. He contemplated his countless fishing rods, while his mind weighed quickly the most real data of the trip. Humidity, the strength of the wind, the night's cold, the clouds—all were carefully taken into account, as well as the waves, which his ears could grasp despite the few hundred yards that separated him from the sea. What fishing gear should he take along? And where should he go? He was undecided. At last he settled on two sturdy reel fishing rods and the Northern pier. The waves were quite menacing and so he had given up the idea of perching on the rock off shore, a common haunt of solitary fishermen.

He stepped out of the house. None of his neighbors had awoken yet. He despised them for their capacity for sound sleeping and for their insensitivity vis-à-vis mighty nature. They live here without bothering about the great privilege of being in the neighborhood of the Black Sea.

The light breeze directed his thoughts toward the hours ahead. It was the beginning of June, and the water was still cold. The fish bit the bait capriciously, but that was the very point of excitement, to wait for them until they would yield and try. He had barely caught anything during the past few days. That was why he hoped that the new currents from the North, the presence of which he could sense, would make up for the dearth.

He walked the still-lit trails with the light, elastic strides of a wild beast out for its prey by night. As he advanced, the sea grew ever louder and soon its sound was reassuringly distinct. His fleshy face flattened, his black pupils grew larger, and even his cropped hair grew spiky like the fur of a beast ready to pounce. He descended the steep cliff with his wonted assurance, bypassing the stairs and instead taking a loamy trail well known to the soles of his feet. Shrike despised the cement stairs built for the ever-increasing crowds of tourists. These were the scourges of the summer season. In September, when they would all vanish, he felt relieved. It was only then that he could go back to fishing again during the daytime without being accosted by curious town clerks or by inquisitive and doting mothers with their brood in tow. He would have liked to talk to the children but they were not allowed out on the pier alone.

Anyway, Shrike hated the crowd in bathing suits, which grew hysterical at the mere sight of the beach. He did not like to sun himself, even on sultry days. Instead, he would take long swims, a distance out from the shore, which from that vantage point looked like a moistened and bloated slice of bread. And now that the hated summer season was upon him, he had changed his fishing schedule in order to secure absolute privacy. He had given up the company of fellow anglers who did not seem to mind the frivolous crowds.

When he reached the northern pier he put his sunburned face up to the rushing wind. The dawn was not yet pierced by the cries of seagulls, or by the human voices from the land that sometimes acquired a painful pitch.

The stars were melting away and the streak of the horizon became a purple thread, gradually growing into a pink ribbon and then a multicolored panorama pouring out over the sea until the waters were clad in a thin blinding skin as of apple blossom.

The cold droplets that assailed his body with the wind were like a blessing and he felt like he was on a high grassy plateau surrounded by mountainous ridges. Patches of morning clouds, with their suddenly acquired whiteness, wandered across the now azure sky. In moments such as these Shrike experienced a state of total relaxation and a dizzying openness toward the universe. The fresh air had cleansed his mind to the point of intoxication and given him a feeling of power and everlastingness.

Shrike was not bothered by time. It rushed by him and yet stood still. He was never bored and he felt that spending his time by the sea was a way of gaining a piece of its permanence uttered here at his feet. Many of his friends were in their eighties yet looked sixty or younger. They were spry pranksters vying with each other in gathering earthworms from the bottom of the sea. To their waist in the water, they scooped out shovel after shovel of sand, unmindful of the temperature of the water, its perils and even the threat of death. They distrusted doctors and did not look deep into the grave. When the day was over they drank wine together in the small taverns at the edge of the cliff and they never asked each other where they went off to sleep until they met again with the rise of the sun.

Contrary to early morning predictions the waves had calmed down. Shrike regretted that he had not followed his first impulse of going to his rocky outpost on the south. He looked over his tackle and put fresh worms on the hooks and unwound the nylon lines from the reels and waited. He stood there on the pier scrutinizing the sea and his fishing rods. He cast dozens of times without catching anything. Yet he remained unruffled. A couple of hours went by and the sun began to burn. When the first tourists came down to the beach he suddenly caught a large gray mullet. He decided to stay where he was.

Straight out from his place on the pier a new sand reef had formed during the past few years, a spot hard to get to from the shore, hence he looked at it with pleasure and proprietary interest. It was occupied only for a week or two out of the whole summer when a black and orange striped towel was hoisted there like a flag. A woman sat on the sand reading with studious intensity as if she were in a library and not relaxing by the sea. He saw her every year with the same feeling of vexation. People have no sense of place, he thought.

Usually she did not appear until July but this year she was early, the middle of June. He could not discern her features from the distance but registered that her figure was ordinary, banal even, in a yellow bathing suit, her age indifferent. Why did he even look in her direction? It irritated him that she should be so absorbed by a book instead of gazing at the sea. Then he suddenly realized that she was no longer reading but was returning his stare. When after catching two more mullets he felt her eyes still on him, he decided to leave.

He had no other choice but to nod in her direction as he walked past and to his astonishment she returned his salute.

For the next few days he avoided the northern pier and chose to fish from the rocky isle to the south. He hoisted his khaki flag painted with a circle, half white, half red. The fish were obliging to the point of boredom. On the fourth morning he went back to the northern pier. When the sun was high in the sky, she was there again with her black and orange towel but not reading this time. She was not in a bathing suit but in a sundress. Shrike was astonished to notice she was coming out on the pier in his direction. For three years she had had her nose in a book. She was breaking with her own habit. She was also breaching the rule of etiquette by disturbing the peace of a fisherman on the pier.

He expected the usual nonsensical show of interest that he was always trying to avoid. Any luck today? What are you catching? Don't you ever get bored? He had little appreciation of women except for their performance in bed after which he quickly got rid of them. He had managed to create a buffer zone around himself keeping the most eager ones at a safe distance. Hell, he muttered to himself, focusing on the horizon. He sensed a pain coming from somewhere out there. Thin, transparent clouds were sailing across the sky. The woman advanced on him, seeming oddly smaller as she came closer. Was it a mirage resulting from the balance between shoreline and horizon?

Shrike almost failed to hear her addressing him as he stood still concentrating on finding answers to his own inner questions. But he saw her lips move and realized something had been said. He mumbled a few words, which he then quickly swallowed. Then he glanced sideways at her from the corner of his eye. He waited, but heard nothing more. She remained silent and sat down a few feet from him and waited. What could he say? He pretended he had some repair to perform on his rod. He looked over the earthworms, searched about in the sand box, and made sure the pole float was at hand, the silvery weight, the Swedish hooks. He had almost forgotten she was there when he bumped against her as he stepped backwards for another launch of the line. She did not react but kept silent and watched.

"Aren't you sunbathing?" he heard to his amazement his own foolish remark. He wished he could have swallowed that too but went on examining her.

She wasn't beautiful, but not exactly plain either, neither very young nor old, her hair somewhere between gold and brown. He could not tell the color of her eyes. Nondescript would be his assessment, of no interest.

But there was something that caught his attention. Her bright red earrings, corals set in gold, and a plain thin gold chain round her neck. She wore no rings on her fingers, which was unusual, as most women seemed to enjoy wearing them.

"You have not been around for a few days. Up till now you have always been here fishing, while I have been sunbathing on the reef during my vacation. It has been at least a couple of years now." Shrike was astonished that she should have observed him and noticed his daily routine. He would normally have been annoyed but he noticed the timbre of her voice, melodious and low key yet with a self-assurance that few women have.

"And where will you be tomorrow?"

Shrike was caught off guard and had to come out with an answer.

"There's not much going on here, so I think I'll move on to the isle."

"To the isle?" she echoed. "What isle? Where is it?" She was obviously intrigued. Shrike pointed to the south to a small island out at sea. A friend would bring him there by boat and come to pick him up at the end of the day. He had his flag to signal when he was ready. The island was essentially a rock with only a small beach at the point on the far end barely visible from where they stood. He pointed it out to her. "Would you mind my coming, too?" And then she said: "For years I have been lying out there on the sand without being afraid because you were here on the pier. I cannot be there on my own. I can't tell you why."

Shrike was again perplexed. He was a free man and he did not do anything for anyone for years. He was a free bird and did only what pleased him, and, like a bird in the wild, he had always taken flight if something nearby seemed to be threatening him. He would never let himself be caught. But of course politeness prevented him from telling her all that. He could only mumble something noncommittal. She seemed reassured and walked away.

The following day he was out on the isle at dawn and enjoyed some good fishing. The sea spoiled him by sending him the large gray mullets that had grown too old and fat to put up a real fight for existence. When the sun got up high and scorching he heard someone call out to him from nearby.

"How are you doing?" Here she was swimming about leisurely a long distance from the shore without seeming breathless in the least. She floated effortlessly in the clear water in front of him, the coral earrings sparkling in the reflection from the bottom sand. He moved his lines aside and waited for some sort of revelation. After a few moments she cheerfully threw him a question. "Who are you?"

A simple question that deserved a simple answer: "A fisherman, I guess."

"A fisherman? That's a big one!" She burst out laughing while splashing water around with her hands. "I am a draughtsman by trade and can tell you with a fair amount of accuracy that by the way you move you are closer to my line."

"All right, I am an architect," Shrike acknowledged reluctantly.

"And so you practice drawing with your fishing rod," she went on brazenly, "or designing palaces under the sea?"

Shrike grew impatient. He took a deep breath, gazed into the distance and with deliberate control answered her that he did not like people, that he chose to be alone by the sea because that was what made him happy. And would she please not interfere with his lines. He chose to be polite but cold and brief, to bring distance between them and disarm her.

"What's your name?" she asked, unperturbed.

"Shrike," he retorted, "Shrike. What else would you like to know?" The Black Sea was not home to any fierce sharks, a fact that he regretted. Had she not been in the water already, he would have given her a push. He was taken by surprise when she flipped over and took strong swimming strokes back toward the shore. He thought for a moment he might call her back but could not think of a reason.

Day after day, Shrike continued to fish from the rocky isle even as the wind changed and it turned colder. He did not know what else to do. One morning he heard his name called from out on the water.

This time she was cold and exhausted and he felt pity for her and pulled her out of the icy water and tossed her his sweater. He gave her some vermouth and coffee and left her to rest. Her hair as it dried looked like a ripe wheat field, he noticed, and her eyes resembled the playful glittering of the sea. She was still shivering and Shrike had to apply his survival skills, necessary in his chosen pastime, as he might be called upon to help someone in need. She submitted to his harsh massage of her thin limbs that were clearly not suitable for long swims in cold water. He passed her a sandwich. Not a word came across her lips, which surprised Shrike and made him wonder about her.

She no longer seemed interested in annoying him with questions. In fact she seemed to want to escape but was obviously not about to go back into the frigid water. The Southerner had blown all night and Shrike knew there was no point in staying as all the fish had gone. He might have signaled to the shore for the boat to come, yet he did not. For the life of him he could not say why.

"What does Shrike mean?" He heard her saying behind him. "What on earth does Sh—sh'**Rike** stand for? What kind of name is that?"

Shrike was annoyed by the question. But not to answer might have been harder to explain. It might bring his whole manhood into question. "It's the name of a bird," he explained. "It is spelled s-h-r-i-k-e. It is a predatory bird, a sparrowhawk or a sparrows' wolf for short."

She burst out in peals of laughter that almost brought her down from her rocky shelf. This fit of mirth seemed natural enough to him. He would have laughed too, had he, for the first time, heard of a man like a wolf to the sparrows. He could not help but join in her laughter. It was as if he heard his own name for the first time.

Soon they were deep in conversation, exchanging opinions on what was their favorite season, what jam was most to their liking, how to best cook spinach, why was Sartre a great writer, which is more delicious: gray mullet or bluefish, what time did they like to get up in the morning, which kind of classical music makes one happier than grand opera, what was the fate of rock music, why did they both dislike the color brown, what did they think about ghosts and life after life, how great it would be to go to Tibet, how nasty white cats are, under what circumstances each had had a little puppy, how much they had been disappointed by their friends, and so forth, and so on. Meanwhile, the sea kept splashing them good-naturedly with its waves, and even the fish started to congregate waiting for their daily ration of worms.

Now Shrike saw the boat coming toward them. He had not even realized that the sun was on the point of setting. Rummaging through his pockets for a piece of string, he came across the sea pebble with a hole in it that he had found digging for worms a few days earlier in the port of Tomis. He handed it to her and overjoyed she passed her fine chain through it and put it around her neck. Shrike for whatever reason felt a tightening grip around his heart. He believed in the forces of the sea, her capricious acts in giving and taking away. If angered, she might take revenge bitterly. Maybe he was being superstitious but he made a fervent wish that the sea would not claim anything in exchange for that pebble, but if she did he promised himself he would be the one to pay the price. It was he who had found it.

They did not talk in the boat back and parted on the shore. That night a storm broke out. Wind and rain whipped up the waves driving a cold wet fog inland that kept Shrike away from his island for three days. On the fourth day when he finally reached the island again he realized that he had half expected her to show up despite the cold. He regretted that he did not know anything about her. Not where she came from, not even her name. He waited for her for the rest of the summer and late into the fall. In December he gave up but began dreaming about her for many nights in a row. After a week or so he heard her voice and laughter clearly and he thought his hand or a part of his body was touching her warm skin. Then, while fixing his frugal meals in the kitchen, he felt her presence in the room.

It was then he began to live with her. He knew when she got up in the morning, when she laughed, when she read or when she went for a walk. In the evening they would watch a movie together and sip cognac. Shrike felt a change within himself. He became less cynical and felt more generously disposed toward the world. He marveled at finding himself sentimental even. He kissed her goodnight.

Shrike told her how he had come to quit his position as an architect. He had graduated ten years ago, but it had been a mistake. His heart was not in it, it was unclear to him why. He was skilful enough. He came down with a disease that was never diagnosed but left him disabled and led him to an early retirement. Because of the disease he could now live permanently where he was happy, in the vicinity of the sea.

He told her about the laws of the sea, of fishing, and of life viewed through the exigencies of the sea. She listened to him but often interrupted him in a state of agitation and with remonstrations. It upset him and they would stop talking for hours on end, sometimes for a whole day. Shrike grew melancholy. Increasingly he felt that she was right. He took daily strolls down the piers, reliving their meetings and anticipating their future. After a particularly cold New Years Day, which he spent alone, he returned from his walk and suddenly felt an urge to take up drawing.

Fishing was for Shrike more than an average male passion. He looked upon his hunt for marine life as a way to learn patience and perseverance. The wait in itself made him strong, tenacious and desirous of his catch. Now it was a woman he sought, her image so strong that he became oblivious to everything else. He was keenly aware that the wait would be worth it. He did not need to rush it.

He resumed the abandoned project of an opera house, a structure where the music would filter through an aquatic world, through the color spectrum of the marine life. Solutions came to him in droves.

She was there applauding him and drawing by his side, displaying a lot of ingenuity. In April, when he went out fishing again, all the drawings were displayed, at her suggestion, around the walls of his apartment fixed with thumbtacks the way the students used to exhibit their year's work. Having looked at them for a while and feeling pleased with them he sent them to Negulescu, his former instructor. To his surprise he soon received a telephone call. His design stood a good chance to be accepted, not as an opera house, but as a cultural hall to be erected in a new health resort along the coast.

Shrike's sense of accomplishment was short-lived. His patience and mental equilibrium were sorely tried. He was tormented by the thought that she was a spirit and had never been anything else. Her image now haunted him to the point of exhaustion, yet he could not sleep. Drinking had no effect on him. On the first day in May the tourist showed up in search of the sun, which gave him renewed hope that he would one day find her on the reef reading her book as before. He alternated his fishing between the north pier and the island. He cleaned up the house. He bought a couple of tracksuits, for he intended to bring her on a fishing trip to the Danube Delta and at the same time he was determined that she should come and live with him. He could no longer endure the kind of life he had led so far. He was thus parting with the sea in order to come closer to people. She might have wanted that. Thinking she might be critical of him for neglecting his friends and relatives, he renewed contacts and visited people he had not seen for a long time. Yet he lived with his ruses and worried about consequences but there was no reaction from her or from the sea.

At the beginning of June, after a couple of days of fair weather during which Shrike caught fish on the south island, out of the blue there arose a sly, violent storm that caught everybody by surprise causing fishing boats, pleasure craft and even large ships to run aground. Land, sea and sky were all a leaden gray, indistinguishable and whipped by the elements. And violent. It turned cold and people huddled and dressed in sweaters and heavy shoes. For several days the sea howled, terrifying man and beast in Constantza and in the towns and villages along the coast. Then the sky cleared as if a sponge had wiped out the whole episode. The sun beat down again as if nothing had happened. The see too, forgetful, displayed her whole palette of radiant blues and soft hues and the tiny wavelets resumed their joyful play around the shores.

On the second day after the storm Shrike went back to the island. As he approached he was amazed to see his khaki flag still waving in the breeze. In the turmoil at the onset of the storm he had not had time to lower it. It had against all odds survived the ferocious winds. He carefully took out his gear placing it on the narrow cement landing strip, which was now overgrown with algae. He arranged his fishing rods in a row according to his ritual and with arms crossed he scrutinized the sea. There was a cold breath rising from the distance and an eerie light that filtered down to the rippled sandy bottom as far as his eyes could reach. He felt uneasy for no apparent reason. The hunter's mood deserted him and he felt himself being hunted. By whom? A haunting presence emerging from out there on the water closed in and hovered about the place where he stood.

He waited stock-still for several hours until the sun had risen in the sky and illuminated the sea in its minutest detail. Then, through the purplish water, Shrike spotted, more or less by instinct, something that kept lunging towards him. When the warm current from the north reached the shore, lapping against the strip of cement on which he stood, two eyes of a murderous crimson stared up at him from the shallows by his feet. In an instant he had a knife ready in his hand, ready to plunge it into whatever it was that the sea had brought him. But quickly he realized that the eyes did not belong to any creature of the sea but were the coral earrings piercing her soaked and swollen ear lobes.

After the initial jolt, a strange calm gripped him. He carefully secured the body, which trailed behind rich plaits of fair hair interspersed with seaweed. Her eyes looked wonderingly at him from the water. Of course, he thought, she had seen his flag fluttering and tried to reach the island in spite of the powerful waves. Maybe she had even reached it but was unable to get back to shore. Now the sea has laid her at his feet punishing him twice: for the pebble polished by the waves, which hung around her neck, but more importantly, because he had given up his watch by the sea.

It was the sea that was hunting him down. He could not pretend otherwise any more. His choices were simple. He could never go back to shore to be among people, and he could never again abandon her to their stares and speculations. He took off his tracksuit, t-shirt, sneakers, and socks. He left his fishing rods in place, fastened the knapsack with care, and placed his knife inside a plastic bag. He kept the watch on his wrist out of curiosity about how long he would be able to endure. Then he slid into the warm water of the northern current. She had been waiting for him and Shrike kissed her for the first time.

He stretched himself on his back beside her in the water embracing her with infinite tenderness. She finally had come; he had not been waiting for her in vain. With a piece of rope he tied her to his body with secure fishermen's knots and began swimming toward the open sea. He had to pull out of the seashore current and reach a spot far enough out to prevent the waves from pushing them back to the piers or to the beaches. They now belonged to the sea.

Shrike advanced, crossing all the barriers of warm or cold currents with great difficulty, whether they ran closer to the surface or deeper down. He left behind the ships' limit, far out in the open, cleaving the water with his strong arms, his beloved beside him. He was at ease now, happily joined with her whom he had awaited for so long. All he could think of was that they would lie together on the clean sand of the deep, alone and undisturbed.

Annoyed by the watch that kept recording the march of hours, he unclasped it and threw it away. He knew, however, that he had still a long stretch ahead of him. When a cramp assailed him he did not stop, but fiercely pierced the calf of his leg with a safety pin that hung from the chain around his neck. The euphoria of his progress grew when several schools of horse mackerel and gray mullet swirled around them with curiosity. He did not stop but kept on swimming forcefully. Soon the sun would be setting, signaling its own fatigue. Then the greatest diver that the sea had ever known emptied his lungs and plunged towards the depths pulling his woman with him. His heart tolled like a cathedral bell. Like a hungry bluefish he bit hungrily into the bait of the sea and his mouth filled with blood.

He was laughing at the wonderment of the sea. She had never hunted a bird like him, a sparrows' wolf. Shrike was overjoyed that he had managed to play a prank on her. He was giddy with happiness. The woman by his side was laughing too. He embraced her and laid her gently on the sandy bottom. He made fast to a rock as tight as he could by dint of a harpoon he had tied at his waist. Everything was settled now. It was warm. He took a deep breath and laid himself by her side content that his dream had come true.

On the Road to Formio

Helen had always been in love with Marcus Tullius Cicero, who unlike her had not been able to escape his executioners. Helen, whose writing bore a marked resemblance to his fluid rhetorical style, was lucky to be alive. The dictator of the country where she grew up and spent most of her life had been deposed and executed only hours before her own would-be executioners were about to kill her.

Shortly after the political turnaround she was awarded a Fulbright fellowship which she accepted without hesitation. Leaving behind both a deteriorating love relationship and the land of her birth, she went to teach Roman civilization at the University of Minnesota. In Minneapolis she met and soon married Hamilton Price, a successful lawyer who had a previous marriage behind him.

It was not Helen's style to indulge her husband's love for her. Even before they were married she had been outspoken and told him that his life ran in hopelessly narrow channels.

Hamilton Price had of course never noticed this but he accepted Helen's pronouncement and even liked her all the more for it. She was the promise of a new life, challenging and full of possibilities.

Helen also kept telling him about a mystery she was eager to investigate but never had the opportunity, for Marcus Tullius Cicero was still part of her life.

Therefore it came as no surprise to Hamilton when Helen one day disclosed her plans to go to Italy on her own in the hope of solving the enigma of Cicero's death.

Hamilton had no objection. Time apart might be a good thing. He would make some improvements to the apartment and work quietly on his cases. Gaiety sparked the relief to be on his own.

They had a lovely place on Willow Street overlooking Loring Park with its peaceful little lake. Helen sometimes liked to spend the evening on the terrace counting the stars and listening to the splash of water in the fountain below, an unusual piece of garden sculpture shaped like a giant dandelion.

Increasingly, since the time of her emigration and marriage, she had found herself enjoying nature, more than reading or going to exhibits and concerts. Less and less she needed to be entertained. It was perhaps a sign of intellectual maturity. It also seemed to her that her mind had reached a level of growth where she was ready to express her own views on life, art and the universe.

She liked to walk alone over the Stone Arch Bridge and gaze at St. Anthony's Falls, but most of all she liked Boom Island Park. It reminded her of Tulcea, the city of her childhood in Romania.

The Mississippi River here looked like the Danube preparing for the ultimate adventure at the delta by the Black Sea. She knew she was viewing the two great rivers from opposite ends, one near its source, the other ready to surrender at last its great burden; one in the middle of a huge continent hundreds of miles from any sea, the other in the shadow of the southern sea yet sharing with the Mississippi of the north light and flatlands and some deeper sense of solitary existence.

Helen could not tell if what she felt was real or only a resurgence of old emotions. She had always thought of the Danube delta as a fertile place where European dreams and follies found peace at last. Her homeland river, she now clearly saw, was tired and cold. This was also true of her memories related to it.

And yet she was haunted by the resemblances between there and here. The sand and the stones by the riverbank looked the same at Tulcea. The water even tasted the same. Downtown on Nicollet Mall she walked on familiar reddish granite.

The trees and the flowers were not any different. The sky and the light was the way she remembered from home. When she told Hamilton about these sensations he remarked that people always see, wherever they go, the place where they spent their formative years.

"A Parisian will tell you that it is the Seine he sees. In fact, I know a Frenchman who feels strongly that Minneapolis looks like Orléans."

Uncompromising, she will see what she sees. Maybe it was too much to ask that Hamilton should understand that each day as she walked in this American city she always thought of her Tulcea, and of her family: where they had spent their lives, loved and suffered long ago.

Helen used the few days before her departure to build an even more immaculate image of Cicero than the one she had nurtured in her soul for twenty years. She welcomed this mental and physical space exempting her from the ordinary rhythms and routines of her life.

Hamilton was more concerned with what he saw as the flirtatious goings-on in Helen's classroom than with her seemingly harmless obsession with Cicero, which meant nothing to him.

Moreover, Hamilton felt she still suffered under some form of "post-dictatorship" stress, and he viewed her trip to Italy as a chance for her to heal herself. His attention was also diverted from Helen's "Roman fever" by a more practical matter: if she was to be tenured, a book on Cicero, or on whatever other Roman topic might now take her fancy, had become an absolute must.

The night before leaving, Helen had a dream while Hamilton held her in his arms. She felt herself swept up on a rapidly rising flood. Her home, she knew with certainty in her dream, was carried away in the deluge. The torrent hurled her over a waterfall so huge it was as if an ocean had emptied into a lake. The huge body of water drove deep into an enormous crater swirling with giant whirlpools. Waves rebounded violently from a massive uprush, churning a turbulent watery chaos of immeasurable force. Above, livid black clouds appeared lit from within by continuous bolts of lightning. Helen in her dream was thinking how exciting Noah's flood must have been. While slowly coming out of her sleep she wondered if this was the glorious Mediterranean pouring into the languid Black Sea?

As she packed, Helen was trying to find a key to her dream. At one moment she saw Hamilton as representing the stability in life, preserving the traditions so necessary to daily existence, while she, the great adventurer, was traveling abroad in search of new experiences. She was the Mediterranean and he the poor Black Sea.

She did not consider a third personage that morning: the one who leaves home and transforms the dislocation and discoveries into art. As it turned out, she would assume that role.

Helen had already discovered that some of her ideas and acts had preceded her; her diaries were full of examples. She was repeating herself, reliving a life, and she did not know why. Could it be that what we wish for today is a premonition of what will actually take place in the future? Or is it perhaps an expression of what we have already done on another level of our personal history?

It could be an effect of writing also. Words becoming reality. Where did those words come from? Balancing between neoplatonism and realism.

It was a bright December afternoon as Helen's rented car sped through the canopy of pines on Via Appia.

Along the road ancient olive groves covered the hilly ridges on her left. The cold blue sky hinted of the presence off to her right of the Tyrrhenian Sea, as yet invisible. The wind shaped all the pines bending from right to the left, as if they were ballet dancers on a stage sixty miles long.

It was her first trip to Italy, and only her second to a foreign land. Before the *coup d'état* in her old country, she had never been allowed to cross its borders.

Now, after decades of frustration and struggle, Helen felt she was at last approaching the reality of what had been slowly but surely forming in her mind since the completion of her last book: the revelation of what Cicero had experienced while facing his killers in his own villa at Formio, near Gaeta. Only the atmosphere remained to be supplied and she would look for it here in Italy. The book was to be something between essay and fiction. Marguerite Yourcenar's *Memoirs of Hadrian* played on her mind.

Cicero had lost the battle, and with it the last chance of ever reaching Brutus in Greece.

Marc Antony decreed his death.

Octavian Augustus, his friend, did not protect him.

Helen remembered how appalled she had been when she first read the letter in which Octavian betrayed Cicero.

Cicero tried to flee, but a storm and unfavorable winds forced his ship back to Italy.

Weary, resigned, he went to his villa and waited for the killers.

They severed his head and hands on December 7 in the year 43 BC. On Marc Antony's order these were displayed on the speakers' rostrum in Rome.

Cicero had been sixty-three years old. The Republic, which he had always upheld and defended, was overthrown.

Helen saw again his tired, unshaven face, and his white hair filled with sand. She saw his eyes as he leaned forward, looking at the soldiers in a pensive mood. She felt so close to him!

One by one, the centuries separating them were swallowed by the speed of the car.

And here he was with her, as he had often been. Even when she made love with Hamilton. It had been Cicero that gave her the pleasure she craved, drawing words of love from her in his own language.

Hamilton's Latin went no further than the legal terms known to lawyers. She could not bear his pronunciation of Latin words as if they were Midwestern American English. But she loved his blue eyes and his quiet ways. If she were fair to herself she would say she had married Hamilton for his likeness in her mind to Cicero.

Now, the old language of Latium seemed natural in the car speeding down Via Appia.

Cicero spoke of how much his career had been the result of cold calculation, and of the moments when the exact opposite had been true. He was amused by her naïve involvement in the plot against the dictator. Their experiences were different. Nobody could say that he had been either stupid or innocent. He had been caught only by the sea and the wind. Had the envious gods been against him? Obviously Zeus had disliked his challenges, but he thought Pallas Athena would have seen him through.

But Helen, Cicero said, had been saved, even though Venus apparently disliked her.

There was the dialogue she should record here about his life, fragments of history. Authentically proving that Cicero had been at war with the gods.

"Why is Venus my enemy?" Helen waited for him to tell her. Cicero laughed.

"Because your beauty is matched by your intelligence." His voice kindled a glow deep within her. Such modesty! She could see why they were alike.

Cicero asked her to tell the story of her near execution. And she started by confessing that it was from him that she had learned the greatest lesson of her life, the dignity of dying.

"Oh, Cicero! Oh, Cicero!"

Helen's admiration collapsed on him. He bore it as it came and came.

But it became too much. Cicero dismissed this with a wave of his hand. It made no sense to talk about "learning to die," he said.

"Wise people learn to live long and to enjoy life." Not that it made any difference to him now, but he was thinking of her.

The powerful silver-green Porsche leapt through space, telescoping cities and villages in its rear-view mirror.

Driving out of Rome had been difficult. Helen had discovered that Via Salaria, now as in Cicero's time, mocked the traveler's efforts to go south. But after several times finding herself unaccountably heading back into the city, she had at last cheated the gods. She had celebrated her triumph with a late lunch at Albano Laziale. Now, with Velletri far behind, she was speeding south on the straight road along the eternal eastern foothills adorned by olive groves.

At last she saw the turn in the road ahead that she knew would open up to the sea. The dazzling afternoon was gently taking on the shadows of evening. She took the surging, dangerous curve at full speed.

A series of twisting tunnels, deeply excavated into wild rocks, flashed extravagant vistas of the sea, previews of the breathtaking expanse that suddenly opened up before her eyes as a gift from the gods. Silky smooth waves moved over the surface of the water and gathered infinite hues in the changing light. The setting sun was leaving a pink luminous strip where sky and sea met. Aligned in perfect order, white clouds made their way across the evening blue sky.

Hamilton had remarked many times that speed intoxicated Helen. With that first vision of the sea she actually thought she might meet her end. It was her past that kept her going through life. Her face had assumed the rigidity of the Roman statues she had always worshipped.

"Slow down," Cicero said.

Helen laughed. "Are you afraid of death?"

He had the answer to her sarcastic remark. *"In istam dico vitam mortalem, aut mortalem vitalem nescio."* We live a deadly life, or else a living death. *"Dementiam nescientem diligere homines humaniter."* It is madness to love people only as perishable. His voice was serious, portentous. "If you don't believe you are eternal, your life is useless."

Still accelerating, Helen was obviously tired. She hated metamorphosis. She knew that some people believe that the human is the last and the highest incarnation. If a person accomplishes all the duties of a human lifetime, the soul goes to heaven. There will be no further earthly life. She hoped that would be true in her case.

Immortality, Cicero said, did not mean to fall out of time. Nor was it a burden one is doomed to carry through time.

Cicero, she suddenly realized, was telling her that her attitude ran counter to intellectual and spiritual evolution.

"Augustine!"

She took one serpentine curve after another as she grappled with Cicero's impossible use of the African bishop's ideas and sentences.

Aurelius Augustinus.

She shook it off, explaining to herself it was a synaptic jump. But the strange sensation lingered. Unable to take her eyes off the tortuous road, she thought that Cicero's place beside her had been taken over by the much sterner and more demanding man from a very different time and place. She was relieved when she felt Cicero's presence again. And she left her mind to linger a while on his books questioning the relationship between gods, human beings, and destiny: *De natura deorum, De divinatione,* and *De fato.*

The needle on the dashboard crept past one hundred and forty kilometers per hour. Would anybody care if she died? She was merely a name to be cited by some eccentric scholar who cared to write about events that had happened thousands of years before.

She glanced over a cliff to the sea far below. Cicero was saying something about the famous *spelonche,* the caves on the beach near Gaeta.

Life and death, present and past, were all one. She sniffed the sea air. She had no real man in her life; Hamilton was a fiction of a husband. No deep communion between their souls ever happened. All true relationships in her life had been fulfilled through phone calls and letters, and through passages in books.

Cicero's voice penetrated the fog of her depression. She slowed down. He was trying to urge her back to the story of her near execution.

"A girl loved by the gods but unable to deal with her life."

This struck her forcibly. He was a lucky man. It is not hard to die; it is only hard, once you have escaped death, to try and to do something different with your life. How did he think his life would have turned out if he had in fact reached Greece? What would he have done had he lived in her time?

She had been born into a wealthy family. Many of her uncles had been jailed when the Russians took over her country in 1944. Both her grandfathers had died in misery stripped of their businesses and estates. Her uncles narrowly escaped execution only to die after many years in jail. And she had spent the best years of her life trying to convey, through her writings about the Roman republic and civilization, that we do not have to obey our oppressors or ever forget their crimes. She had herself never despaired of freedom.

"It was a December afternoon." Helen began to speak in lucid and elegant Latin, befitting the dignity of her story.

She had learned to control her voice, breathing, gestures and diction. She knew that natural talent is the greatest asset to oratory, and she was glad she had this particular gift. She wanted Cicero's admiration.

"The streets were empty as always. In front of my house the secret police car stood there as on any other day. The black car wheels sank little by little deeper into the ground, and I fully hoped one day to find a big hole in the road in place of that car. I had been under surveillance for more than two years, and had grown accustomed to it.

My contact with friends, calls, letters, my walks in the park or in the streets—all were carefully reported to the bosses of my stalkers. In time their watching my every step became part of my life.

"I was banned from teaching. My books were removed from the bookstores and libraries, and my name could no longer appear in print. Yet from another point of view I was considered fortunate. Many friends were in jail or deported. One of them disappeared; it was rumored that he had killed himself after being tortured in prison. My freedom, if you can call it that, was a privilege due to the fact that I had been invited by an American university to teach. My case required special handling.

"Then one particular afternoon—I remember a particular fragrance of winter—a group of men entered my apartment and ordered me to follow them. I said nothing; just tried to grab a few things with me in a bag. 'You won't need anything,' one of them said. They pushed me towards the black car, which was waiting with opened doors. We left Bucharest and headed south in silence. In the back of the car, squeezed between two officers, I tried to grasp what was going on. The driver took his orders from the man sitting next to him. Soon it became clear that we were headed for the southern border. I began to understand that I was to be caught 'trying to leave the country' and to be killed outright. Such a scenario, although shocking, would have been plausible to anybody, even to my closest friends.

"It was not yet dark when we arrived at a village close to the Danube. All four men escorted me into a nondescript house. In a small room I was told to sit on a chair. The driver, who did not look particularly brutal, cursed loudly because he was hungry. His complexion told me that he was of Gypsy ancestry. The leader of the group silenced him and left the room.

"Another man, with a narrow face, the one who had sat on my right in the car, lit a cigarette. He was thin and long-legged, with a large head, plenty of hair and a brown face. He had combed back his oily black hair, like the young Elvis. He was good-looking, and he knew it. I noticed that he kept his hand to his back, pushing it as if it hurt him there. He wore a kind of permanent sneer. I wondered if he was in pain. For a minute he stared at me as if he wanted to tell me something. Then, turning abruptly, he too left the room.

"After another minute the other two also left. I was afraid they were planning to rape me before they killed me. I looked around and saw a radio. I turned it on and played with the tuning knob till a loud, clear voice announced that Ceausescu had fled his palace, and that his regime was over. The whole country was free, the voice went on, and the revolutionaries were intent on having the dictator tried for his crimes.

"The slender officer entered the room and ordered us to leave. Again they forced me into the car, which now took the road back towards the capital. The good-looking one eased himself along the seat until he was firmly squeezed up against my thigh and leg.

"The car stopped in the middle of nowhere, with cornfields both right and left. Everything was cold and still. This was to be the last minute of my life. I was told to take a few steps toward the field. I stepped through rain puddles. My shoes were instantly wet through. I went on, climbing a small stony ridge, expecting bullets in my back. I felt almost curious about how it would feel.

"But no shots came. The sound of the car's engine behind me changed, and I turned my head and watched it drive away. I was numb, but as soon as I was sure they had gone I crept back over the stones and through the wet field to the road. I found a village, and at the post office I told some lie about an accident. I was put through to my friends in Bucharest. I don't know how long it took them to get to me. Other friends were in my apartment, already mourning my death. It turned out the whole episode had taken only a few hours."

"And here we are." Helen stopped the car. "It seems that myths are events of one population told by another population. I forget the name of the person who wrote this sentence."

She spoke with the gloomy relish of one who had lived long enough to see history prove her right. A road sign pointed to Ter-racina, which they had already passed.

"Let's go on to Gaeta," said Cicero, his voice heavy with fondness. "It is already night."

A minute passed before Helen started the car.

She felt like hiding her face under her long curly brown hair. Any-one watching her would have noted the ivory glow of her skin over the graceful lines of her jaw and neck, the angular bone structure, the straight nose. Her sensual lips and the dark night of her eyes (they were her grandmother's) lent her a delicate mix of beauty and power. She was dressed in jeans, a red sweater, and sneakers. A black duck-down jacket lay on the back seat. Italy was cold, its December sun was not the sun she had read about in books. The day was rapidly coming to an end.

The road dropped precipitously in serpentine curves until it bot-tomed out in a narrow valley. She took a sharp turn into Gaeta. She proceeded slowly along a commercial street and stopped at the first gateway to the seashore.

She walked onto the beach and could feel the sun's warmth radiat-ing from the sand. She scooped up a handful and put it in her pocket, afraid that in the morning she might discover all this had been a dream. The streetlights did not reach as far as the sea. To her left, on top of a lonely outpost at the end of the crescent bay, a light-house pierced the darkness with its measured sweeps of light.

Back in the car, she retraced her way to an Irish pub she had noticed driving down to the shore. Inside, ghostly music was playing to an empty saloon. Helen ordered a Campari and a cappuccino, and wondered what she was looking for. She craved the coffee, but clearly she needed to find something to eat, and a room.

Following the Irish barman's directions, she drove in the gathering dusk down toward Gaeta's promenade.

The streets were quiet. Some of the shops and seafood stores were still open, but largely empty. The promenade itself was lit but deserted. Out at sea, she could see points of light, ships at anchor waiting for permission to enter the harbor.

In Gaeta's historic center, she saw at last some street vendors of strange *frutti di mare*, and also the *carabinieri* at the entrance of the customs and patrol borders building. This was not the place she had imagined. A huge potted plant with carnivorous-looking leaves attracted her attention, and she stopped the car and took one of its leaves. The scent was strong but unfamiliar. She continued to drive back and forth through a maze of streets.

Finally she saw two human beings on a wooden jetty that faded into the night toward the sea. She could not make out what they were doing. She stopped the car and got out.

There was an odd sensation on the shore of a cold wind mixed with a warm breeze. She zipped up the black jacket, and even put on the gloves that Hamilton had insisted she take with her. She also put on the fancy little green hat he had bought her from a flea market.

Two women in long fur coats were intently scanning the sea in the now almost complete darkness. They paid no attention to the pleasant-looking Corso or to the shops behind them, nor to the gentle hill rising from the cliff with Castello Agioglino on top, a medieval structure lit up like a Christmas tree. But they must have heard her, as both of them turned when Helen approached the jetty. They looked friendly but oddly out of place, she thought. One was probably in her late fifties, while the other appeared to be in her early forties, like Helen herself. They had long dark hair and Helen saw they wore silk dresses under their open fur coats. They also wore elegant summer sandals, which struck Helen as odd in this cold weather.

"You are a tourist from America," said the younger one, in perfect English. It was, of course, about Helen's presence. The way she walked. Exulting independence. And it was also about the way she was dressed. Taking in Helen's sneakers, jeans, and black duck-down jacket, both of them laughed in a friendly way. Of course no Italian woman of Helen's age would walk about dressed like that, in the anti-feminine American style.

Helen did not feel embarrassed. Elegance separated their worlds. In her years in America she had overlooked that. Merely by sacrificing elegance for comfort she had branded herself as an American.

They introduced themselves and the conversation was easy and natural. Helen asked the name of the leaf she was holding. It was *Gerano malvone*, a rare plant that bore beautiful flowers in the spring.

If she wanted to see the flowers, she should visit the nearby *Giardini di Nimfe*. Other visits were recommended: *Grotta di Tiberio* near Terracina; Cicero's grave near Formio—*Tomba di Cicerone*—looking out onto *il Golfo di Gaeta*; *Grotta di Magna Circe*, the famous witch from the Odyssey; *Mura Ciclopica* and *Faro di Torre Cervica*. But they told her the ruins should be visited at night. Only then, under the floodlights, could they truly convey the history and mortality which they represented.

Octavia, the younger woman, was from Canada; Cornelia was French. They were both married to Italian men. They professed being happy with their lives, enjoying the comfort and beauty of the place. They had no desire to return to either boring France or cold Canada. Octavia was an interior decorator; Cornelia was a specialist in recreating social events from the era of Caesar Augustus, even to the food and recipes enjoyed by aristocrats of the Roman Empire.

Cornelia was of course very impressed by Helen's field of expertise. They exchanged a few sentences in Latin, as if it was a secret jargon for the initiated, then continued in French and English.

Octavia and Cornelia had been gossiping on the dock, waiting for their husbands who were amusing themselves casting off out on the sea beyond the halo of the streets' lights. The two women, whose real names were Suzy and Belle, understood right away why Helen was in Gaeta and what she was looking for.

"We have a villa for you," Octavia said. "The rent is low, less than for a hotel room. *Professoressa*, you deserve some joy and beauty in Italy."

She called out a few words to the two invisible men, and then asked Cornelia to phone the man with the keys of the house from her cell phone.

A short while later Helen was pulling up in front of a villa surrounded by fields of violet ice plants illuminated by spotlights. Just steps away from the white sand beach, the feathered branches of a cypress tree cast a soft shadow.

She was so bewildered that she stopped the car in the middle of the driveway. The villa was connected to the wild fields by a narrow boardwalk, positioned atop a rocky ledge and surrounded by a thick spruce forest. Helen's first view of the place was bathed in the light of the full moon, just out from behind a cloud. The only sound was the tide washing in and out over the rocks.

In the living room, a gas fire took the chill out of the December night and made the whole house inviting. The small reception room with marble floors and a comfortable drawing room was furnished with a sophisticated look. Going up the stairs Helen had the illusion she was coming up out of the sea. Murals on both sides of the steps displayed all kinds of creatures from the sea, swimming upwards from rocks on a sandy bottom towards the surface.

Cornelia and Octavia showed her the bedrooms named *il mare, il vento, il cielo*, and *il sole*. Helen chose *il sole* where the bed, tucked into an alcove and dressed with a white comforter and silky pillows, had windows at its head and side. Small cotton rugs were thrown over the tile floor, matching the robin's-egg blue walls which were covered with scenes from Greek mythology. Zeus and Leda made love under a cypress tree whose branches turned the corner of the wall. In another scene Zeus caressed Europa.

The villa, Octavia and Cornelia told her, was owned by a wealthy man deeply involved in Italian business and political life, Signor Cicerone Tiramollini, a friend of their husbands. But this was not Tiramollini's residence, which lay further down the road toward Formio, but a smaller villa looked after by a boat dealer and the person in charge of the historical site at Formio, where lay the great Cicero's tomb.

The two women were now conversing so fast that Helen began to feel uneasy about this place where she so abruptly found herself.

Uninterrupted by Cornelia's endless chatter, Octavia gently guided Helen back downstairs to the kitchen. She opened a bottle of red wine, filled three glasses, said cheers, and swallowed hers so quickly that Helen felt obliged to do the same. Cornelia produced a variety of cheeses and fruits and, eating greedily, talked to her friend ignoring Helen. Listening to her Helen had an uncanny feeling that they spoke in a dialect stemming from a time before Cicero and the Empire of Augustus, a dialect never recorded in the books she had come across.

Obviously these women saw in their guest an occasion for some extra excitement in their lives. Mystified and drugged by wine and sleepiness though she was, Helen could still tell that their exercise in hospitality was a way of dealing with boredom.

She stopped being the grateful lost tourist. She just wanted to sleep.

Octavia handed her a set of keys to the house, telling her that both of them would come at nine sharp the next morning to give her a tour of Gaeta.

In her room suffused by warmth from a fire and with the sliding door facing the sea drawn just enough for her to hear the sound of the waves, Helen fell asleep.

The sunrise and the garden greeted her as she woke up. Even in that December climate flowers were everywhere. Geraniums glowed and birds sang for her, gradually drowning out the crickets. She stepped out on the terrace and could see the racing flags of a regatta. To her left was the lighthouse she had noticed the night before, on the same forested hill. Pigeons and seagulls patrolled the blue winter sky.

In the living room she turned on her laptop and typed a few sentences about the villa and her encounter with the ladies of Gaeta.

Fifth of December 1998. Just about the two thousand and fortieth anniversary of Cicero's death on the Seventh of December. She was very close now to his tomb.

She felt ready to go to Formio by herself, without telling her new friends. But like a bad dream they both appeared, resuming their stormy dialogue. They were wearing fur coats of different colors, sandals of course, and even silk scarves and silk gloves.

The moment she saw Helen, Octavia blurted: "We have great news!" Had she guessed that Helen was planning to go alone to Formio?

She opened her orange fur coat, revealing a close-fitting camisole and skirt outfit matching the strap silver sandals. Her dark and wildly curly hair adorned her pale face.

"And you are invited!" Cornelia added. Vivid Cornelia, reminiscent of a Pompeian painting.

"Today is the birthday of your generous host, Signor Cicerone Tiramollini. He knows all about you and dearly wants to have a chat with you about his namesake, his life's obsession, too. So we have a lot to do to get ready."

Again Helen noticed that Octavia and Cornelia sometimes lapsed into a dialect, closer to Latin than to Italian. Cornelia was moving around as if trying to find something she had lost.

"Tonight we are having a party!" Cornelia unbuttoned her fur coat, which was green, not to be outdone by her friend.

The brightly colored fur looked perfectly natural on these two women. Helen examined Cornelia's corset-style purple dress and the diamond necklace she wore, in the shape of a butterfly, and wondered absently about their apparent wealth. They were nestling shoulder to shoulder.

Helen disliked parties, especially when she did not know the guests. She was also exhausted from jet lag and her long drive. She wished to be left alone to focus on the project for which she had come. She tried to make them understand. But what registered with the two women was that Helen was unprepared for a party.

"You do have a credit card on you, don't you?" Cornelia's question betrayed a slight undercurrent of sarcasm.

Helen nodded. This was becoming too much. She should not have accepted the offer of these strange ladies. She had come to Italy to be on her own, free even from her husband. Her impulse was to leave the villa right away and go to a hotel.

"First, you need a fur coat. You must have one. You cannot go to the party in your jacket. Believe me, Helen, this will be the party of your life."

They burst into chattering. Then followed an extended charade in which a plan to lend Helen a fur coat had to be abandoned because Helen was quite a bit taller than either of them. She would have to buy one.

"Even if you already have one at home," Octavia concluded. She was measuring Helen for size with a chilling gaze, insensitive to the fact that she might be intruding or causing discomfort.

"American fur coats are not in good taste. And you'll have to buy an evening gown as well. I am sure you haven't brought one with you, have you? And sandals, of course. Well, I shall lend you one of my evening purses, one of my pearl necklaces and some earrings. I hope my husband will not notice. We must go to have our hair and nails done, as well as the makeup. The appointments have already been made, and there is not much time left."

As Cornelia hurried away, Octavia swept Helen off to get dressed. Helen did not have a chance to object or to tell them of her plans.

But as she was putting on her winter jacket, it struck her that perhaps this really was a significant occasion.

She suddenly decided to let herself drift with the current. Working against such tides, she thought, might be the root of her troubles. Not only did she often seem to disobey her instincts, but she actually seemed bent on diverting them. Maybe in all its absurdity this was the moment of her destiny.

She had come to Gaeta to discover something new, and to explore the mystery of which she had always dreamt. Cicero's grave at Formio would still be there tomorrow, and the day after. She would have time to see it. But these women and the auspicious party would soon be gone. She could not have foreseen how this day would change her life so completely.

Helen joined in with the excitement for the evening, buying a white dress with a high bodice up to her neck and bare back exposing her shoulders. She felt a glow in her face when she saw it was flattering to her natural beauty.

In a black fur coat she had just bought from a famous furrier at an excellent price, she had taken her new friends to Gaeta's most expensive restaurant for a lunch matching their moods. Octavia's pearl necklace and earrings, and the makeup, enhanced Helen's lovely lines, and her long brown hair exquisitely framed her face and swan-like neck.

"You look like Fausta, Cicero's lover," Octavia said.

"Which Cicero are you referring to?"

"Oh, the great Cicero."

"He had no mistresses." Helen spoke with authority. "He had two wives. He divorced Terentia because she was unfaithful to him. She had cheated on him with Clodius. I believe Terentia was plotting against him. The second wife was a rich virgin whom he eventually abandoned—because, I think, of her profoundly idiotic innocence."

But Cornelia laughed at her. Her mouth contorted: "You don't master your subject very well! It takes quite a while to know such a complicated man. About two thousand years, or more!"

"How would you know?" Helen retorted, snatching Cornelia's arm. They were in Cornelia's car. The two women were going to meet their husbands at the party.

"Certain things remained unwritten," Octavia fired back. "Things that have been transmitted by word of mouth down the generations. Missing or hiding. Around here we know more about his last years. Made very happy by his secret lover, a beautiful lady named Fausta. She died the day after he did at the hands of those who had killed him. Because she knew as much as he did, they were afraid she might disrupt Octavian's and Antony's plans."

After a second she added: "The only portrait we have of Fausta is preserved in Gaeta in secrecy. Tonight you will see it, in our host's villa. He bought it for a great deal of money."

Cicerone Tiramollini's residence was larger and more opulent than Helen could ever have imagined. A high-ceilinged foyer with fantastic flower arrangements led to a large open living room with an imperial stairway leading to a gallery which ran along the sides. To the right of the foyer an octagonal sunroom housed potted trees. The ten-bedroom house combined a feeling of old Roman tradition with contemporary airiness. Some of the upstairs rooms recalled the Renaissance style of the Palazzo Vecchio of the Medici in Florence; some were closer to colorful Pompeian opulence or to Napoleonic grandeur. Rich colors were set off by a background of sober tan and white. Despite the size and opulence the house offered a sense of comfort and intimacy.

The party was being held in a large room with recessed paneling, wide cypress-plank floors, and very tall doors, the lighting soft and inviting. Three sets of French doors connected the living room with a brick patio, a back garden, and a billiard room.

Octavia, displaying an ostentatious dragonfly etched with body paint and rhinestones on her bare back, showed Helen around as if the place was her own. She had been hired to decorate many of the rooms.

The inescapable Cornelia, in a little black cocktail dress, came with them. As they entered Cicerone Tiramollini's own sanctum, Cornelia pointed out the antique chairs flanking the fireplace. Aubusson rugs hung on the walls, and a seventeenth century French painted leather screen stood between two stone arched doorways. But the most striking features were a grand piano, several paintings by Impressionist masters, and a view of the sea.

An entire wall with baroque cabinets displayed many editions of Cicero's writings by various publishers from different centuries, as well as commentaries and biographies. Helen blushed slightly discovering her own work. A marble bust of her lifelong companion looked down at her with that provocative look of his. What was she up to?

Octavia and Cornelia introduced Helen to Signor Anthony Coccini, the mayor of Gaeta, and to their husbands, owners of big factories in the North, and to many other people besides.

Everyone exuded an aura of elegance and opulence Helen had never before experienced. She was presented as the American *professoressa*, author of books on Cicero, in Gaeta incognito to carry out research for yet another book on her favorite topic.

Finally, she was welcomed by Signor Cicerone Tiramollini himself, who kissed her fingers in the gracious European manner.

He looked younger than his sixty-three years; around fifty, Helen figured. She saw prominent cheekbones, a strong lower jaw and chin, and a dominant forehead with some gray hair at the temples. His winning look was a product not only of his features, but also of years of running political races and battles.

He spoke readily, and in a few moments she had pieced together, from what he said and from gossip she had heard during the day, a picture of the main features of his life. With charm and a natural genius for politics he had gained influence and power in big business and political circles.

He was married and divorced and with a number of discreet love affairs and minor scandals behind him which had in no way harmed his reputation. The great number of people who had come from Rome and from all over Europe to be present at his sixty-third birthday celebration bore this out.

He liked Helen's over-the-shoulder look, which reminded him, he told her, of the portrait of the great Cicero's Fausta in his secret vault.

People around them engaged in shallow conversations, hungry for connections and curious about the others. Dry and thirsty.

Helen's ready-to-become festive mood was suddenly shocked into alertness by a face in the crowd. The narrow-faced officer who had sat on her right in the car on the day she was supposed to be killed was there lighting a cigarette by the doors opening onto the back garden.

There was no mistaking the thin, long-legged man with his large head of black hair and his brown face, though he no longer looked like young Elvis. But he was still good-looking, and still aware of it.

Even as she watched, astonished and afraid, his fist crept behind his back in that characteristic gesture, as if something hurt him there. To judge from his elegance he had apparently been successful. Cicerone Tiramollini followed the eyes of his companion to see what had transformed her features.

"Signor Doncea is one of my business partners from Eastern Europe," he explained and went on to describe Doncea's success; he had originated some of the most stupendous commercial contracts of Tiramollini's career.

The fall of communism had brought a lot of business opportunities to Eastern Europe. Although some French partners had warned him that Doncea was a former high-ranking member of the secret police, Tiramollini did not care about this kind of gossip as long as

Doncea was a reliable businessman. Over the years he had found neither proof nor reason to complain.

As Helen assimilated her shock, trying to put it aside for the moment, and as smoothly as she could returned her attention to Cicerone Tiramollini, she became aware of his admiration for her.

And to her amazement, despite all the tremors that had shaken the very foundations of her security and self-control in the course of the past twenty-four hours, she found herself responding to the powerful attraction of this man, this new Cicero. She saw him smile as he chose to ignore her wedding ring.

"Would you like to see her portrait?" Cicerone asked.

"I have heard about it. My book would be incomplete without including some information about it." She tried to be academic and professional, but her laughter was a little too loud.

"You laugh like a little girl, with all your four eyes! I mean your eyes and your hands."

On their way to his private office, Cicerone suddenly asked: "Do you know him personally?" He spoke softly. Perhaps he was always aware of uninvited guests and hidden microphones. Helen felt he was anxious to probe the ground as much as possible before proceeding. She was not sure how straightforward she should be with him but decided there was no reason to hide anything.

"He was designated to be my killer in December 1989. He was one of my executioners. He was in the secret police and I believe that he still is. Perhaps he is laundering the dead dictator's money in Italy." Her voice was alive with the emotion she had experienced in the cornfield.

When they reached his office, Cicerone opened a hidden vault and carefully removed a wooden box. With ceremonial reverence he unlocked it and asked Helen to look inside.

There she saw a portrait, evidently very old. But the face did not resemble hers. She saw a middle-aged lady gazing at her with big eyes, set off by shaded contours that emphasized energetic lips and thick brown hair.

"I assure you he is not here for you." Cicerone locked up the box and the vault. "How did you escape?"

"It so happened that the dictator had been executed by the time I was taken away. That changed everything."

"Good timing! You are a lucky woman." He was trying to cheer her up and allay her fears.

He went on: "It is the old story of politics and money. In your case, I believe, only politics. In my case, both. It may sound like a false confession but I am sick and tired of it all. As for Signor Doncea," he said with an exaggerated whisper, "I can tell you he is powerful and well-connected. But too much money too fast has spoiled him."

Suddenly he seemed to have a great deal to say to Helen. He felt, he told her, a strong impulse to change the way his life was going. He felt old and awkward. Her presence, he said, had strengthened his conviction. As if to fill the emptiness of the room, he went on about the futility of seeking a perfect relationship. He was referring, of course, to Cicero's mistress. They had found each other too late.

"But what could 'too late' mean?" he asked. "Everything important we wish to accomplish seems to come too late, does it not?"

He sipped the scotch he had been carrying with him. Helen saw that he interpreted her silence as an invitation to talk about himself.

He began making confessions about his marriage. It is difficult, he said, for a strong and successful Italian male to be with a woman who is equally successful. On top of that, he suspected that his wife had had an affair with one of his political rivals. It was his weakness to accept that and to forgive. Indeed, his divorce had made headlines for quite a long time.

Helen had learned from Octavia and Cornelia that he had subsequently acquired a mistress who had vanished under mysterious circumstances. Helen had also learned that he possessed a huge estate, land near Gaeta, and homes in Rome, Venice, and Paris; that he was a heavy investor in American, European, and Russian stocks; and that he was busy romancing a string of beautiful women.

He showed her some newspaper articles about his political successes and acknowledged that it was only a matter of time before he would become prime minister. He could count upon the support of his political party, even though his enemies were trying to destroy him. An old story was being repeated.

He seemed to reach the end of his personal revelations, and Helen felt she was being drawn into a competition.

She could not explain to herself later why she had begun to talk about herself. Perhaps it was because at that particular moment she had ceased to care about him or want anything from him.

She told him her own stories. She had always been the one who ended the relationships. Despite everything, over the years, she had mastered the skill of dealing with loneliness. Helen told him about the political turmoil in her former country, and of her escape to Minneapolis, where she had built an entirely new life. Now, she was in Gaeta to finish a book on the man who had always obsessed her and gave her life whatever coherence it had.

"But it is time to be rid of Cicero," she said, staring at him, shocked by her own words.

Her eyes must have revealed the simultaneous discovery and regret. "I cannot explain how, but I feel that I am finished with him now."

"My name is Cicero as well." His whole manner was suddenly light and airy. "So, what's next? Are you going to run away from me, from this very room? Will you allow me to drive you back to your villa tonight?"

An artery was pulsing in his broad forehead, glistening as it slipped under the gray hair at his right temple. His eyes held her gaze, as if commanding her not to refuse. She turned and began to walk back toward the ballroom. He did not follow her.

But Helen was glad of his invitation. She did not actually know the address of her villa, nor had she written it down anywhere, and Cornelia and Octavia were going to leave with their husbands.

"Such an unexpected pleasure!" It was her countryman, lighting another cigarette. "Helen, I would very much like to spend some time in your company in Rome. What about dinner together?"

The admiration was unfeigned. Bowing ceremoniously as he spoke her name, he had the air of a former lover encountering her after many years.

"I hear of your success in America. But I cannot understand your bitterness and your strange manner of talking about your native land. I think you should be more generous and forgiving. Well, the past is always controversial, is it not? History in the making is only a matter of interpreting events."

The would-be executioner drew on his cigarette with visible pleasure.

The past and the matter of violent death were pleasant topics of conversation, were they not? Helen perceived that he wanted her to feel guilty. He was a patriot, and she a traitor. This at a time when he himself was stepping oh so carefully.

Helen could not speak. It seemed to her that the executioner knew about her current book, a memoir about her final years in her former country.

"But no matter! Who cares about you and these kinds of writings? Neither your enemies nor your friends. I advise you to take up Cicero's offer, whatever it is."

His eyes told her: *You have no right to a destiny. You come from a long line of victims of history. Your inheritance has marked your blood. History is written by the victors.*

But it was her story, the story of her kind that she had to write. She was the one who could give posterity the victims' knowledge of recorded events. Otherwise there would be no real history, only the justifications of those who murdered and destroyed and manipulated lives and souls. If she refused to listen to the inner voice compelling her to do so, history would rely on the interpretations of those who had masterminded the cruelty and degradation.

She saw herself there, in her native land, like a horse running a race. Her legs bound at the starting point.

Every generation is like a horse race. Individuals are ready to start with energy and dedication. But she—and others like her who chose not to be like Doncea—could not ride off. She could not fairly compete in the race. For she was not allowed. Or she was allowed as much as the rulers wanted. Her legs were hobbled. And they wanted her to believe that this was still the case. Her name had been forgotten. It was like ancient times, when emperors would order certain names to be effaced from all records. Controlling the future.

Doncea bowed in his tuxedo and walked away. He and his kind were still in power in Eastern and Central Europe. Something wrong was still there, terribly wrong. And this insidious message had come there so forcefully, floating on the air of this Italian villa full of important guests. Was Tiramollini one of them? Did they annex him, as they did certain influential people all over the world?

It was not easy for Helen to find an answer to what she had to do next. The first and quick response came from her bones and flesh, the deepest levels of her being. She had to outlive them. To be alive when Doncea and his kind are biologically extinct. And then she will deliver her message, hoping it will be listened to and understood. She could do it. The new country where she lived would grant her this passage. Her inner voice was digging an infinitesimal but strong path. It was a mission she hoped to achieve.

Scanning the crowd, Helen discovered Cornelia talking to an elderly man wearing sunglasses and a huge gold-and-diamond medallion around his neck. Helen had met him earlier, one of Cornelia's husband's biggest clients. Octavia was standing next to the mayor of Gaeta.

"We are going to win the elections!" Cicerone Tiramollini was raising a champagne toast to a circle of guests. Helen thought it was imprudent of him to make such a prediction publicly.

"You have always been a man of big ideas," the Mayor said with his camera smile.

"Thank you for believing in me." Cicerone took it as an endorsement.

"I'm going home now," said Cornelia to Helen.

"I've looked for you all over the place." Cicerone was next to her again. "Where have you been?"

Helen tried to put her thoughts together.

"I'm going back to Rome," she told him. "Tonight."

"I want you to relax," said Cicerone. "Let's eat something."

She sipped some red wine, but took a whisky when a tray came past. It would send blood to her heart.

Her executioners were everywhere. They were now businessmen, politicians, cabinet members, ambassadors; they spoke of democracy interlacing their new ideological pronouncements with grim tales of their sufferings at the hands of the communists.

They were still in power, scooping up whatever was left. She knew that she should disappear quickly not only from Gaeta and Italy, but even from Europe. But she had to see Formio, however briefly.

She was still holding the glass of scotch when she saw Cornelia and Octavia through a window climbing into a limousine. She said nothing, and made no move to do anything. She felt extremely tired.

Cicerone was watching her. She sensed it was on his mind that she would be spending the night with him. It was such a powerful thought that he could not hide it from her. It was as if he were trying to tell her a very dangerous secret he could not say in words. All he saw was something like a frightened smile.

Cicerone drove her to the villa, taking a shortcut through his estate. He parked the car and invited her inside with proper politeness. Helen had already learned from Octavia that the villa's owner would not dream of charging Helen for her stay. She was to be treated as his guest.

"Which bedroom did you choose?" he asked with childlike curiosity. His wide-open gaze seemed to be waiting for verification that his guess was correct.

"*Il sole.*"

"My favorite," he said, satisfied.

"Your favorite is always the woman's favorite." Helen stepped toward him.

"How right you are." Cicerone acknowledged her wisdom with a smile.

With natural ease he took her in his arms and they kissed at the bottom of the stairs. Still holding her, he led her up the stairs to the bedroom in which Europa and Leda wanted the same man. And now Helen saw that, on the ceiling, Hera was also present to lay rightful claim to her husband's perfection.

"Venus is not as beautiful as you," murmured Cicerone. "Nor can Pallas Athena compete with your intelligence. You have the right to know that." And he continued, careless that the goddesses might hear him: "Zeus would love to have you in his arms. Pity him!" Cicerone laughed, dragging her to the bedsheets. "Those ladies"—and he pointed to Europa, Leda, and Hera—"cannot challenge you."

For a moment, it was Helen who feared that profanity. She said nothing and soon she forgot that the ancient gods' revenge is always delivered.

Next morning Helen slipped out of bed as Cicerone slept and made coffee in the dark kitchen. The sun had just begun to rise out of the sea.

She switched on her laptop in the living room and wrote. "December 6th, Gaeta. Cicero is with me. Is it right to say that true inspiration lies in the quest for the transcendent?"

What to say next? But he called her upstairs. They spent the whole day sharing stories of their lives and their mutual obsession with the great Roman orator.

He had entered politics because of his spiritual mentor. Helen told him about her dream to write and be like the great man she had admired with all the passion of her young heart in the worst days of her country's history. And she told him that her would-be executioner had threatened her life again.

"Me too," Cicerone said, "I have felt as if under a death sentence. I don't want to tell you why. The less you know the better."

Vividly she saw herself leaning over in bed and she heard her own thought: I believe a two-thousand-year-old man and a forty-one-year-old woman are a sexually perfect match. The same thought was in his mind—she knew it—as he held her as if she were Fausta. More than once she asked him if he had learned to please women all the way down in time. It was as if through all those hundred of years, holding women in his arms, he had been perfected just for her.

But in the middle of the night he awoke with a shout. He was clinging to her, trembling, crying out in the darkness. Certain dreams had tormented him for years, he explained breathlessly. His death was so real, he couldn't tell at once that it was just a dream and not a real terror in the blinding dark.

A few hours later Helen was awoken again, this time by an urgent shaking. Cicerone commanded silence and hurried her with him into a hidden room behind the painted walls. He kept her in his arms, tight against his chest, whispering patience. It was before the dawn. The surveillance camera had discovered an intruder.

Through the secret room door they heard a sort of scuffling and muffled shouts. Releasing her, Cicerone issued short orders. Armed men were swarming all over the villa. He was agitated, and complained that his bodyguards had not been vigilant enough that night.

Cicerone agreed to show her Formio early in the morning and after that go straight on to Rome. He was thinking now, he said, about leaving politics for a while and going with her to the States. He was ready to make a public statement about dropping out of the election. He needed to distance himself from his business partners, at least for the moment. It was a matter related to East European money being laundered in Italy, and to his own key role in the fraud.

He left for his estate. One of his people will come to bring her to him shortly. She was to pack and be ready to leave Gaeta as soon as his messenger arrived to pick her up. The bodyguards went with him. But one was left there to protect her just in case.

Helen packed in a hurry and brought her luggage out next to the doorway. The bodyguard in the living room pretended not to notice her. She decided not to wait for Cicerone.

She will go on her own to Formio to visit Cicero's tomb and from there straight on to Rome. Without Cicerone. Time will decide what to do with this unexpected adventure.

Cicerone was dangerously close to Doncea. And she knew now too much about things she did not want to know and interfere with. Their issues with Doncea were totally different. Coming too close to Cicerone, she put her life one more time in danger. His fight was certainly not hers.

The laptop had been on for twenty-four hours in the living room. The diary file was open and she wrote hurriedly: "December 7th, 1998, Gaeta. Cicero's death. Today, I'll see Formio."

With a brutal, unnatural noise Octavia rushed in, a wild expression on her face, opening and closing her hands, shaking uncontrollably. Her husband had just called her with the terrible news. Cicerone had been murdered in his house. His head was cut off.

Helen stopped and read what she had just written: December—death—Cicero. The real Cicero. By the beautiful Tyrrhenian Sea, she had been trapped in some circular logic of history.

"Cicerone is dead!" Octavia howled. "My God, why Cicero?"

Helen looked again at the laptop screen and the words she just had written. Was her turn next? Fausta's death, the Eighth of December. Could she escape? Just as she had defied death in that other December. She saw that she had only one chance.

The first time she had escaped death by pure luck and evaded it by exchanging Europe for America. But this time, in her stupidity and ignorance—or simply because of a twist of fate—she had actually conveyed herself to the very site to fulfill a weird destiny.

She packed up the laptop and dragged her luggage through the doorway. Everything was suddenly clear. She must be deaf and silent if she were to escape. She paid no attention to Octavia's ravings about Formio, Cicerone's funeral, Cicerone's love for her, the possibility that she might buy the villa for nothing. In Gaeta's vortex between past and present, Cornelia and Octavia were nothing but goddesses involved in her destruction. Formio was her tomb. The last destination.

Octavia snatched at her, beaming a stream of hate. Helen felt sharp fingernails scratching her arms as she struggled, moving ahead as quickly as she could. The bodyguard, despite Octavia's calls, did not interfere. He left in a hurry through the back door, vanishing like a ghost in the light.

Octavia got to the Porsche first and blocked the doors. With all her strength Helen shoved Octavia aside and threw her luggage into the car and herself after it. She turned the key in the ignition and accelerated, even though Octavia was still hanging on.

At the first intersection Cornelia rushed into the road. Helen swerved, and Octavia went flying off the car.

Now Helen was on the road to Rome, speeding far beyond the limit. It was time to do exactly the opposite of what was expected of her.

Several times she had a vision of Cicerone's face entreating her. The artery was throbbing on his broad forehead like a heart, pulsing under the gray hair at his right temple. They were meant to be together, he was insisting. He was not prepared for a lonely eternity. Why had she come so late into his life?

At Albano Laziale, Helen noticed a car following her. In Rome she left her car at the rental office and asked for a cab to the airport. She would stay at Fiumicino the whole night waiting for the first flight to the States rather than sleep at a hotel in Rome. As in a nightmare she saw the elegant Signor Doncea at the airport, talking in the hallway with a group of men and staring at her.

An intercontinental flight was ready to take off in less than an hour for Los Angeles. Helen purchased a business class ticket to Minneapolis via Los Angeles, checked in, and boarded the plane. The next few minutes were a mixture of hope and panic. Once over the Atlantic she could relax and see her life clearly. First it had been the obsession with Marcus Tullius Cicero who had been her mentor and model. Then it was the near escape from death in her country in the same month her mentor had died, many centuries before, under similar circumstances. The miracle of her escape had not helped her to understand that she could live a life of her own. She had felt trapped in an endless cycle of events that required her participation.

Helen felt suddenly free to live. Really live. Humanity meant being endlessly trapped in cycles of destiny. Could there be another way out?

What an annoying question!

Limitation.

She covered her shoulders with her fur coat, switched on her laptop and wrote in her diary: "December 8th, 1998. Tomorrow is today. I am Helen, not Fausta. And my lover is not Cicero, nor is it Hamilton with his blue eyes. I am ready to live my own life."

She was not hungry despite the fact she had not eaten properly since lunch two days before. Back in Minneapolis, she promised herself, she would go to the Nicollet Island restaurant and have a real dinner and she would stroll every day around the lakes that looked so much like Herastrau in Bucharest; and eat breakfast at the coffee shop on 11th Street and Lasalle Avenue, where they served big scrambled egg bagel sandwiches.

She would move out of Hamilton's apartment and have her own rooms on Kenwood Parkway or on the Lake of the Isles. The Lake of the Isles and Calhoun Lake were surrounded by linden trees, fir trees, and flowers of geranium. There were places there that looked like Predeal, Brasov, and Câmpulung Moldovenesc, her favorite Carpathian towns.

Helen knew that all she had in Minneapolis was her job. Wonderful streets where she could walk. Casual friends. And her book, the interpretation and account of the past, the suffering of her country. And the other book that she will write about the way she was transformed, and how she herself transformed the reality of her experience into art.

The present was an eternity waiting to be filled with living. She had cheated death for the second time in her life. A languid game, but unsettling. Such a narrow escape was not in her agenda again at least for the next few centuries.

As she bathed her face in the airplane bathroom, Helen noticed that she was still wearing Octavia's pearls. Were the necklace and earrings really losing their brightness and color? Maybe they were fake? Whatever the case, she would return them to Octavia as soon as possible. But to what place exactly? How could she return them to a goddess? No, these pearls were hers, a souvenir from Gaeta. Their metamorphosis into ordinary stones simply meant she had escaped death.

She touched the pearls, and they recovered brightness. On her neck, close to the left ear and covered by hair, she seemed to discern a hitherto unnoticed dragonfly. She touched the skin near it and violet shadows glittered, as if the dragonfly was illuminated by the light.

"*Libellula.*" Helen murmured the dragonfly's name in Latin.

In the airplane seat Helen was no longer afraid to close her eyes. Her life swept over her like a torrent of events all in the past tense.

She decided to move the past out of her mind for a while and to be conscious only of the present, to use the present tense, and keep her eyes firmly on the endless possibilities of the here and now. She promised herself not to forsake reality. Curious and craving, Helen released her mind and soul to begin the goddesslike journey toward the next moment of her eternity—*ad vitam.*

The Loneliness of
Magnificent Women

On a whim one afternoon, Paul Larson had taken himself to see a classic motion picture, *Julie's Secret*. It was one that he had first seen as a romantic young man of twenty, more than ten years before. He had tucked a copy of a romantic "fictionalization" of the movie into his pocket and paged through it with renewed interest on the subway ride from his apartment on the Upper East Side to Lincoln Center. Now, in the intimate little theater for film buffs and nostalgia seekers, he relaxed into his seat and abandoned himself to the unfolding story.

Back out on the street the evening was deepening and the air had new warmth to it. Instinctively people slowed their steps on Broadway. Paul's thoughts were on the triumphal course of the movie over the years. He was a journalist and film critic and he needed this kind of distraction to get into the mood for writing an article. Always conscientious, and marked with the confidence typical of a man still young enough to see life without limits, he nevertheless struggled now and then with getting into the right frame of mind.

Smith & Wollensky's on Third Avenue and Forty-Ninth Street was already crowded. Paul had a couple of drinks at the bar and exchanged greetings above the noise with fellow journalists from other papers. Finally he got a table in the dining room, where it was less crowded and the noise level a few decibels lower. Around him he watched people devouring big steaks, prime-rib cuts and giant lobster, all served with baked potatoes, sour cream and asparagus, and downed with house wines in long-stemmed glasses. A sense of celebration colored the mood of the diners this April evening. Spring was decidedly in the air.

Paul was still absorbed in the gothic romance of the movie and amused himself by contemplating the difference with which he, and others, had understood the metaphors of *Julie's Secret* back then a decade ago. The director and the lead actress had worked together, with the conviction of artists, to give of themselves and to bring their own true nature into their work. It was their passion for personal honesty as an obligation to the public that had brought them together, a passion that eventually spilled over and complicated their personal lives and artistic commitments. Neither the film nor the book shed any light, of course, on this private conundrum that so often come into the lives of public persons. In time the film had become a classic, the director had died and the actress had for unknown reasons not appeared in any other major production. The role she played later in a film about ghosts and magic was unmemorable and in Paul's opinion a blemish on the reputation of a myth.

He put the book back in his pocket and, trying to shake off his analyzing mood, he settled into his own reflections. Apart from his job as a critic he was not in the habit of judging public figures. As an interviewer, on the other hand, his skill of subtle and revealing ruthlessness was well known and appreciated by his readers. But after seeing *Julie's Secret* this time he came away with a deeper appreciation for Heloise de Grenville as a woman and a person with hidden sensitivities. Her persona had in fact reminded him of the age-old lesson: Eros is the beginning of both troubles and obligations.

Paul Larson was a tall and well-built man with regular features and dark wavy hair framing a calm forehead. He was well dressed in an English tailored suit, a designer shirt and tie. One might say it could be deduced from his appearance that he was careful to avoid trouble in his life. He got out of his love affairs if things were becoming too complicated, the truth being he was happier on his own. His handsome figure and straightforward glance gave him a look of sincerity that was somewhat misleading but nevertheless useful in getting close to his journalistic targets. Although he had no wish or intention to deceive anyone he was determined to put his career first. Betraying his subjects was just an unavoidable part of his job though not necessarily of his character. Scruples he could ill afford.

"Have you got a chair for me, Paul?" It was Tony's voice above the crowd. "I'm not too late, am I?"

"Only half an hour or so." Paul waved him on.

Tony Brook made his way through the room, shaking hands with colleagues. He stopped, before reaching Paul's table, to kiss the fingers of a woman surrounded by a noisy group of journalists. To Paul she looked haughty and businesslike. At first glance he took her for a widow of vast wealth or perhaps the owner of a foreign newspaper from somewhere or other in the world.

Middle-aged and with graceful gestures, Tony Brook was a tall, thin fellow with pallid cheeks and large observing eyes. A seasoned journalist, he had risen through all the ranks in his career and now spent his days coaching others to achieve higher ratings within their various media. He was full of ideas, exuded enthusiasm and had excellent connections. He extended the same civility to all journalists, the experienced and the hopeful alike.

Tony was searching the crowd for a friend who was supposed to be there. The waiter told him that his friend had been seen earlier with the group surrounding the conspicuous lady at the Time Warner dinner nearby. She was seen surveying her surroundings with a look close to derision, her short upper lip raised above the crowd.

"You've got a good view of the diva," Tony said with a wicked laugh, as Paul was about to make a comment. She seemed familiar but he couldn't place her.

"Do you see her face?"

"She is good-looking," Paul said noncommittally. "And she seems also intelligent."

"Look at the lofty expression in her eyes. Everybody adores her, but nobody seems to have the courage to be with her," Tony said in a conspiratorial tone.

"Beauty and intelligence combined scares me off, too." Paul seemed confused.

"You don't know what you are saying." Tony himself was unable to take his eyes off her.

Paul let his eyes wander in the same direction. He sipped his red wine while Tony started on an Armagnac. It had been two years now since Paul had been appointed senior columnist, but his ratings were going steadily downhill. It was high time for some improvement, and Tony was supposed to give him a hand—in exchange, of course, for a substantial fee. Paul was on the lookout for new, cutting edge ideas and hoped Tony could help—Tony, the famous healer of tired journalists, the one remaining hope for so many squeezed dry and burned out by years of writing and the struggle of finding good subject matter.

"So, who is she?" Paul was humoring Tony.

A plate of prime rib was set in front of him but Paul felt unable to eat. He looked suddenly as if the whole world weighed on his shoulders. This was after all about his career and his future. In his heart he was deeply worried. He felt utterly removed from the spectacle at the other table. His was a situation he could not just walk away from, although more than once he had dreamt of escaping to Europe and taking a job with a London newspaper.

Tony grinned with a kind of secret satisfaction. "How can you not recognize her?" He rubbed his hands in delight while Paul's face remained blank. "That's another count against you, Paul! She is Heloise de Grenville, the star of *Julie's Secret*. You should know! They call her Elsa."

Paul tried to pull himself together. He had pictured Elsa as a much older woman. After all, he had been a young man the first time he saw her on the screen.

Paul pulled out the book again and checked the dates. She was twenty-five when the movie was made. That made her not more than five years older than himself, but she did not look to be a day over thirty. The woman Paul now had before his eyes had an elegant simplicity about her. A tight black dress enhanced her warm skin color and soft brown hair. She was clearly a confident woman, consciously calling attention to her charms and at the same time there was something inaccessible in her demeanor, an allure men found difficult to deal with.

Tony was full of information. "She is unmarried and there is nobody in her life except for a few friends. She has been invited to shoot a movie in the States. I heard she signed a contract in Hollywood. Right now she is holding a press conference and in a few days she is going to New England on a short trip. That's where they will do the filming and she wants to have a look and become familiar with the locations."

Despite his good nature there was something surreptitious in Tony's behavior. Never one to restrain his tongue, especially when talking with a peer, he launched into what Paul felt distasteful gossip.

"Have you ever noticed how many good-looking, intelligent and successful women are alone?" Tony asked, looking at Paul with his teasing grin.

Paul did not understand what Tony was after, but he started to think about actresses, women in the media, singers and writers, both dead and alive, who seemed to fit this profile that obviously intrigued Tony. He looked up. "Quite a few," he conceded.

"Have you ever wondered why that is?" Tony cut musingly into his prime rib, without moving his long pale face.

Paul did not really care to find an answer. To him it was just a way of life.

"How about trying to find out why?" Tony persisted. Before Paul had time to make a comment Tony laid down his knife and fork and began developing his idea for a series of articles.

"How about doing a number of interviews with famous women around the world to be published in our syndicated magazines? To show that fame isn't everything. You know, it could be a revenge on the stars for ordinary women struggling with the daily routines of children, shopping, bills, diets and boredom. Yes, their revenge on rich and famous women who appear to have everything in their lives. You would be the one to show in your articles that they are actually missing something important in their lives, that they are pitied by the rest of the world. These women don't seem to be able to make anybody happy. They have no family; there are no significant men in their lives, no children. They work hard and suffer a lot, some becoming drug addicts, alcoholics and what else. You, Paul, take them down from their pedestals. Of course, the subjects will not know your objectives. You can ask them anything you want and publish only what fits your scheme. I myself would be dying to read these stories. At the table over there is your very first—I should say, classical—subject, the perfect profile.

"She has been divorced twice," Tony went on. "Her last love affairs were pure disasters; the rumors go that she finds no satisfaction in bed, and that she is cynical, jealous and mean. The rumors also have it that the last guy she was in bed with was a hotel attendant, the only one who dared approach her last year after she was honored at the festival in Cannes. Anyway, that's the gossip. Would you have the guts to take on a project like that?"

It was a farfetched idea as far as Paul was concerned. It would be hard to get celebrities to reveal their private and innermost thoughts. Still the coincidence of events that day had piqued Paul's interest. And this was what he paid Tony big bucks for.

Tony had been prepared to give Paul other ideas but this proposal invented on the spur of the moment was by far the most intriguing.

Tony was speaking in a low voice as if afraid that some colleague from a nearby table might steal his idea. The callous attitude to people as fair game for journalists did not really bother Paul. This was his meat. The interviews themselves would be a subterfuge. He saw himself in control, using his casual charm to disarm his victims. Paul was suddenly hungry and started in on his dinner.

"Get me a list of celebrities with contact addresses," he said, "and work up a contract."

After some bargaining, more wine and dessert, Tony took Paul over and introduced him to the famous Heloise De Grenville. She looked at him with a rather cold and distant air but held his eyes for a moment and finally agreed to talk with him after the press conference in the presence of her agent. Paul and Tony listened in for a while. She spoke in a soft French accent and at times seemed unable to understand what everybody was saying. It was obvious that her vanity forbade her the use of a translator. She wanted to show she was in command of the English language.

"This lady is indeed keen on making her life miserable," mumbled Tony leaning forward. "I can recognize the French style."

It proved impossible to talk to Elsa after the press conference, and the day after was no better. Since she was scheduled to spend a few days in New England her agent told Paul that he might have better luck if he went along. Even though she had a busy schedule there would be more time for an interview in the mountains. And Paul did not delay booking hotel rooms for himself.

A few days later two limousines carrying Heloise de Grenville, her staff and her wardrobe headed north to Connecticut followed by Paul's Toyota. They stopped overnight in Riverton, a village close to the Massachusetts border. The Old Riverton Inn built in 1796 was a bed and breakfast place with exquisite rooms, wonderful old bathtubs and a low-ceilinged dining room made for romantic dinners. Paul indulged himself with a long hot bath, sipping from a glass of

wine and dreaming about Elsa. Making love right out of the bath tub
excited him and, if not Elsa, he promised himself he would bring a
woman up to this place at some later date.

Paul got a chance to see Elsa in the morning. He had just finished
his breakfast when he saw her through the window on the bridge
walking briskly toward the other side of the river. She entered
"Hitchcock Fine Home Furnishings," but soon she left that famous
store with its exquisite furniture manifesting the elegance of past
ages. He dashed out and followed her as she entered a path leading
up through the forest. The sun played on the ground through the
fresh greenery. Billowing clouds moved fast across the pale blue sky.

She wore a red dress and a broad-brimmed golden hat sheltering
her from the sun. It was a scene out of the past, like a little girl, he
suddenly thought, gathering flowers for a dinner table, or on her way
to a secret patch of wild strawberries; a far cry from the star he had
observed a few nights before, spoiled by the public and the press. As
he caught up with her, the rippling shades on her red dress and
golden hat, brought on by the chromatic play of the sunlight, had an
intoxicating effect on him. He was reminded of the morally charged
atmosphere of the forest scene in *The Scarlet Letter* where Hester and
Pearl, clothed all in red and gold, are suffused with the green of the
wilderness around them.

Elsa did not speak to him. He was content to walk behind her. She
did not slacken her pace as she moved off the path and into the forest, heading for a brook winding through the undergrowth. The
green weeds and pebbles in the riverbed seemed to sparkle with a
light all their own. Nimbly Elsa leaped on to a rock in the middle of
the flowing water.

"Look at the hue of the loosestrife," said Elsa as if talking to herself. "What a glorious purple!" The riverbanks were lined with purple flowers.

"The contrast with the green of the forest is very dramatic. In his
theory on colors Goethe suggested that red is thrust and that, with

the complimentary green, the colors vitalize each other through a dialectic of attraction and repulsion. He also wrote that orange and scarlet are a high-tension combination. Colors as 'acts of life'." She turned to him: "Mr. Larson, do you like flowers?"

"I am indifferent," said Paul. "But I studied them in college. I majored in biology."

"And you gave up biology for journalism? What a pity!" Elsa teased him with a roguish smile.

During his last year in college Paul had been chosen by a magazine editor as an advertising part-timer. He worked for a few years as a pen for hire, always on the lookout for an idea to sell and a way to minimize research. Interviewing stars and writing movie reviews had fed an idea to publish a book about friendship with dead actresses. It got the attention of an editor anxious for an idea with public appeal. In *Romance of New York* he was in one chapter the intimate acquaintance of Greta Garbo, revealing her private thoughts during her years of success, as well as during the Oscar ceremony and other events—most of it of course pure fiction. There was a "sensitive" quality to his "memories" of Marilyn Monroe, Grace Kelly, Greta Garbo and others that made his writing attractive to living actresses, some of whom saw him as the ideal interviewer. He still remembered with a faint blush the Hollywood lunch, where he had been introduced as a journalist to be trusted.

Elsa jumped off the rock and hurried back to the inn before Paul had a chance to talk to her. It wasn't long before the motorcade headed north through Massachusetts and into Vermont. They stopped in Arlington in front of the Norman Rockwell Museum. By then Paul was hungry and nervous. He wanted to know when he would have the chance to begin the interview. Elsa's agent had promised to make arrangements for that evening. He had been invited to join them for dinner so he could be informed of the day-to-day schedule. Elsa was busy studying the screenplay. This was not a vacation for her but a working trip meant to prepare her for the movie.

The road went on through the forested mountains, crossed covered bridges, entered gorges and passed signs indicating the presence of moose. It was a sunny day and Paul was caught off guard by how much his spirits rose in response to the beauty of Vermont. Following the limos without thinking he suddenly found himself come to a stop at a dead end in front of a trout hatchery. It was an unexpected place with hundreds of ponds and basins where mountain stream fish were feeding, growing and breeding.

The air was still and hot. Elsa's group took refuge in the museum of local wildlife while she herself walked out to the fishponds. The strong sunlight bathed every inch of the ground. Paul followed Elsa not only by a journalist's instinct, but also out of a genuine sense of chivalry. She tacitly accepted and seemed to be at ease in his company. They strolled in front of a basin swarming with fish, a few dead on the surface. They leaned over and dipped their hands to check the temperature of the water. Their shadows immediately attracted a rush of fish expecting to be fed. They came to an open place where a huge white pine towered majestically. Elsa hugged it as if it were a friend, walked around it and spoke in her meditative way about the greatness of trees. She had spent her childhood in a small village playing barefoot among old trees and dreaming about her escape into the real world.

Suddenly Elsa was heading for the forest with quick steps. Apparently she already knew the path through the wild terrain. For a moment Paul lost sight of her. Careful to keep in the same direction, he found her standing entranced in a clearing edged with pine trees. The ground was covered with flowers in the soft new grass, and humming insects filled the still air. He had a sudden vision of himself and Elsa making love in the middle of that clearing.

"This is the most enchanting spot I have ever seen," said Elsa softly. "No forests anywhere in the world compare with this."

Instead of responding to her he reached out to touch her arm. But he checked himself instantly, thinking the whole episode was the device of a highly experienced woman out to seduce him. He remembered the cardinal rule of journalism: never get involved personally with your subjects! Get to the interview and be done with it. If you are going to flirt with intimacy, between what is fair and what is not, writing becomes insincere, a betrayal both to the victim and to yourself.

"I have some advice for you." Elsa interrupted his thoughts. "Don't let yourself be mastered by the narratives that demonize our lives. I particularly refer to the lives of actors, or the lives of movie stars if you will—your favorite topic. I have read your books and articles. You tend to think in stereotypes. No wonder you have had such success with the public."

Paul did not answer. He was working by another maxim: let the subjects explain themselves, even if it hurts you. They often feel better and talk more freely if they think they can humiliate the interviewer. And it turned out he was right.

In Woodstock, Vermont, the limos stopped at the nineteenth century Canterbury House. After settling in, Paul found himself at a dinner table in Spooner's restaurant known for steaks and prime ribs, his favorite food. Despite a strenuous day Elsa looked fresh and energized and with a naughty grin plunged into a discourse on "the grand unified theory of the universe" while sipping her Johnnie Walker. A professor of physics had recently announced that the infinitesimal size of sub-atomic worlds with more than three dimensions could be large enough to be observed. If he could prove this in his calculations, he would be able to reconcile the contradictory assumptions of quantum theory and the theory of gravity, thus explaining by a single stroke both the laws of the sub-atomic world and those of the cosmos.

Paul loosened his tie. He was not in the mood for physics. The wine and Elsa's perfume invaded his senses and drew his eyes to her décolletage and the harmony of her soft creamy skin meeting the silky dress. He felt languid as if from a hot bath and knew that the moment to begin his interview had passed. This did not worry him. There was still time and he sensed she was well on her way to telling him whatever he might dare to ask. Savoring the atmosphere he relaxed deeper into his chair and, reaching for his drink, pretended to be the quiet listener.

Persistent loud sounds disturbed his sleep. Barely opening his eyes Paul saw it was only seven. He usually slept till nine. Someone was moving around noisily next door and out on the porch. He cursed and tried to go back to sleep but in vain. Through the curtains he saw Elsa wrapping herself up in a blanket and settling down in a lounge chair with a mug of coffee and a manuscript. The morning was not his best time, but he judged that now was as good a time as any to get going with the interview.

Before Paul had time to shower and pull on his jeans and a shirt, Elsa had left the porch. He saw her disappearing into the dense vege-tation on the slope toward the river. Farther away lay cornfields and pastures in the misty air. Paul walked down a country road and wan-dered around in the lush vegetation of the riverbank for a while. Here too the loosestrife was abundant and attracting all kinds of insects and butterflies. A rich variety of fragrances rose with the warming rays of the sun. But Paul was mindless of the glories of the morning.

Nature was not his cup of tea. He was beginning to feel annoyed. Even if she was the great Heloise de Grenville, he did not enjoy chas-ing her around at all hours so far from his routine comforts. He returned to his room and went back to bed. No celebrity had ever treated him like this. Who did she think she was? A French actress who had not made a film in the last thirteen years, who read physics, made a racket at the crack of dawn not caring who she disturbed, and treated him as a nonentity. He began to regret ever having enter-tained Tony's suggestion. He had been successful in the past and able to build a reputation. Why not repair his flagging career on his own terms? All he needed was a vacation.

Lying in his king-size bed Paul thought about inviting his girl-friend in New York for a few days relaxation in New England, even though he was thinking of breaking up with her. No woman had ever really been able to satisfy his sexual appetites. He was a man in need of variety and surprise in his love life. In his defense, he was always up front with the women he became involved with, always letting them know early on that he was not the marrying kind and had no desire to commit himself to serious relationships, and therefore separations came easily. Right now he was thinking of the good-looking blonde he had met at a cocktail party after a movie preview in New York, a senior analyst on Wall Street who seemed equally uncommitted in her personal life, married as she was to her brilliant career. He had seen her on and off for a couple of months and was now thinking of her with growing appreciation.

Suddenly a new vibration in the air awoke him from his reverie. Elsa was standing by his bed coolly surveying his room. There was nothing untidy. Paul was a man of order and accustomed to the impersonal hotel rooms he occupied on all his travels. In fact his own studio in the city resembled a hotel room. There was nothing for anyone to uncover about his personality, his women, his passions or hobbies. The only vaguely unique thing among his personal possessions was a collection of crafted mugs inherited from his mother.

Paul wanted to get up. Elsa was sprinkling dew over him from a bunch of grasses she was holding. Very relaxed, she sighed and undid her ponytail, freeing her soft brown hair.

"I was hoping you would join me down there," she said. "I found a four-leaf clover. Are you married?"

Paul did not particularly like being humored in his present situation.

"I am not," he answered, surprised and wondering what she had in mind.

"How many lovers do you have at the moment?" she asked with a small chuckle. "A man like you is supposed to take full advantage of women's liberation." She was not sarcastic; merely displaying a sort of sympathetic curiosity the way men do when sharing stories of their sexual conquests.

"What is it you would like to know about me, in addition to what has already been reported in the media?" she continued.

He looked at the ceiling, embarrassed, pondering the best reply to her question.

"As much as possible about your lovely personality."

This was apparently not the most advisable approach, for she did not look at all flattered.

Elsa was dialing and ordering up breakfast in Paul's room. "And how do you want to proceed?" she asked. "Do you have a written questionnaire?"

Paul nodded. He did have one, just in case. He had drafted it on his laptop and printed it out on the portable printer the night before. "It is there on the desk."

Elsa moved to the window and pulled the cord to open the slats of the blinds before sinking into the armchair to look through the pages. There were more than forty questions. When breakfast arrived, she folded up the pages and put them in her pocket without comment, then sat for a while absorbed in thought.

Unshaven and irritated at being humiliated on his own territory, forced to have breakfast in bed balancing a tray on his lap, Paul was stripped of his journalistic prerogatives.

"Aren't you curious to know why I am alone and why my personal life and love affairs have been disasters?" Her voice resonated with a wounded sensuality. On her face one might have read her sadness at the thought that Paul, like so many journalists before him, was merely intent to uncover the source of pain in her life. She leaned against the back of the chair as if a storm was bearing down on her full force. She tied her hair back and looked searchingly into his eyes.

"I have found an explanation," she said, her figure bathed in the morning sun. Through the window behind her the slope of a mountain separated land and sky. "Life's trap for a woman is a combination of beauty, intelligence and success, a curse magnified by her will to break out from the cycle of cooking, cleaning and servitude. The Greek gods in their envy punished such women by killing them or changing them into animals or trees. Pallas Athena changed the beautiful and gifted Arachne into a spider, because she dared to win first place in a contest where the goddess came second. In our time such women are rejected by men, pure and simple."

Paul frowned. He looked back at her in silent protestation, disapproving of her narcissistic speech. Yet he had no wish to contradict her.

"My explanation," Elsa continued, "is that the decent man, *bien sûr*, is always intimidated by beauty, intelligence and fame in a woman. It can indeed be very intimidating. In a way, beauty and sex appeal are signs of superficiality or carnality, betraying the core of a woman's intelligence."

Apparently she felt free to share her thoughts with Paul. She took a sip of tea and looked in his direction.

"Other men turn violent to overcome their inhibitions with women like this. Their inferiority complexes are alleviated by the act of humiliating them. God alone knows how many hidden failures men carry around, and in the end it is sheer envy of women's accomplishments that has such devastating effect on them. As for me, I really don't think it is a matter of competition; it is just that men think differently. So, the only man who approaches this type of woman is the 'jerk'. He has no fears and is not troubled by complexes. He doesn't care about feelings or wisdom or beauty. He simply wants a woman's body. When she is tired of being alone, the beautiful, intelligent and talented succumbs to the jerk hoping that she will be able to change him. The results are disastrous. In time this woman comes to accept that the only way to have a life of her own, to feel alive with her sanity intact, is to accept loneliness. I have reached that stage. I have lost hope that there will ever come a man who will be able to break this *fatalité*."

Paul wasn't sure how to react to this theorizing about the sexes so early in the day. For one thing he did not agree with her; he could not see himself belonging to either category of men. On the contrary, he would have been delighted to discover a woman such as Elsa described. She was overreacting. Suddenly he wished she would go away. He needed a shave and to get dressed, for God's sake. She was too much.

In Paul's car, as they were heading for New Hampshire, Elsa continued to talk freely. This time she was being ruthlessly self-critical of her own professionalism. In order to survive as an actress her work had to measure up against her greatest achievements in the past and if possible surpass it. She had known rewarding moments of self-confidence, as well as the sense of betrayal when brought down by critics from the heights of fame.

Listening to her stories Paul could tell that Elsa had lived an enchanted life and that everything had been done with style and excitement. She was precisely the kind of woman he would like to know and be with. He did not feel in the least guilty that the conversation was being taped by his hidden video camera. Work and pleasure were surely allowed to mix under certain circumstances.

In Woodstock, New Hampshire, they stopped at the Three Rivers Inn, where a large wooden moose welcomed them. After a short walk along the riverbank and down Main Street they had dinner in the restaurant car of an old steam train puffing along a scenic railroad. Animated by her surroundings Elsa talked about her love of ballet, that form of theater where "nobody speaks a foolish word all evening," in Edwin Denby's perfect phrase. Ballet meant good-looking bodies, graceful movements and music. She had met Georges

Balanchine. She described scenes vividly and, using the terminology of ballet theater, discussed technicalities of *Les Sylphides, L'Après-midi d'une Faune* and *La Fille Mal Gardé*.

Paul felt slightly at a disadvantage. He would have preferred a conversation of intimacies or to sit back taking in her sensual beauty. He was culturally literate in a superficial sense and got by sufficiently well at cocktail parties. Elsa on the other hand was full of knowledge. He could appreciate her accomplishments, but it was her charm and her body that kept him there—and, of course, his commitment to Tony. A warm glow emanated from Elsa as she talked about her years training as a ballet dancer before giving it up to become an actress. "And now," she said, "I am ready to go in front of the camera again."

"I wish I could believe you." Paul leaned forward. This time he touched her arm.

She steadied her glass of wine on the table and placed her hands in her lap.

"You ought to," she said, her eyes vaguely evasive but sparkling in the candlelight.

He shook his head, wondering what were the reasons for the fears he could read on her face. Despite her place in the public's esteem there had been some unflattering comments, but no successful actor or actress was immune to the vicissitudes of stardom.

Paul tried to press her to admit that her work with masks and disguises put her in danger of exposing herself, which is what he had thought seeing her again in *Julie's Secret*. Elsa grabbed the rudder and changed tack. She made comments on the marks of perfection in some of the greatest American films, revealing her studious interest in the matter. This greatly impressed Paul. She was an artist reaching for unattainable goals.

They kissed in the car. The next day, after a trip along Koncamagus Road, a visit to Bretton Woods and a ride on the Mount Washington Cog Railway, they spent the evening in his room. Late in the night Paul called Tony asking to release him from his commitments.

"You've got caught," Tony grumbled with deep concern. "The beast has gotten you. Now I will have to find something else to improve your ratings. Damn! It was such a great idea!"

Lake Winnipesaukee was the next stop on their itinerary. Their room faced the dark waters and the forested mountains beyond. For the next three days and four nights Elsa enjoyed every minute they spent together, delighting in Paul's sense of humor and tasting the sweet pleasure of sleeping in his arms. She felt she belonged to that place, discovering not only New England but also America through his eyes. She admired the land and its people, their ambition, imagination and hard work, the kindness she met everywhere, and most of all the straightforward and childlike character of the American people, which seemed to allow them to live every moment to the fullest. Paul delighted her with stories, with his command of the English language and his wonderful patience explaining new words. She seemed to acquire a new sort of energy bringing her a new outlook on life. Paul, rather unexpectedly, turned out to be a perfect companion, caring and loving, ready to fulfill her every desire.

Paul had never met anyone like Elsa. He could not figure her out. Her instinctive capability was simply astonishing. She always seemed to have her sensory antennae out. Paul tried as hard as he could to be on the lookout and to anticipate her reactions, but he only got tired. Her powerful presence at times threatened to overwhelm him and triggered in his heart a mixture of admiration and envy and sometimes almost hate. She seemed to know him better than he did himself. Jung wrote that a human being consists of both masculine and feminine traits in varying degrees, possessing both animus and anima. The ratio of each determined the nature of one's soul. Paul wished for more anima in himself, a lot of anima, but on condition that his appetite for sexual encounters would stay the same.

One night he actually dreamed he was a woman, beautiful and intelligent, in love with a handsome man. They were making love in the forest, on the grass, surrounded by trees, and he even felt the pressure of a body penetrating his. In that dream he plunged into a pleasure never before experienced in his life. Through his skin, mouth, breast and genitals the sensation grew like a river flowing without end. He visualized this pleasure as a luminescent vibration casting two bodies into a solid block of light. The sensation was so intense that Paul woke up in great distress. It made him wonder if even in lovemaking Elsa was the more powerful.

On the last day by the lake, Elsa woke up at five, showered and opened the door, calling out to Paul to come and watch the sun rise among the glowing clouds filled with the promise of a new day. Birds were singing all around at the height of their voices. From time to time the sun's path on the lake was broken by the wake of an early motorboat, the waves gently rustling under the wooden dock.

It did not occur to Elsa that waking up Paul at five was upsetting for him. For who would prefer to sleep on a morning as glorious as this? She was ready to go to work right there, that minute. Elsa had breakfast. She read and did her exercises. She checked her appointments for New York and Hollywood and announced to her crew that she was ready to go. Paul was still sleeping and she had to hurry him up. They had to leave New Hampshire and go back to New York. She had an event to attend there that same evening.

Paul was disconcerted. For him it was too soon for their vacation to be over. He wanted to stay in bed at least another hour and make love to her right away. He craved her body next to his. And she had to obey him. Paul grabbed Elsa murmuring words of love in her ear. He swung over and pulled her closer. For the first time in his life he had found a woman capable of fulfilling his sexual desire. Her breasts were soft and heavy. And he was struck by how attractive she was at any hour of the day.

"I love you." His voice was blunt and unfocused, almost begging.

"You love whatever woman you happen to have in bed with you," Elsa replied, kissing and rejecting him. She was ready to go now. But because she realized that her sarcasm arose only from fear of being in love with him, she sweetened her remark. "I mean, you are a man with the mind and heart of Haroun al-Rashid from the *Thousand and One Nights*. Before he met Sheherazade. I hope I'm wrong."

Paul knew that the cynical Caliph of Baghdad had his women beheaded one by one after taking a night of pleasure with each. But one of the women, Sheherazade, survived by spinning such wonderful yarns every night that she bewitched him with her storytelling. By power of the word she was able to ward off her execution and his departure, and to keep their love alive. Art and wisdom changed both the mind and the heart of the Caliph. During those nights listening to her stories, he had fallen in love with her.

On the way back to New York, Paul decided he would join Elsa in Hollywood. But could they really get away with it? Both of them were known to the public and being seen together might compromise their careers.

That evening Paul stayed alone in Elsa's apartment and watched her live appearance on HBO. She talked to the camera and was applauded for her charming speech. He was asleep when she came back, but thirsting for each other they were soon in each other's arms. Before daybreak Paul felt her slipping out of bed. By nine she was gone.

During the next month Paul and Elsa saw very little of each other, tied up as she was with filming in Hollywood. Paul flew out on weekends, sometimes only to be told by her agent she had no time free. They talked on the phone and promised each other things would get better. Paul was in the grip of a sweet and tortuous tension, desiring Elsa as he had never desired anyone before, and at the same time worrying that he might lose her. No woman had ever had such power over him.

After the movie's première Elsa signed another contract in France. It was a trying time for them but nothing could diminish their love. Paul believed he was the man who could efface Elsa's private misfortunes and make her happy. He traveled to France to be with her, although they were still careful not to be seen together in public. It was a strain they could have done without. When Elsa mentioned marriage, Paul by habit told her of his reluctance to commit himself. To him marriage meant family. As it was now he felt they did not have a true life together. Elsa did not agree. They did have a life together but he was unwilling to change it.

Paul thoroughly disliked this kind of discussion. He wanted to keep his personal freedom, even though he had to admit that he was sometimes hurt by Elsa's own form of independence. Her life was lived in many directions and he often felt relegated to a subsidiary role. The tension of being around Elsa on a daily basis took its toll. Soon he was yearning for his empty apartment in New York. In time he realized that he would not be able to conform to a life under the pressure of her work schedule, nor was he always charmed by her insights and penetrating remarks. He knew he would always be in her shadow.

Most evenings Paul preferred to wait in her apartment on rue de l'Université, close to the Seine and the Eiffel Tower, while she attended the social events he could not be part of. Often he set out on foot, crossed the Seine on the majestic Pont d'Alma and strolled up the Champs-Elysées. He made notes for his columns at café tables and amused himself with the *Astrophlash* horoscopes at Galérie des Champs. He was at those moments a contented man. He believed Elsa was happy as long as she was committed to her profession and her audience. She was a diva in keeping with the times and she was good at it.

Back in New York, Paul found a more relaxing relationship with a former girlfriend while continuing his telephone conversations with Elsa. He saw no conflict between his love for her, the true love of his life, and dating another woman. To him it was a privilege of manhood. The frequency of Paul's visits to Paris decreased over the following months. Rumors in France about their relationship had become too threatening to his position as editor of a glamorous magazine, and he was tired of not being able to be himself. Elsa remained a strong force in his life. They spoke nearly every day assuring each other of the constancy of their love.

Then one day Elsa was free to move to New York. She was involved with writing a film script set in the States. She was going to both direct the film and play the leading role. Paul felt his whole existence, so carefully orchestrated to his satisfaction, coming unglued. Instead of living from moment to moment he would have to make decisions. It was distasteful to him and upsetting, and he had no one to rely on but himself. He tried to discourage Elsa. Life in Paris suited her; she had much more of a presence there and even her career in America depended on her image as a Parisian celebrity. To his utter surprise she confessed to him that it was her personal life that meant most to her and that had guided her.

His silence lasted a bit too long and was met with questions he was at first unable to answer. He was evasive, knowing full well this was the beginning of the end. Yes, she was the most wonderful woman he had ever met. He loved her. But their relationship was difficult for him. He had started seeing another woman. He suddenly felt no need to dissimulate and told her all about it and how long it had been going on.

The silence between them lasted several days. Neither of them knew what the other was thinking. The unsettled feeling grated on Paul and he did not know how to overcome it. When Elsa called asking him to come to France one more time he was glad to accept. It had been too good to end with a telephone call. Making love, or so Elsa believed, was also a way of saying goodbye.

Elsa had chosen to bring Paul to her place at Saint-Malo on the northern coast of Brittany, a counterpoint to New England, a place where they could gently but surgically sever all bonds between them. It was Christmas time and it was their last vacation together. For hours on end they watched the tidal motions of the sea with its calming rhythms, and contemplated the permanence of certain things.

They tried to identify the many islands guarding the bay, some barely visible in the haze; La Conché, La Petite Conché, La Plate, Le Grand Bé, Le Petit Bé and many others where the famous pirates had ruled supreme three hundred years ago. They feasted on *galettes* at La Grignote on Chaussé du Sillon and on *langoustines* and *fruits de mer* at Les Embruns prepared by Thierry, *le patron* and a friend of Elsa's. They paid homage at the lonely tomb of the stormy and romantic Chateaubriand out on Le Grand Bé, reachable at low tide, and they strolled through the old city quarters.

"You will have to go back to New York," Elsa said one morning. They were lying in bed in her house on the Promenade du Sillon, near the beach.

She slipped through his arms, pulled on a coat, opened the door and quietly stepped out of the room. A bit unsteady on her feet she crossed the street and walked until she found the steps leading down to Plage Paramé. According to legend, kings in the middle ages sent their soldiers here to heal their wounds after battles. Exposed to the salt, the sand and the sea, the soldiers recovered. Perhaps it was this salubrious and miraculous effect that Elsa had sought for herself and Paul during those last few days by the sea.

It was low tide. The ocean lay more than a mile out. Strange creatures sprawled on the wet sand. The cloudy sky brought cold winds from the Channel. It was beginning to rain. Elsa could think of nothing more to say to Paul.

Paul did not understand what was happening. It was all so wonderful and he had no wish to leave. He had hoped she would allow things to continue as they were. He was confused and stared through the rain at the blurred horizon. Deep within him he knew that Elsa was still exercising power over him and an irresistible force compelled him to go.

One afternoon late in the fall, as the wind was sweeping leaves and dust through the streets of Manhattan, Paul turned up the collar of his tweed coat and headed across a busy intersection. He wanted to have a bite at Smith & Wollensky's before the preview of *A Perfect Day to Part Forever*. A movie preview was routine for Paul, but this time he had read the announcement several times; directed by Heloise de Grenville, screen-play by Heloise de Grenville, and with Heloise de Grenville in the leading role. It was a French-American production. The preview was held simultaneously in Paris and New York.

After Saint-Malo he had tried hard to restore his universe to his usual demand for order and neatness, and he had been confident that everything was under control. He straightened his designer tie as he made his way to the grille but could not brush off the slight trepidation that had come over him since receiving the announcement. The usual group of journalists from the daily papers showed up, Tony Brook among them. He had disappeared without a trace after that midnight phone call from Vermont. Paul tried to avert his eyes but Tony was already at his side.

"Remarkable!" Tony exclaimed loudly. "Both of you here!"

Paul frowned at him. He did not want to get into any discussion about the past, but turning his head slightly he caught sight of Elsa among the group of journalists. He was so precipitously thrown back to the previous occasion in the same place that he thought for a moment he was reliving the past.

"I'll see you at the preview." Tony clapped Paul on the shoulder and shook his hand. Then he seated himself at Elsa's table, on her right.

As the preview of *A Perfect Day to Part Forever* started to roll, Paul was shocked to see it was subtitled *The Loneliness of Magnificent Women*. He was further astonished that Elsa played his Elsa just as he had known her. He himself was played by a famous screen actor under the name of Henry and their love affair began at the very same restaurant he had just left and where he had first laid eyes on Heloise de Grenville in the flesh.

With a sense of panic Paul gripped the arms of his seat. Here was his and Elsa's love affair played out in every intimate detail on the screen to an audience of film critics, actors, directors and journalists. It was a story of a woman living her life under the curse of beauty, intelligence and fame. A French actress adored by fans and critics, but in herself lonely and unhappy, is approached by an American journalist who wants to interview her. They fall in love and their love blossoms during an enchanting trip through New England. The action continues with the hectic travels, the arguments and misunderstandings, Henry's infidelity and the final farewell between two individuals who by fate are being pulled in different directions.

Paul's entire being was flooded with embarrassment, anger, betrayal and even, in the end, a sense of shame. He was grateful for the dark. She had spared nothing. His stories, his dreams, his gestures of love, every line was his, but seen through Elsa's eyes.

After their first night of love in the mountains, Elsa had found out from Tony who Paul was, and about his plan to expose her. It was then that she had decided to beat Paul at his own game. She would make a full-fledged screenplay of their encounter. She carefully prepared her revenge but, like Paul, she fell in love. Against Tony's advice she was willing to give Paul a chance.

In the end the movie showed the gray clouds moving in over Brittany on that perfect day when the lovers part forever. The final scene was a panoramic view of the dining room at Smith & Wollensky's with Henry having a frugal meal by himself.

The audience broke out in a spontaneous burst of applause. The salon was immediately abuzz in comments comparing the movie favorably with any number of screen romances in recent years. Not since Demy's *Les Parapluies de Cherbourg* had there been such a romantic movie. Heloise de Grenville had surpassed herself and turned out a performance unlike any in the postmodern motion picture arsenal on the subject.

It was an astonishing feat and the audience clamored for her appearance. Elsa came out on stage and to Paul she was Sheherazade incarnate. Who was he but that rascal Haroun al-Rashid?

Paul did not remember how he got out of there. He needed to walk. Oblivious to the cold wind he walked for blocks on end without knowing where the next step was taking him. He felt a void and a weakness that brought him back to the death of his mother and how he had felt when he buried her ashes. He had become aware then not only of an irrevocable loss, but also of how close he had been to her, closer than to any other human being.

Back in his apartment he sat for a long time in the dark with only the streetlight casting shadows across the room. He had not realized that Elsa had been the first person to fill that void in his life. Suddenly he wished he could tell her that, and much more. Few things in life are forever, Paul mused and switched on the light. It was so like her to overly dramatize things. He would tell her that...

The Life Manager

That Tuesday noon, Margaret Staundinger arrived earlier than usual at Shirley Shone Hall. She chose a table at the far end of the row facing the windows, in the nearly empty dining room that resembled an old English club. She wore a creamy white suit with a black silk shirt and a string of pearls. Her profuse brown hair with its luxurious sheen brushed her shoulders, half-revealing her pearl earrings. A barely noticeable red contour highlighted her smile. The foundation she wore lit up her large brown eyes. What she could not see or imagine or control was a reflection of tiredness in her expression. A kind of torpor close to that mixture of desire, distaste, and sex appeal seen often on the faces of city courtesans; viciously deepening the pallor of those fine lines around her coyly curved lips to a confounding shell of light. Making men sweat. Pumping adrenaline to their hearts. Raising the heat of their bodies.

It was the last faculty lunch of the spring semester. Easter and Passover were close at hand. The war constituted the lunch agenda. The standing of the speaker, a key player in the peace process in Northern Ireland, required the audience to be formally dressed. Three judges from the European Court of Justice, coincidentally attending a conference hosted by the Law School, also appeared, which enhanced the general nervousness. Everyone knew at least in a vague sort of way that it was considered discourteous in Europe to go on eating while the keynote address was being delivered.

The Dean introduced the speaker. "It is a great honor for me to welcome Senator Ashton, a former federal judge and ambassador, a man of extraordinary breadth of interests and experience…"

The company beamed and applauded. Seated around tables according to scholarly concerns and personal affinities, they represented an identifiable section of the New York intelligentsia, eager to socialize with the rich and famous. Many were the Dean's personal friends. The Dean himself was the next in line for president of the University. He had raised millions of dollars and recruited the best legal minds in the world. A recent photograph in *Time Magazine* showed him bowing to a rich lady at a banquet in Chicago. His ceremonious kissing of her wrist brought in, they say, some fifteen million dollars. A similar kiss, on the wrist of the wife of an eminent professor of European law, had garnered the School a major adornment that would otherwise have graced a rival university.

During the brief moment of silence before the speaker began, most of the other chairs at Margaret's table were abruptly taken by half a dozen latecomers. Margaret knew all their faces. Far from being sheltered, she was now surrounded by the most influential people in the room. The Dean himself came over and sat next to her. She grew nervous as they were all staring at her as if they had never seen her before in their lives.

The man at Margaret's right complained about the food in a loud German accent. Alternately, he also distinctly muttered his disagreement with the speaker. It was the typical American point of view, he told the table. As for the food, it was the same tasteless *dreck* he'd had to eat for the last two months. He did not care if the Dean could hear him. He leaned back in his chair and looked away and then turned back and gave Margaret a sort of compliant smile. He was eating like a European, holding the fork with his left hand.

Looking at him, Margaret realized she had been curious about this man, the famous Bruno Heinrich Schönfelder, for some time. Herr Schönfelder, a visiting scholar this semester, was a recognized authority on the euro and a worldwide eminence on bank fraud. Margaret, a specialist in international and foreign law research, knew of his work, although she had no clear notion of his ideology. Schönfelder was regarded as an extravagant advocate of the poor and underprivileged, a kind of scholar that held little interest for the elegant and influential people crowding her lunch table. But here he was, a grizzly beard engulfing his jaw, his jowls and his lips, wild hair covering his ears and tumbling over his forehead in utter defiance of New York academic etiquette. He wore a blue suit with a black shirt and a red tie.

Margaret had not slept well for weeks. As the speaker's stream of words droned on, she returned to the deck of the Staten Island ferry at a late hour on a frosty Saturday night in February. She was alone with the freezing wind and water. The salty frigid air blew in her face. The waves splashed against the relentlessly forward-moving vessel. The crests seemed to arch to reach her, as if they knew that was what she wanted. Lower Manhattan shrank away as the darkness triumphed. That night she had wanted to cool her body and her soul, to freeze her boiling thoughts to numbness. Jules had bought tickets for a Broadway show. But she had abruptly left him as they were on the point of setting out, catching her own cab and telling the driver to take her to the Staten Island Ferry.

Who was Jules? An irresistible (she thought) and passionate bachelor, about her age, a successful trader on Wall Street; as independent as she was. Perhaps they were too alike? The South Dakota plains with the thirst for freedom they engendered were in his blood. Although he had fled at an early age from the homestead his ancestors had established many generations before, he remained a solitary man of the prairie.

They were getting dressed. And Jules had told her, answering her question, that he was not sure she was the woman he would spend the rest of his life with. And this was her dilemma too. How could she tell if it was love she felt? What she thought she felt was a need to end the quest; and it also was about the chemistry of freedom. The chain of molecules of the soul saturated in mutual love. Was this what she experienced with Jules?

Again in her mind she watched Jules as he got dressed. She saw his tall well-built body, his athletic legs, his blue eyes, his chestnut crew-cut hair, the salt-and-pepper shadows on his temples. She had just kissed his lips again. His smile revealed his strong white teeth. What was freedom without love? Was she in love with him?

It was deliciously cold on the ferry's deck. Her sleeveless evening dress was a blessing. It let the icy storm reach her skin, her slim waist and breasts under her unbuttoned coat. She had taken off her hat and shawl and gloves. The glacial wind loosened and lifted her hair steadily until it was reined by the ferry's arrival at its destination. But she had returned all the way to Manhattan at the same spot on the deck, playing the same game with the waves and the wind and the icy spume. And so did her hair and her cheekbones, and her legs dressed in glimmering stockings. She didn't freeze. All she got was a sore throat that went away without any medicine. She had slept well that night, although her body was cold and her soul too. But it didn't help. Soon after she awoke she was under pressure from the same bursting thoughts. Did she want to spend her life with him?

"You are very strong," Jules had told her that night when they separated. "You will find another man." But what she heard was a sarcasm that made her feel unlovable.

Margaret was vaguely aware that the people around her were engaged in criticizing a recent European Court of Justice decision. The Dean yielded the floor to a guest from the European Court. It seemed the two sides were irreconcilable. Bruno was looking at her crossed legs and arched body pushing her breasts forward. Margaret noticed now how obviously absorbed in her own thoughts she must look to anyone.

"I don't understand what all of you are doing over the weekend," Bruno suddenly shouted. He was visibly displeased with the end of the speech. He was consulting his watch and smoothing down his tie with ladylike hands. He asked the waiter to fill his glass with red wine.

Nobody else drank wine at the table. For Bruno this was a sort of disgusting "political correctness." His American colleagues were chaste professors going back to work, hard working professors tacitly telling the Dean that they would not spoil their afternoon classes with a glass of wine. Bruno sniffed. How could someone eat without sipping wine or beer?

"Are you Americans doing anything else beyond work in this country? What do people do during the weekend?"

But nobody paid any attention to his question. In a lower voice he added: "New York looks to me like a labor camp."

This did elicit a response, quiet but icy.

"Is he making a comparison with the Nazi labor camps that his country developed during World War Two?"

It was a voice on Margaret's left, belonging to an eminent lawyer and professor who had prosecuted this issue and secured a big settlement in the victim's favor. The almost whispered question had actually been addressed directly to her. Margaret, now fully alert to her surroundings, was not sure if Bruno had heard, but she felt obliged to challenge this rudeness.

"Shopping, watching TV, doing laundry, cleaning, cooking, going to museums and seeing shows on Broadway," she said half in English and half in German for all to hear, looking at Bruno.

Bruno looked back. "Fraulein Margareta, let's have dinner together." He spoke in German. Margaret saw that he was genuinely worried that another weekend would pass by in complete loneliness.

"As old friends do," he added, still in German. "I'll pick you up at your office on Friday at 5 PM. I am bored with museums and exhibitions. I deeply dislike those tasteless shows on Broadway, so childish and loud. To tell you the truth, I have not had much opportunity to meet real people here."

It turned out to be seven o'clock, not five; an unexpected symposium, he said. But it was better. Hunger and the warm evening made the conversation easier. They looked at each other with relief after devouring the appetizers at the Grand Ticcino on Thompson Street. The main course, something *grandioso*, was supposed to come soon. The Pinot Grigio was excellent, and cold.

To find the Grand Ticcino in the Village, at the same location for more than a hundred years, one must know that it exists. Anyone passing by could easily remain forever unaware of the abrupt, small stairs that led down from the sidewalk to a sub-basement with one tiny window and an unfriendly door just big enough to slip through. The sudden darkness there is a sort of trick to scare the newcomer. At first only three tables can be discerned; the visitor perceives the real dimensions of the room later on, after adjusting the eyes. The room is a cross between an Italian pasticceria and a German cellar. Dimly revealed on the walls are relics of famous artists and writers who have dined here: paintings and sketches, autographs, dust jackets, candid photographs of famous personalities engaged in eating and drinking.

"Let me fill your glass." Bruno tendered his service with studied chivalry. "New Yorkers believe that their city is the center of world culture, just like Paris used to be. What a joke!" Margaret saw that he was still fuming, especially on account of one of his German colleagues who always failed to give him enough attention.

"He has gotten them, yes, he did, with his humble attitude, a shame for Germany," he went on. His tone sought revenge. "I cannot stand to see him. I have a studio on Mercer Street, not far from his, but he pretends he hardly knows me."

Lucky fellow, thought Margaret. A room in the dorms on Mercer! Foreign scholars and visitors rarely get to stay on the overcrowded campus. And the cost of rooms in the neighborhood has gone through the roof. Yes, a studio on Mercer was quite a luxury.

Bruno's voice resonated in the vault. Margaret said nothing, enjoying the sound. She will temper his anger later; now she wants to know more about it.

"Everything is false in this lovely country. I get nowhere." Banks, bankers, non-profit associations, financial disclosure, penalties for the poor: all his frustrations came out. Politeness, always mere politeness. "New York it's a nice place, though. Nice weather. Still I cannot wait to get back home. My Germany is cool and wet, but I like it." And then suddenly: "Do you sing?"

Margaret made an ambiguous finger movement.

"I play the violin," he said, sipping his Pinot. "I carry it always with me. I have it packed on the bicycle parked in the School's courtyard. I had studied music and played for pleasure. During my traveling, I like to give violin concerts in parks, intersections, public places. I like to make people happy, and also capture their generosity. The biggest amount of money I ever collected was in Venice, in Piazza San Marco, and here in New York ten years ago, at Columbus Circle."

It was a different man Margaret saw now. His eyes were sparkling. He was deeply happy. He had no preconceived ideas or any sense of the inappropriateness of violin playing for money in the street. He too must have seen the change in her expression. She felt his obvious pleasure in watching her there, in her black velvet suit and silk creamy blouse and pearls, her hair tied back in a girlish knot, her face following his thoughts with a new freshness after a long day. A purple silk scarf with little flowers of all colors hung around her shoulders and gave her more life. Yet he seemed stiff to her in his dark blue suit and black shirt. Only the red tie gave his liveliness away.

"Let's drink a glass in our honor," he encouraged her. "Long live friendship, long live the thirst for knowledge!"

"Do you still play the violin at the crossings?" Margaret spoke from behind her wine glass. She was filled with a strange mixture of sorrow and envy. She felt she would have liked to have been among the people in his life, attending his performances.

"Yes, I do." Bruno was proud of her concern and interest.

"Would you tell me about your repertoire?" Has he ever played the Andante from Berlioz's *Symphonie Fantastique* on the Champs-Élysées or Park Avenue, she wondered?

"Haydn, Mozart, Beethoven, Schubert. It depends on my mood also but people like classical music. I got good money in New York."

He moved on to the dinner prices on the menu.

"How can you people survive in New York? I paid today five dollars for a hamburger with French fries that costs in my home town one dollar something."

The entrée came, as well as another bottle of Pinot Grigio. The fish and pasta were tasty. Despite this, Bruno complained about American junk food, he dislikes it, while his kids adore it. He motioned his head. And he went on with German accuracy.

He was born in München or Munich, the way Americans call that city, he told her, where his family (meaning his sisters and cousins) still lived. He had been married, but he divorced his wife of twenty-five years because she was obsessively jealous; he has three daughters and a son; he has had many love affairs in his life, and now he was settled with his girlfriend in Köln. He had decided that he must stop fooling around with women. This was a voluntary decision, he told her, based on boredom and the pressure of responsibilities.

Bruno produced pictures of his family, former wife, permanent girlfriend, and children. He has been successful: teaching abroad at many universities, in many languages, and writing books. The institute that now sheltered him is the most zealous watchdog and adversary of the EU banking maneuvers. He had a Ph.D. in law, and another one in business administration and accounting, an M.A. in philosophy, and a B.A. in music, specifically in violin playing. He grew up surrounded by women, so he learned early that they are the most powerful and intelligent beings on earth. He very much valued the company of women, and he knew that the best part of his mind and soul had more *anima*, the eternal feminine, than *animus*.

"The eternal feminine beckons to us." Bruno declaimed the sentence, assuming (Margaret could tell) that she would recognize the last line of Goethe's *Faust*.

"Is your husband of German descent?" he abruptly asked, pronouncing her family name, Staundinger.

It was not her husband's name, but her maiden name, Margaret explained, as a big cat, the restaurant's guardian angel, gently touched her legs under the table. She wanted to change her last name, she said, as nobody seemed able to pronounce it in the U.S. She was thinking of having it changed to "Standinger" or simply "Stand."

The cat didn't want to leave, growling when Margaret tried to remove her, climbing up on her lap and chest. It was an unusual black short-haired Siamese-looking cat with a golden collar around its neck. Orange dots sparkled on the cat's forehead. She rubbed and purred in a feline show of affection.

The owner of the restaurant, a man in his sixties introducing himself as Glenn Irwin Hoyt, a true Manhattan-born American, barely holding his belly in with his belt, assured Margaret in a low voice that the cat (whose name was Madame Blavatsky) had all the necessary shots. It was safe to let the cat nestle on her lap. He had more to say too. Tightening his belt, he imparted that the cat had mysterious powers, proven over the years. However, Madame Blavatsky never sat on anybody's lap. She did not generally like people. She has two buddies, dogs that she plays with. It was a big surprise for everybody in the restaurant that the cat liked Margaret. No offense, but it was hard to understand why. But he was sure Margaret would find out herself sooner or later.

Margaret listened politely. She caressed the cat and went on with her story, after this interruption, to a much-focused Bruno. She was surprised how ready she was to talk about herself. Glenn Irwin Hoyt stayed, pretending that he was watching his cat.

Margaret had been in the States for about a decade, she was saying. Her ancestors migrated centuries before from a small German state to Transylvania, an autonomous province of the Hapsburg Empire. Many of them went back to Germany during the harsh years of Communist dictatorship during the nineteen seventies and eighties. They were bought up, like the slaves of ancient times. They were delivered one by one to their relatives in Germany who paid big money in order to get them out of Transylvania. She followed her parents, but she did not fit there. So she came over to the U.S. She had been born in Transylvania into a middle-class family, in a town named Sibiu. The Saxons who had settled there a few centuries before had called it Hermannstadt.

As Margaret spoke, she realized that there were many parallels between her life and Bruno's. Bruno shook his head. His mustache and beard engulfed his face and allowed a smile to evolve on his lips. He too had some relatives there, he said, in Dracula's homeland.

Margaret did not wince at his remark—she was used to it—but concentrated on family details and legends. Her grandfather had studied engineering in Germany. And the sister of her great-great-grandfather had graduated in biology from the Sorbonne early in the nineteenth century. Margaret's relatives had been barons in Poland and aristocrats at the courts of Maria Teresa and Franz Joseph in Vienna. Margaret could still remember her grandfather teaching her the Gothic script.

Her mother was quite the opposite. She belonged to an old Macedo-Romanian tribe from the Pindus Mountains, many of whom had migrated back to their native country north of the Danube at the beginning of the twentieth century. They called themselves Aromanians, Macedo-Romanians, or Armâni. They lived like their ancestors, going back and forth to the mountains in summertime and wintering in the lowlands.

Their language was still similar to that spoken fourteen centuries ago by the Dacians before migratory tribes from the East had taken over parts of the territory. Margaret learned that language at her mother's knee, listening to the way her grandmother talked to her mother and uncles and aunts and cousins. Her mother was the first to break tradition by marrying a man outside her tribe. Margaret felt sure that her soul was paying a great toll to the mixture she sprang from.

Her education, she told Bruno, was similar to his. Margaret Staundinger attended a reputable science high school, but she did not go on to study mathematics as she was supposed to, to the disappointment of her teachers. She held a B.A. in comparative literature, an M.A. in historical linguistics, and an M.A. in journalism. Information science and legal research were the fields of another Master's degree in the U.S. Her recent book, issued by a North American legal publisher, had attracted attention among her peers.

"Why couldn't I do, in my whole life, what you have succeeded in doing here in a couple of years?" Glenn phrased it in such a way that one could not tell if there was admiration or irony in his voice. He was listening closely. And when Margaret said nothing he went on: "Are you a hundred years old or something? You must have had plastic surgery?"

Glenn tried to keep his humor up, as well as his belly tight. Margaret saw Bruno's discomfiture. He was disgusted at Glenn's obvious attraction to Margaret.

"You shouldn't forget the life pattern of your ancestors, the settlers. The way they adjusted to this land." Margaret's impolite tone addressed the spoiled Americans who had no idea what was outside their world and took everything for granted. "If you forget that, you have lost your America."

"What pattern?" asked Glenn. His face looked solemn, quite the opposite of his body's clowning movements.

"Could you, please, let her end her story?" Bruno was annoyed. "What have you done in the country you were born in?"

To Bruno's relief, Glenn was forced to leave the table, as the restaurant had become very busy. Margaret told Bruno that in her homeland she had been a published writer as well as a respected journalist. She had also studied music, mastered early in her life in order to become an opera singer, but had switched to writing. She divorced in her native country and subsequently took care of her son, now enrolled in a faraway college. As to her very recent history, she had just ended a relationship of many years' standing. And she added that she felt tired of carrying on with her life.

"If he did not love you, he did not deserve you," Bruno said. After a silence he added: "I am fifty years old." Perhaps Glenn's question was echoing in his mind. Perhaps her account linked to events in his life. "How old are you?" It was against American etiquette, but normal for a European to ask.

"I am fifty as you are," Margaret answered. She was only slightly embarrassed. She knew she had already entered another stage of her life.

"This is impossible," Bruno exploded. "You cannot be fifty." It was unthinkable for him to flirt and spend an evening with a woman of his own age. So she must look as sexy and attractive as a thirty-something! "You are lying to me."

Margaret knew that a woman of her age was old in Europe. In one of her recent novels, published in her native Romania, she had developed a theory that time runs differently in Europe and in America.

"What is the place your parents live in Germany?" Bruno then asked.

"Munich." Margaret started to answer. But she could not continue because something appalling was happening.

A man with a black dog entered the restaurant. The dog, of a non-descript pedigree—something between a German shepherd, a Rhodesian ridgeback, a Labrador and a greyhound—headed straight for their table. Margaret screamed in fear. She did not like dogs. The man assured her that his dog was peaceful and friendly. Bruno looked deeply unhappy. A black cat and a black dog were too much for him.

All of a sudden the restaurant was filled with a whiff of the ocean.

"Wagner, come here!" The man tried to persuade the dog to come to where he had seated himself.

"C'mon, Wagner," he kept saying.

He was a tall and distinguished-looking gentleman in his sixties, blond hair, gold rimmed glasses, soft gray flannel slacks, a light mauve pullover, and a brown cashmere sport coat.

Wagner did not obey. He lay between Bruno's legs, calmly watching Madame Blavatsky.

"They are friends," the owner of the dog said. "Cats are usually rude to dogs, but not Blavatsky to Wagner." His bluish eyes, crowned with full, glossy eyebrows, seemed bemused by the event.

"Wagner cannot entice Madame Blavatsky out of your lap! Unbelievable!" He smiled, obviously in the best of spirits. "You must possess extremely special qualities," he congratulated Margaret and Bruno.

"Could you take them out of my table?" Bruno disliked the moment, and especially the cat that had claimed Margaret's attention. He wished to take Margaret to another restaurant. He wanted to pay the bill. *Zahlen.*

Then Glenn appeared and declared that nothing could be done. "*Au contraire*, matters will get worse if we try to separate them."

"The dinner will be on me." Glenn tried to persuade Bruno, speaking with clear urgency. His obvious need to remedy a bad situation drove him to keep talking. "Blavatsky and Wagner are friends. Baron Marini believes that Edgar Allan Poe is reincarnated in Wagner, while Blavatsky is indeed the famous Madame Blavatsky. Although some of us say that Wagner—who, as you see, is all black—is descended from the white dog that healed Madame Blavatsky and taught her the way to theosophy. Wagner and Marini go every year to the White Dog Café at 3240 Sansom Street in Philadelphia, where Madame Blavatsky used to live. And Baron Marini comes here every Friday for dinner so the dog and the cat can play with Goppollone—oh my God, where is Goppollone? He will appear any minute from nowhere! I tell you, I've never had a situation like this. Usually they sit quietly under Baron Marini's table."

Glenn made an exaggerated gesture of the kind that signifies "abracadabra" or "hey presto!" Margaret remembered him saying once that in his early years he had worked as a magician in the Cirque de Soleil and had bought this restaurant after his partner died during one of their shows.

"Circus!" Bruno muttered.

"Who is Goppollone?" But Margaret didn't have to wait for an answer. A creature with the head of a cat and a dog's derrière appeared abruptly, playing with Wagner's tail. A washed-out-looking beast, it did not comport well with the elegant fur of the cat and dog.

"I don't know where Goppollone comes from, but he always arrives to play with his friends. I believe he lives in the cellar safeguarding my wines." Glenn spoke with bravado. He was still embarrassed. "Another mystery of the Village. The dog is very sensitive to people's emotions. Anyway, the dinner is on me, please stay and let these creatures enjoy your company. Apparently, they are in love with both of you."

"Absolutely," Marini intervened. "Plain to see."

"This is a zoo," Bruno complained, between dalliance and frustration. Margaret could see he was relieved that he did not have to pay the bill. "This is a loony bin, not a restaurant!"

Bruno's words were drowned out by the racket of a group of youngsters who entered and took all the available tables. Shouting and joking they ordered pitchers of beer. With the cat still purring in her lap Margaret read Bruno's mind: his dinner was ruined, Margaret was his own age (he couldn't see himself in bed with a fifty-year-old woman!), she indulged the cat, the dog called Wagner was in love with his legs to the point of embarrassment, and now Goppollone also captured Margaret's attention.

To make them happier, Glenn ordered Zambalione, a special dessert prepared from cognac Massala.

"These are my LLM students." Margaret spoke loudly to be heard.

A tall handsome student approached her with a warm hello and took a seat at the table, to Bruno's obvious displeasure. He continued to gaze at Margaret as he introduced himself to Bruno.

"Jerome Joinville."

"Jerome is a lawyer from France," Margaret added. "He has just earned his Master's degree in international business transactions—I mean, international taxation." This event was, she suddenly realized, the LLMs in international taxation graduation party.

Bruno deeply disliked the combination of the words "taxation" and "lawyer." All tax lawyers were crooks who twisted the law for the benefit of their filthy rich clients. Worse, Jerome was displaying signs of natural charm and masculinity, a demeanor that made him irresistible in women's eyes. Margaret saw all this plainly written on Bruno's face. Jerome had combed his brown hair with golden glow straight back. He had wide features, a Roman nose, a strong neck, great biceps, and firm pectorals. Bruno's shape could not compete with that of Jerome, who diligently worked out daily and lifted weights at Cole's, the university sports center.

"Are these animals yours?" Jerome asked Bruno, holding his breath. Then he grinned as Goppollone jumped on his lap. The creature sniffed his elegant cream-colored sweater and sneezed on it and on the impeccable white shirt. Baron Marini came over. "These animals are friends, and their friendship is so special that nobody can interfere with it," he announced.

"Why?" Jerome wanted to know more.

"It is hard to explain, but you will find it is true."

Bruno was on the verge of exploding. Uninvited, Baron Marini took a seat and introduced himself. He was from Italy. He had lived in Rome, Paris, London, Hong Kong, Nairobi, and New York. His fields were philosophy, theosophy, and theology. At present he was studying reincarnation and magic. For many years he had worked for the Vatican as general manager of the Holy See's business. Wagner was his dear friend. He came to the Grand Ticcino every Friday to give Wagner a chance to play with Madame Blavatsky and Goppollone. "Madame Blavatsky grants people's wishes. Wagner and Goppollone do too, but somehow on different levels or planes. Anybody here will verify this."

"I like Goppollone." Jerome seemed to be truly attracted to the oddity of the animal.

"French foolishness," Bruno whistled. He was really annoyed. And to Marini: "Could you put these goddamn dogs somewhere else?"

"Are you German?" There was a sort of illumination on Jerome's face. "This would explain everything."

"Frogs." Bruno was trying to get away from Wagner. All French were frogs to him, Margaret supposed.

"And we are *maccaronari*," said Marini jovially. "What else? How about you, Fritz?"

A shadow of pleasure crossed Bruno's face. He did not dislike Marini's humor. The cognac after the Zambalione helped him to accept all these events as unexpectedly artistic.

"Tell me a joke about German people," Bruno challenged Marini.

"Shitty German, stupid moron, put your gun down!" Marini sang, stupid English, stupid melody, continuing in this vein to Bruno's great enjoyment. He also managed to play with "Moron" and "Marini".

"Be careful with Wagner." Marini went seamlessly into a harshly voiced warning. "He has recently developed benign warts or growths, and he is in pain. In his case homeopathy is the best treatment. Warts can be inherited or viral. I must go online to www.AcadVetHom to learn more. Tomorrow I have to bring him to the Sutton Dog Parlour on 60th Street and 2nd Avenue for a hair cut and a bath. They have an excellent hairdresser there."

Internet for dogs! Hairdressers for dogs! Bruno looked sick. But Marini had already moved on, describing loudly his latest bargain, a new car for only $32,000, a Lexus ES400 listed at $100,000.

"So much money for a car?" Bruno was contemptuous.

Baron Marini was unperturbed. The car was luxurious—210-horsepower V6 engine, automatic transmission, plush interior, polished wood front panel. All the controls within easy reach.

"I prefer to ride my bicycle," Bruno retorted. "I want to preserve the environment and respect the money I earn. I brought the bicycle with me from Germany. I avoid the subway. I feel very happy and comfortable riding my bicycle."

Baron Marini didn't believe him. An internationally renowned scholar riding a bicycle in New York?

"My bicycle goes with me wherever I go," Bruno declared. "It is in the Law School courtyard. And so does my violin."

Margaret wondered if he would disclose his street musicianship. He didn't.

"Don't you ever take a cab? Surely you cannot ride the bicycle wearing a tuxedo—I mean when you're going to a concert or a business meeting, and you have to dress in black tie?"

"Never. I ride my bicycle even in tuxedo." But enough of that. Bruno turned to Jerome. "What do you want to do after graduation? Are you going back to France?"

"I don't know what to do with my life." Jerome was clearly glad to capture the attention of Bruno and Marini, not to mention their sympathy.

"I hold two Master's degrees in law, one obtained in France and one here. I am now thinking of pursuing medicine or philosophy, or a Ph.D. in law. What's your advice?"

Margaret was pondering the lure of learning for this well-heeled young man from Toulouse. He was a descendant of the Comte de Joinville de Grand Pré, a family whose historical account goes back before the year 1000. They fought in the Crusades. Some had died at Acre and at Kalaat al-Horn, and some later at Carcassonne cleansing the earth of Albigensian heretics. Jerome would have made a good crusader. He didn't like to work in the real world, to hold down a job as modern times required. His "contract" with his father earned him money as long as he was enrolled at a University to study; the real fortune will come to him only after both his parents have died. The graduation date on the calendar has always been a cruel deadline because he must always have another degree program lined up. But in fact he preferred student life to lawyering in an office. Now, however, the sands were running out. He was well past his thirtieth birthday. Jerome was opening his heart to all of them, asking for help. With Goppollone in his lap he admitted again that he didn't know what to do. He had hoped to find guidance with Margaret. She was a charismatic teacher, he told them. Margaret glanced at Bruno. All this bullshit, Bruno's face said, was the youngster's strategy to get Margaret into bed.

"Law is a waste of time." Marini sipped his wine.

"Time slips away so fast, you need to use it rationally and not abuse it," Bruno declaimed. It was a line from *Faust* in Martin Greenberg's translation. Margaret was not sure if it was addressed to her, to Jerome, or to himself.

"I believe so." In this vague way Jerome responded to the remarks of Marini and Bruno. And the conversation stopped.

Then, as if remembering something in a dream, Jerome said: "Are you that Marini involved in the Vatican's latest financial scandal?"

"Yes, I am," said Marini.

Jerome glowed. "What a New York moment! The real thing, as they say—on the spot! Mister Marini, I was just talking about you with my colleagues. Is it true that you stole all that money?" Nothing could have stopped Jerome from asking.

"My dear friend, it might be true. The good life is for the clever, not for those who hold degrees. I count at this table many Ph.D.s, a dozen Master's degrees, a stack of books, hundreds of articles, but not much money in the bank. I graduated from the Law School in Florence, but what could I do with my degree? So I enrolled in l'École Normale of the Sorbonne. I went into business in the Vatican and became very influential. I am doing now what I like the most, finding out what comes after life."

Marini did not care if he was impolite. He had apparently achieved that state of mind and wealth when one can say anything without concerning oneself about the consequences.

"Why are you trying to find out what's after life? You will find out in due time as we all will." Bruno's insolent response trailed off into mumbling about idiots exploring what is on the "other side" instead of concentrating on what they have here and now.

Feeling compelled to cover Bruno's remark, Margaret turned brightly to Jerome. "Why don't you finish your paper on network effects and the Internet market? Jerome's thesis," she explained to the group, "is that in a virtual network all known antitrust laws are irrelevant."

A "winner-take-most" effect was the natural equilibrium in these markets, even over and above monopoly. Huge inequalities in sales and profits were inevitable in markets with network externalities and incompatible technical standards.

Jerome himself added that he had developed the ideas of a professor who worked at Stanford University and at the Stern School of Business of New York University.

"You really must get it published," Margaret insisted.

"Monopoly maximizing social surplus," Bruno said, rubbing his eyes. "I am involved in this matter. A relevant case will be filed soon with the European Court of Justice."

"I adore this new law," said Marini. "Comte de Joinville, don't bother finishing the paper. Maximize your profits buying shares on the Internet stock market!"

Jerome had to remind Marini that he had no money. All his money was his father's, and that old-fashioned count wanted nothing to do with the stock market.

As this conversation was in progress Wagner had slid smoothly under Marini's chair and Goppollone had jumped into Bruno's lap. It was as if the animals were checking them out to see whom they might prefer. Bruno cursed. Glenn begged him to be patient. "Something extraordinary is about to happen," he said.

Meanwhile, Marini continued advising Jerome. "Medical School is too hard for you, obviously. I can also see that you don't have the patience for philosophy, or even the stock market. Theology? It is not in your blood. You need some excitement, my dear young friend. How about becoming an actor, a movie actor in Hollywood, a TV celebrity, having fun, lots of women, and, of course, fame? Money doesn't seem to be your goal."

"I don't know how to act." Jerome was embarrassed. Bruno laughed much too loudly. A "frog," his attitude said, was a natural born actor; he agreed with Marini. Margaret shushed him. Jerome was too delicate a man to be laughed at like this.

"I have perhaps to honor my father's wish for me? To go home and take care of my family business?" His family had tax troubles. The property needed a lawyer.

"Come on," Marini said. "I am not joking. I speak seriously. You are a good actor. You have been able to get money from your father over the years, convincing him of your love for study. On the other hand, however, you do not possess the shark-like qualities of all these

American or French or Italian lawyers. You need pleasure. As a celebrity, your family will give you all the money you want."

Jerome fidgeted. "I don't know what to do with my life. I mean, what is important? What am I here for really?"

He was looking down, humiliated. Margaret knew that his girl in Toulouse was getting married. And he had to leave New York and move quickly to enroll at another university.

"Get money. Enjoy pleasures. What else?" Marini's voice grew, as if he spoke for everybody. "If you need fame, I can get it for you. Failure is death. Success is immortality and spirit. Will you become an actor?" Suddenly the issue had become a kind of challenge to Margaret and Bruno.

"I don't know if I want to." Jerome was groping for the right answer. His eyes pleaded with Bruno and Margaret.

"The task of a human being is to make the lives of people around pleasant and meaningful. And to pass on or transmit knowledge." It was Bruno, trying to give Jerome the essence of his lifetime experience.

Margaret felt he spoke for her too. Bruno seemed to gather strength as he went on.

"The first task, I believe, is related to love. The second one, to the struggle of teaching, writing, preaching, and raising children. It seems that there is nothing beyond. Nothing lasts. Nobody will talk about us in one hundred years."

He shook his head: "What is writing? Throwing paper onto a pile of sheets. There are too many books around. And almost no reaction to them. A striving for perfection. Scared by oblivion, death, aging, sickness, we keep trying to leave something behind. To survive despite our mortality. What a contemptuous stance lies in the act of writing!"

"You make me laugh." Marini's disagreement was pompous and crude. "You are so wrong! I can prove it! You speak from your own frustrations: no wealth as you wish to have it, three or four children, no real fame, even though you have written many books. You are sick of seeing your name on them. But there is another way around, my friend."

Goppollone jumped over onto Marini's lap. Wagner came back to Bruno's legs. Margaret was holding Jerome's hand.

The noise in the room had become very loud. Bruno did not react visibly to Marini's words. Wagner gave him a sort of discomfort impossible to escape especially after the dinner was clearly on Glenn, but Margaret could feel his mind working laboriously. All he said was:

"Nothing will remain from all of us in one hundred years. My doings, my projects, struggles, nothing. What do I have then?"

"Perhaps the joy of doing them." Margaret spoke as she stroked Madame Blavatsky. The cat's orange dots sparkled on her forehead. A strange happiness suffused Margaret's face.

"Another stupidity." Marini was relentless. "Bruno can write books that will become cornerstones for the future. His name shall never be forgotten. Every important work of art and spirit becomes a piece—smaller or bigger—of the human spiritual creation on which future generations rely. You, guys, need a breakthrough, a personal manager to tell you what to do and how to get visibility and money."

Was this true? Could his work become a cornerstone of the future? Bruno was not sure but did not know how to phrase his uncertainty. Artists and thinkers had always needed examples in the past to prove their new message. On the other hand, humanity was tired of new messages and also craving for them; and it was also afraid of mistakes and impostors. Beyond any doubt, the human species had been reluctant to carry too much in its cramped luggage as it toiled through time. But in order to solve paradoxes, a few were chosen. They would certify anything valuable the human mind would invent at any time.

Could he be one of those? Bruno took a deep breath. But he had to accept the truth. He was sure he would not get in the human species' backpack. And what would really last from those wonderful effects, compositions, intellectual discoveries of the chosen ones? Ideas, ideology, anything that belongs to a specific time are wiped out by the wild winds of changing generations.

Closing his eyes, Bruno tried to embrace those messages coming to him from the past. When he opened them again he saw Margaret, Jerome, Marini, and the crowded restaurant. Wagner's presence between his legs did not bother him anymore. And suddenly, the framework of a love and war story came to his mind; and a smile on a woman's face in a painting, and the sculpture of a young body, and two lines in a play, followed by a small philosophical sentence, and the tension of a musical theme. The most general and simple or universal, if you want, human things and things of nature. And what was truly special was the hard and sophisticated intellectual work of the original composition behind them all.

He looked at himself as if discovering who he was. And he was aware of the magnitude of the moment, as Wagner held him immobile in his chair.

"The quest of my life"—Margaret found herself speaking, the words tumbled out—"was to find my soul mate. I wanted to wake up in the morning, feeling the warmth of my man by my side, listening to his breath, embracing his body, remembering that he was with me in my dreams. Instead I got books, some recognition, and a void inside myself. I did not get what I asked for, apparently it was not for me. I convinced myself that what I am missing I actually possessed once. This way I am free."

Abruptly she knew she did not hate Jules any more. She accepted as fact that she was still in love with him, even though they were apart forever. There was nothing she could do about it.

"False freedom." And Marini added: "Why don't you just say you are burnt-out?"

Margaret relapsed into silence. Jerome, who had impatiently endured her interruption of his conversation, leaped into the gap.

"What do you mean by personal manager? How much would you charge for this?"

"You have to give me some credit if things work out," Marini answered.

"I want to hire you." And addressing Margaret and Bruno: "What do you think of this?" And to Marini when they were both silent: "What do you mean by credit?"

"A sort of statement that the dissenting energy or power or whatever you name it of the Universe is not so bad after all, as humanity claims while in fact believing the opposite. Hypocrisy and schizophrenia. I'm studying this aspect and I see how greatly what is called negativity behaves in the dialectic of matter and human lives. I need followers on this."

And Marini added, theatrically brushing his hair with his left hand while pointing with the right at each of them: "A written statement, an article, a character in a movie, or a thesis signed with your full name. You do this when your accomplishment becomes real and you feel fulfilled. One of my followers, an eminent physicist, conceived a well acclaimed theory on the increasing universe expansion rate attributed to dark energy."

"I have heard about the negative way of redemption—I think the Albigensians were good on that theory. Isn't that why they were destroyed eight centuries ago?" Margaret asked, still holding Jerome's hand.

"I love them." Marini smiled. "They were adorable."

At this interesting juncture Bruno asked Margaret: "Are you an Aries?"

Margaret nodded absently, her mind on the change in Marini's features when the Albigensians were mentioned. It was as if he had known them and was an adept in their heresy.

"So we are both born in the same month, in the same year, in the same zodiacal sign. What day?" Bruno persisted in his alternative conversation.

"The eighth of April." Actually it had been the tenth, but she preferred the eighth; she had always believed it was the day on which she was actually born, that the tenth was merely the day on which her father had declared the newborn.

"I'm April ten," said Bruno. "It is worse than I thought. We went through the same turbulent lives: totalitarianism, '68 militantism, anti-war manifesto, sexual revolution, and now abstinence."

"Interesting, indeed." Marini grafted the conversations. "The quest is on."

"I see here a lot of stuff for a good romantic novel." This was Jerome, wriggling out of his embarrassment. It was obvious that he knew something about Margaret's love life.

But Marini stayed on track. "French jest. You all need a person like me to put you on the right path and accomplish what you are unable to do otherwise."

Bruno's disgust exploded. "You make me sick." He was violently scratching his hirsute beard. Wine and cognac had eroded any politeness he may have preserved. "Don't play Mefisto with me. You are an Italian banker. A fraud. A *maccaronaro*." Wagner barked rubbing Bruno's legs.

"Mefisto is never German. I despise your arrogance." Marini's face was a dangerous-looking yellow. His gold glasses scintillated under his glossy eyebrows.

"I know that gods are immortal, and that men die." Bruno challenged Marini. "Try to change it and you will end up worse off. And that man is imperfect. And that you—who want to perfect Jerome—are imperfect too. Imperfect beings cannot make perfect decisions."

"I feel like eating something special." Jerome was trying to dissipate the tension.

Glenn saw his chance at last as Jerome continued. "Some *Rousquilles fondantes* prepared after *des recettes authentiques depuis 1874*. Or an ice cream, just like that in a pastry shop on Saint Germain de

Près. Flore, my dearest Flore!" Jerome referred to the famous coffee shop on Saint Germain, praised by so many writers.

Marini grimaced as he cooled off. "Too sweet for me. I would prefer pasta at Trattoria da Nello on Borgo Pinti in Firenze, or a Brazilian *feijoada*, black bean stew, with sausage, dry beef and pork, and at least two strong *caipirinha* with lemon after this discussion that has made me sick."

No one said anything. Glenn looked discouraged. Marini went on:

"I know a Brazilian grille on Eighth Avenue and 48th Street. They have *casquinha de siri*, baked crabmeat, and *frango passarinho*, fried chicken sautéed with garlic, olive oil and white wine. There is nothing so great as *caipirinha* and *cachaça* sipped in a small village on the *cerrado*, in the middle of the night while watching the Star of the South, right there on a green *cerrado* with an oasis of *buritti*, imperial palms, as well as gigantic red termite nests!"

At the end of this gourmet discourse, however, Marini divulged that he would settle for a modest restaurant, *Annone Veneto*, in Brasilia DF, around CLS 212 in Brasilia's system of numbered quadrants. From a pocket he produced the restaurant's card and read the address loudly, as if he had just enjoyed a meal there and wanted to pay homage to the chef.

Goppollone and Wagner sniffed Madame Blavatsky in Margaret's arms.

"Why not vodka and Russian caviar Astrakhan Augustovskaya, my favorite brand, in Hotel Rossia in Moscow, close to the Red Square?" Bruno joked uneasily. What was going on? Margaret watched him deeply surprised. He must be familiar with caviar prices in New York. On the other hand, many students coming to Germany from Russia had spoiled him with caviar. But enough of this. Obviously, under normal circumstances, Bruno would have left this table right away. Was it Margaret herself that detained him? She did not deserve, he perhaps thought, to be left there? There was something that stopped him from saying goodnight. She could see he was not sleepy. And he was still hungry. Glenn's food did not fill his stomach.

"The day after tomorrow is Easter," Jerome reminded everybody. "To tell the truth, I miss my family in France."

"We are a family." Marini once again pushed on into a new reality. "We can have a nice celebration at my place, if you like. I have a four-bedroom apartment on Fifth Avenue and 12th Street, just across Washington Square Park, beyond the Arch. I'll give you a ride in my new car, and we'll have lunch and dinner together tomorrow. On Sunday I'll order a special Easter lunch. Or we can have lunch here, in this restaurant."

He spoke rapidly. He clearly wanted no one to refuse his invitation. They were all lonely in this glamorous city where almost everyone was alone. He went on to say that they didn't have to sleep at all. They could just go on with whatever they liked to do together from this moment until Sunday afternoon.

"I'll have a beer," Bruno called the waiter. "A German brand."

"I'll have a strudel," Margaret said, thinking of her grandmother in Sibiu, who had been born in the Pindus Mountains. But could she also get *cozonac*, the Romanian pastry for Easter and Christmas?

"Do you have spinach pie, by any chance?" Margaret was hopeful. It was her grandmother's best pie, filled with *spanac* (spinach) and *brânza* (feta cheese) in handmade fillo, baked in the huge oven in the middle of the courtyard were wood burned every day to bake bread.

As a child Margaret's passionate appetite for feta cheese (*brânza* it was called) had been considered a clear sign that she belonged to the Macedo-Romanian tribe. She had spent many summers at her grandmother's house, even though it had been quite close to her parents' home in Sibiu. She remembered the smell of the evenings there, and those tales about fairies and brave heroes fighting monsters that her grandmother, Zoë, had told her as she braided her long hair.

"How about the real pie and the real *cozonac*? We can go to Sibiu and have them now. Just like that. In a minute."

There was an open challenge in Marini's eyes as he met Margaret's astonished gaze. But all she said was: "I wish I could."

She was thinking of her mother and both grandmothers, their gracious food prepared with fathomless love, recipes as old as the language they spoke. *Plăcinte, cozonac, prune, mâncare de pui cu gutui*—pies, pound cake, prunes, chicken with quince: remembered dishes redolent with the sweetness of life.

"My soul has always been torn apart like Germany's mystical waters: the Rhine flowing up North and West towards the Atlantic Ocean while the Danube keeps all the way down East and South until it reaches the Black Sea."

Margaret's almost voiceless comment made Bruno murmur "der Geist!" She continued: "I was born in a land were most rivers run southward. What a shock to see the waters of the Rhine flowing northward."

Marini turned to instruct the waiter. "I'll have pasta fettuccini."

None of this food talk had distracted Jerome from his life-plan concentration.

"May I call you 'manager'?" he asked Marini. "I like your idea. Could you be the manager of my life?" And addressing Glenn, who was respectfully waiting for his decision, he ordered ice cream with cognac.

Margaret's pie arrived. Strange ancient words, almost forgotten, blew in her mind. But the jarring sensations caused by this pie, which was merely a pizza topped with spinach and mozzarella cheese, dislocated her thoughts.

"*Nu potu s'mâcu aista.*"

"What?" Bruno was sharply concerned.

"I cannot eat this, it doesn't have *brânza*, I mean feta cheese. This is only *pită*, I mean crust bread."

"Are you sick?"

"*Nu potu s'mâcu aista.*" Margaret was trying to rise to go to the bathroom but she could not dislodge Madame Blavatsky, who was securely anchored to her lap and her right arm. "*Nu potu s'imnu,* I mean I cannot eat and walk." She smiled vaguely, as if she was asking for help.

"What's wrong?" Jerome slowly returned to the moment. Gentlemanlike, he stood up and tried to remove the cat, but without success. Margaret sat back down.

"*Tiaharauâ.* I mean, I feel fine." The old language of her mother tribe was taking possession of her. She could see that Jerome and Bruno accepted this as both strange and normal. New York was multinational. Lapses of this kind were common to all of them.

Then, suddenly, Madame Blavatsky startled everyone by leaping away from Margaret. In a flash she shot out through the main door. Cuddle time was over, Margaret smiled to herself; playtime had begun. The Village noises and smells and lights had lured the animal out in the night. All at once, as Goppollone and Wagner rushed after their good friend, Marini quickly slipped a golden collar that the cat had dropped over Margaret's wrist.

"What's that all about?" Bruno shouted. "She is not a cat."

"This collar contains an orientation device. We cannot afford to lose that cat," Marini said. And with a hint of anger: "Madame Blavatsky is almost blind. Haven't you noticed that?" And then, with an air of finality, Marini turned to Margaret: "Will you join me? The cat likes you."

Margaret felt a weight of responsibility fall on her. The collar on her wrist was a message, one she did not understand. Did she want to understand? So much of her life went in the pursuit of mystery.

Glenn, quickly sizing up the situation, begged Margaret to go with Marini. "Madame Blavatsky is a real character, a living treasure," he pleaded. "We must find her. And Wagner too," he charged on. "His warts medication must be given at certain hours." He scurried away and reappeared immediately with a box-like device, a space locator he called it. Blavatsky had a corresponding mechanism in her tail, an implant that would help to locate her. She could only survive about twelve hours on the battery in her pacer.

It was twenty minutes past eleven.

Bruno fretted and rumbled. Jealousy, Margaret thought. Marini and Jerome and Glenn were without doubt all three after Margaret, so Bruno's duty was to watch over her. And Jerome! Sleeping during the night was not his habit anyway.

It took no more than a minute for all four of them to be installed in Marini's luxurious car, ready to begin the quest for the animals.

"I hope that you can all deal with spatial and temporal distortions," Marini warned.

Glenn, remaining on the sidewalk, near the car's opened window, poured out more details about the locator. "Blavatsky suffers from spatial disorientation. And she runs with awesome speed."

Bruno clearly bought none of this. It was all a scam, like tax evasion maneuvers. But he would watch over Margaret; she was so very like his sister in Bonn, he had told her.

"It will not be unlike what you experience in dreams." Marini was still talking about the spatial and temporal distortions they were about to experience. Marini's Lexus was sweeping up Sixth Avenue. In an eerie silence, the angry snarl of taxis and trucks parted before them like the biblical Red Sea. Margaret sat still in the front passenger's seat with the cat's collar on her wrist and the locator in her lap. Marini appeared to be using the erratic green lines that shot all over the locator's screen to navigate, even though they had no identifiable connection with streets or bridges.

"Keep right!" Bruno shouted. He could not contain his rage. He also spoke loud and clear for the wide-eyed Jerome.

"It's a one-way street. And anyway a cat doesn't follow avenues and highways." Marini was more than cool; he was icy. But Margaret keenly felt his thought as his admiring glance touched her: as always, women are the courageous ones. The fabled bravery of the male is nonsense.

Like Bruno. "Slow down, Marini! Jesus Christ!"

The cars horns were left behind and they were out in a sort of unknown-before expressway.

"I am listening," said Jerome. His voice quaked. "You are my life manager. What do you want me to do in order to get an Oscar?" Did he need proof that he would survive this ride?

"Play the devil's advocate. You will get the main role," Marini answered.

Margaret saw the Lexus ES400 leap up in a way she could hardly feel, as if it was not moving at all. A dim unfriendly light leaked into the interior.

"How about me?" Bruno's voice was recovering its sarcastic tone. He was returning to the attack on Marini's preposterous pretension of managing other people's lives.

"You will get your bestseller, Margaret will get her man," Marini almost sang, one hand on the steering wheel, the other waving elegantly in the air, ballet style.

Margaret felt cold fresh air surrounding her. She stared at the locator. They would find the cat, and she would go home and get some sleep.

Marini turned his head and looked straight at Bruno "When the wire transfer for your first big lump sum shows up in your bank account you will publish an article in the *Financial Times* about Baron Marini. He did not steal the Pope's money. You will prove it with clear documents I will provide. I have them in my possession."

"You are a big fool." Bruno almost spat. "Your reputation is ruined."

"And Margaret will write something about the beneficial dark powers of the Universe to return my favor. I will secure a contract with the best publishing house in the entire world."

As Marini turned his face forward again Margaret was suddenly aware of this very interesting man next to her. Marini hit the accelerator and sent the Lexus into a tunnel, perhaps the Lincoln Tunnel, not caring that he was supposed to do the opposite, to slow it down. He drove the car with style. His well-built body, his eyes and voice, his composure all exuded sexuality. But the cold, distant voice contradicted all the other signs. Not a friend. Not a lover. More of an adversary in some indefinable opposition. Margaret knew they all sensed it. Who was he? Why were they all caught up in these absurd circumstances? Surely Glenn would call the police if they didn't return soon?

The car windows were now completely dark. It was cold.

"It is the spatial-temporal distortion," Marini announced. "We are on the right track. Blavatsky is close by."

"This is not a starship, and we are not a bunch of idiots from Epcot Center in Florida." Bruno now spoke with harsh determination. "Stop the car, please, and let me go home. I am tired of this." The sweaty locks on his forehead shook with the car's vibrations.

Jerome had apparently decided to deal with the crisis by trying to fall asleep. Margaret too experienced something close to stupefaction. She had fallen into deep reflection on her past and the life path she was on. The hatred of Jules was not there any more. He had re-entered her life, he was with her all the time. The revelation caused a pang in her womb, there where she located the emptiness of her life without Jules. It was herself she had been denying. Hate is winding down, love does not go away.

Marini pressed a button and all the doors opened. "Here we are. Get some rest. We'll meet in the lobby in four hours sharp." Jerome had to be urged to get out of the car.

"We need a plan," Marini went on. They were walking across the opulent lobby of an old-world hotel. "Wagner is here." And he added: "The hotel is on me."

It was not yet noon on Saturday when, after they all gotten some sleep at the Grand Hotel, they spread out in four directions from the center of Warsaw. Marini had given each of the others a map. The locator indicated four different possible positions for Blavatsky. Marini looked grim. The frisky cat was faster than the locator could handle, he said. And Wagner and Goppollone were deliberately confusing the locator with swift erratic movements.

Margaret followed the Wista, turning right on Krucza and heading for Al. Jerozolimskie, where she turned right again. She passed through Rondo de Gaulle to the Most Poniatowskiego, the old bridge across the Wista. She walked for more than two kilometers along the road. She passed the Museum of War. It was part of the old main road that ran through the heart of Poland from Gdansk to Krakow, a road of many stories from the Second World War and the Solidarnost era. Margaret knew that some of her ancestors had lived in Warsaw. She was perhaps the first of her kin to return there in about two hundred years. She scooped up a handful of soil and put it in her purse.

Here at the edge of the city passers-by were infrequent. They paid no attention to her, as though she belonged there. She felt she was not alone. It was as if her ancestors spoke to her in that language she could not speak. Retracing her steps she went back to the city and wandered around old streets looking for the cat. As she entered the garden of Warsaw University, by the Law School, she felt she had been there before. She lingered for a while in the garden. Under the lilac bush, daffodils and lilies and pansies brought a rush of childhood memories of her parents' garden in Transylvania.

A wooden bench in a grove of blooming willow with its lovely tiny yellow flowers appeared unexpectedly at a turn in the path. Margaret sat down, absorbing with all her pores the melodious fluidity of the moment.

An oval steel barrel floating on the ocean's surface seemed to materialize in front of her, glistening in the sun. The ocean and the sky were perfectly blue. The top of the steel barrel slid open and she could see a golden seed inside. She was that seed. As she watched, a fragile golden stem emerged and climbed straight up toward the sky.

Golden leaves sprang from it as it grew bigger and stronger until it became a tree. Branches reached from it in every direction, looking for something that Margaret soon saw: a garland of golden branches and leaves surrounding Earth. Margaret was the tree, weaving her leaves and branches in and out of that gracious golden belt. This gave her strength and she went on growing. Unfamiliar white flowers blossomed on her branches. She continued to reach upwards, discovering more golden girdles to entwine herself among, each one giving her the power to rise ever farther. But at last an intense light filled her with awe and fear. And there was a sound too: vibrating music she could not remember ever having heard before. Stars glittered in a deep dark blue firmament, moving with a wave that seemed to usher them toward an entrance, an invitation.

But with her fear a withdrawal began. The tree shrank all the way back, becoming a stem and again a seed. The top of the steel barrel closed. She opened her eyes.

Margaret was the first to return to the hotel. She didn't wait for the others, but crossed the street to have lunch at a bar called Lockomotjwa. A noisy table of young men fell silent as she entered, and then broke into a loud laughing conversation. It was about her.

"I am not a whore," she said. Instantly the laughing stopped. Then one of them spoke directly to her.

"I am not an actress either," she answered. She felt giddy, as if she was high on something.

Obviously, she was dressed too elegantly for lunch in this place. She was still wearing her black velvet suit, creamy silk blouse and pearls, and the purple scarf across her shoulders.

A man alone at another table leaned toward her.

"They don't understand why you answer in English if you speak Polish," he said politely.

"I don't speak Polish," replied Margaret.

"You just did," he said.

"Are you also joking at my expense?" Margaret realized she was enjoying this.

"It is not a joke. You understood their remarks about you. You look like an American actress from a soap opera, I cannot remember her name, but she is mostly a kind of whore, I am sorry to say this. They are wondering why you are here and alone. They speak only Polish as you see. And you answered in English. But just before you spoke to me in Polish."

Margaret looked at him. She could not remember speaking to him at all. He was a stocky man in his late thirties, brawny and thick around the chest. He said a few words to the group of young men, and then came to her table and introduced himself as Piotr Miedzeszynski. He was working with the Poland Ministry of Foreign Affairs for the Commission on European Union integration. He was also enrolled in a weekend course for a second master's degree related to politics and he had just stopped here to have a beer on his way home. Margaret told him that she had just arrived in Poland that morning.

The restaurant was set up to look like an old wooden wagon from the early days of the railway era. Parts of a steam engine were displayed on the walls. The benches, on a sort of podium by the window, were supposed to create the illusion that the bar was moving past the people on the street outside.

"Margaret Staundinger." She pronounced her name in a German manner.

"Contessa Staundingera?" Piotr seemed pleased. "We have many old stories about love affairs between German grafs and Polish countesses," he added with a smile. Margaret kept looking at him. His head was clearly illuminated by a light that hung above the table. Her memory sifted through her father's stories, but the only Staundinger she could recall from them was a very distant relative, author of a famous *Kommentar* on the German Civil Code.

"How do you know the name Staundinger?" she asked.

"From history books. Part of the Staundinger clan settled in Poland a few hundreds years ago."

"I believe I am the first of my family to come back to Poland in more than two hundred years," Margaret said slowly, trying to pull this sudden complexity of sensations together.

Somehow she had to hide that ridiculous quest for a cat, a dog, and an animal that was neither. She was listening to the conversation in Polish behind her back. They were still joking about her. Polish must have been there, in her genes, all her life.

"You have a family here," said Piotr. He seemed to bow his head as he asked: "Contessa, would you like another beer?"

"Are you from Sobieski's szlachta?" The question tripped off her tongue. She had not heard him.

Piotr nodded. In the cone of the light he looked familiar.

"I don't know why speaking to you makes me think of Constantinople and Sobieski visiting the Sultan, and those horses covered with gold, purposely losing the golden horseshoes on the street. And you grandly throwing gold to the crowd. And the Turks coming to Poland to steal its treasure. And the war and you and I dancing at the ball." Margaret spoke quietly and slowly. It was all there, rising inexorably to the surface.

They were in Krakow, in Sobieski's palace. It was about 1675, at the height of the Ottoman invasions. For centuries, the armies of kings and princes had been engaged in battles according to European rules of chivalry. But the Turks did not respect knights' rules and the laws of war. They were savage barbarians and they wanted everything. And Sobieski's szlachta were so haughty and so arrogant they believed they could turn back these Asiatic hordes.

She stood with him in the corner of a huge ballroom. Piotr was in love with her, and she loved his love. He was the King's cousin and she was a Bavarian countess. A perfect match. Their marriage would be a warranty for the Northern Alliance against the Turks. Bavaria and Poland were committed to fighting side by side. The Turks had overrun the south from Constantinople all the way up to Krakow. The place of the battle was to be decided. Tartars were also ready to attack Poland's Eastern flank at the Turks' signal. Tartars in the east and Turks in the south. Poland was not able to fight alone on two fronts. The Bavarian army had not arrived yet. Piotr pivoted to give orders to his officers and then turned back to her. "Go to Danzig with your family and wait for me there," he said.

"As you wish." She liked to salve Piotr's worries. Her Parisian dress sparkled with nuances of creamy brocade and golden embroidery. A pearl pin held her hair away from her shoulders.

"I leave tonight for the Moldavian border. You must leave Krakow tomorrow."

"As you wish." She repeated those words again in the garden. Piotr kissed her and pressed her to him. Their life together lay ahead of them. The wedding was to be soon after the danger had passed.

As Margaret stared across the table in the Lockomotjwa she wondered if Piotr remembered the bloody field thick with Polish and Turkish corpses. The breeze of the Carpathians must have made death seem far away to him as he rode south and the Tartars destroyed Krakow. He died the next day in the battle. The Turks continued to proceed north. Her entire family, trying to escape, was trapped and killed.

Piotr's embarrassment was palpable. She could see that he felt guilty and unsettled by strange images and uncomfortable feelings. Of course he felt they should spend the night together, as they were supposed to have done three centuries before. He did not care that now she was fifteen years older than he.

Margaret let him kiss her in front of the hotel. "Life goes in circles," she said.

These words too came from nowhere. Slowly she had become aware that Jules had been in her mind all the time. She wanted to be with Jules. Her desire for Jules had surfaced as the crucial element in a sensation she recognized as guilt for betraying Piotr. But must there be anything more to this mutual destiny? With nothing rational to give her full confidence, hugging Piotr she repeated, instead of goodbye:

"*Moyí drogy*, my love, we will meet again: *Kokhany, spotkamy sie jeszcze.*"

It was eleven o'clock in the morning at a café on Boulevard Saint Germain. Margaret played nervously with Madame Blavatsky's golden collar and a little napkin that proclaimed *Café de Flore* in green designs. Not a meter away, the cat was licking her fur, but Margaret dared not approach. To wait for Blavatsky to come to her, Margaret felt, was the only strategy possible at that moment.

A waiter brought hot chocolate and some cookies. All three animals obviously liked it here. Goppollone and Madame Blavatsky, sniffing and purring, had settled under a table where Wagner had lain down to rest. Margaret was tense and poised, ready to perform the double duty of replacing the collar and the battery of Blavatsky's life preserving device. The beasts clustered at the feet of two gentlemen engaged in animated conversation. The café was crowded and alive with talk and laughter. Everybody seemed to know everybody else.

Margaret expected Bruno, Jerome, and Marini at any minute. The pets had only to be taken gently one by one and loaded in the car. Journey's end.

"Dominique!" The name was spat with contempt by one of the men. Blavatsky draped herself across the shoe of his right foot. "I will not give him back my *Cahiers de L'Herne.*" A ripple of mirth ran around the café, saying this man was foolish but well-liked.

"Don't be so sure," his table companion said. "His offer is very good. At least he'll not do what you're doing now. You're washing the whole venture right down the drain."

"Jean, I am not the idiot you think I am. He put you up to this clumsy attempt to discourage me. Lack of imagination, both of you. *Les Cahiers* are doing better than ever."

Both men were quite advanced in life, but they had nothing else in common. The plump one addressed as Jean—the defender of the *Cahiers* from the other's freewheeling course—fairly crackled with an alarming ingenuity that streamed from his electric eyes. His lips barely moved when he spoke, so it seemed like his voice came from his flying hands, as if his tongue wagged between his fingers. The other, white-haired, very thin and still, smoked a cigar and coughed quietly and regularly. His slow rhythms brought to mind the movement of the tides. His face was a map of a continent crisscrossed by rivers and mountain ridges.

"Is monsieur Jean Parvulesco publishing another book with monsieur de Roux?" the thin one said in response to the other's remark. "How much did he promise you?"

"Costa, I don't think you can match it. You are too greedy." The plump man looked all around, his eyes sparkling, and got the approving laughter he expected.

"And you're a beggar." Approval of Costa's remark was about the same. Everyone was amused. It seemed these two had been crossing swords since time immemorial.

But here was Jerome. To Margaret's surprise he fell on Jean Parvulesco's chest and trapped him in a hug that was clearly unwanted. Everyone loved it.

In his instantly embarrassed way, Jerome became effusive as he explained the unexpected scene to Margaret. Jean Parvulesco, a mentor of Jerome's at the Sorbonne, was a living legend of European literature—mystic, poet, novelist, literary critic, connoisseur of political intrigue, revolutionary, friend and confidant of celebrities from Ezra Pound and Julius Evola to Raymond Abellio and Arno Breker. He was a visionary, Jerome said, a direct and inspired contemplator of spiritual spheres, always ready to open to the chosen the deeper truths behind the sullen and trivial appearance of the profane contemporary world.

The avalanche of words did not embarrass Jean Parvulesco. *Au contraire*, he augmented and clarified Jerome's screed with his own impenetrable comments.

Margaret was wondering whether Parvulesco really remembered Jerome. The proof came soon. When Jerome's words sputtered out, Parvulesco asked carefully weighing up his elegant cream-colored sweater and the impeccable white shirt: "Are you still *dans le deuil de la beauté perdue*?" Margaret recognized this coded anti-revolution-ary nostalgia for lost French nobility. She saw how someone like Jer-ome would satisfy a yearning for the restoration of the kingdom's grandeur.

"Are you still feeling the *incendium amoris*?" Parvulesco got more personal. "Are you still in the *aedificium tantricum de la fournaise absolue de la châsse d'accompli le désir*?"

Jerome was overjoyed to tell everyone around about his hunt for love and the deceit of his girlfriend in Toulouse. She did not wait for him while he was getting his LLM degree in the States, he told his old teacher. "In the Middle Ages a lady would patiently await her knight's homecoming, no matter how long it took. Time was not important." Jerome explained that he was here to keep an appoint-ment with Margaret. He pointed at her as he ordered *rousquilles fon-dantes*. They had visited Foucault's pendulum at the Panthéon, he explained, and stopped at 140 Rue du Bac to visit la Chapelle Notre-Dame de la Médaille Miraculeuse. When they separated, they had agreed to meet at Flore.

Margaret felt engulfed as Jerome threw himself down in the chair next to her and launched into another breathless disquisition across the two tables, this time an attempt to explain the identities and roles of the animals at their feet.

But Parvulesco interrupted him. "*Écoute donc*, Jerome, are you saying that she is your teacher in New York?" Margaret looked at

Parvulesco. It wasn't only his glittering eyes; his gross presumption lay thick upon the air between them. "Is she married?"

Jerome's next rush of words recounted Margaret's love affair with Jules and its demise. It was a *médisance* or gossip the room absorbed thirstily. Nothing could have had less relevance than Margaret's feelings. As he spoke he devoured his *rousquilles fondantes* with such speed that a woman at the next table told him to slow down, no glycemic coma in her presence, thank you.

"Margaret, you are wearing *un cosmique manteau de ténébres ecstatiques mais, en même temps, foisonnantes*," Parvulesco addressed Margaret with great gestures. Obviously, her elegant black velvet suit had inspired him. But Margaret's attention had been drawn to the woman who had just spoken. She thought she had known her slightly at some time: a poetess in exile, age hard to define, in the zone between eternal youth and caustic age. Nobody knew where she came from. Her literary taste was unquestionable.

"You might be a good writer, Jean, but you are a bore when you talk," the poetess (as Margaret dubbed her) said.

Margaret felt something move over her hands, still clutching the golden collar. It was Costa. "If you are not married I will marry you," he said. He raised her free hand and kissed her fingers. "I have a big palace, waiting for my lady love in the middle of Paris. I am rich. My children are married, my wife is recently deceased. I need a woman like you in my life. You are a wonder of this world. The males of your generation pee in their pants when they encounter a woman of your beauty and intelligence. None of them dare assume the risk of loving you. Jerks. Morons." She felt his assault from three different directions: his dispassionate voice, his febrile words, his piercing eyes.

"Why do you want to marry her?" It was Parvulesco playing to the gallery again. "First you have to clean the toilets in that palace of yours! Have you any idea how disgusting they are? I would fire that housekeeper of yours."

Crude laughter ran off Costa like rain off a tin roof.

"How about what's-her-name? She thinks you're going to give her an engagement ring," the ageless woman said. She was sipping latte. A kind of black light shot from the sockets of her white face.

Costa asked Margaret about her family history, and Margaret was too polite not to answer. He found out about her Macedo-Romanian roots. Amazing! He belonged to that tribe as well. They were relatives! Costa was a distant cousin on Margaret's mother's side. Marriage between cousins was a tradition in their tribe, was it not? Almost a rule. Indeed, that is how they had preserved their blood and tradition for two thousand years.

"I want Margaret," Costa proclaimed. "She deserves a good husband." It was his duty, he said, to marry her in order to prevent her mixing her blood with someone outside of the tribe. Together, they could even repair damage done in the past.

But this was too much for Jerome. "Friends, please, stop this show, this is not customary in North America. Ladies there have a different psychology."

"For God's sake, she is a European, not an American," said the poetess.

"I'm not joking. I will marry her tomorrow." Costa's voice swelled far beyond what his frame seemed able to support. His hand trembled at his breast. With fierce smiling energy the poetess held a glass of water to his lips and forced him to drink. Choking, Costa thrust the glass away from his face.

"*Faut-il rire des femmes savantes?*" He glared at the poetess.

"*Qu'est-ce que l'art? Prostitution.* What is art? Prostitution." The poetess translated for Margaret. "Charles Baudelaire said it, dearest."

Parvulesco broke in with an access of jocularity and dispersed and reassembled the scene. The poetess was distracted by a man softly singing a song in some unfamiliar language. She laughed as he translated it for her word by word.

Costa seemed to be waiting for Margaret to speak, but Margaret addressed Parvulesco. "Are you an initiate?"

Parvulesco said yes, at least that was what they all said about him. She told him about her vision in the Warsaw University garden.

"You must read *Zohar*, the most important part of the *Kabbalah*," Parvulesco said. "You will learn there that each thing in this world creates its own mystery. When you name a thing, you hide its mystery." He added: "Sex is a yearning for unity."

"What do you feel about me?" She wanted to know.

"You are an initiate too. With unlimited powers."

This was spoken with great solemnity. Margaret smiled. She was not, she said. Everything she had ever done was merely for the sake of survival.

"You are afraid to express what you want to do," said Parvulesco. "You can do anything you want. Dare to will what you want into being. That's what the great initiates tell you through your vision."

"I can't believe it, I need proof."

"You will have it. You must be prepared for what you wish."

"There's Prince Murat," Costa said, pointing.

"Aristocracy of the Empire," Parvulesco sneered. "Two hundred years old! Give me a break. Napoleon!" Immediately Parvulesco's mocking mirth was all over the room. Had it ever been gone?

Of course Margaret understood that the Murats are not real aristocrats like Jerome with his thousand-year pedigree.

Marini appeared in the doorway. He strode to Wagner and administered his anti-warts medication.

"We're leaving," he said. "First we go to Mont Saint-Michel as planned. After that we go home. Get Goppollone and Blavatsky." Margaret changed Madame Blavatsky's battery. The cat meowed and stretched as if giving up all her adventurous intentions. The orange dots on her forehead sent a luminous message to the room.

"*Au diable*, why do you need to see the swamps of Brittany, those grim quicksands?" roared Parvulesco. "Are you really obsessed with leaving now for the Northwest a few hundred kilometers away?"

Marini shouted back as if Parvulesco was deaf. "Don't worry, we go straight to the Castle's Terrace. We won't touch the beach. It is only noon."

And then in a flash Goppollone and Madame Blavatsky jumped from under the table through the open door. Wagner escaped Marini's tight hands and charged after them. Margaret leaped after Blavatsky, golden collar in hand, and Jerome did the same despite Parvulesco's cry to stay.

In the front seat of Marini's car they found Bruno sitting in silent rage. Apparently he had spent the last hour with Marini in a restaurant near the Comédie Française.

Margaret was thinking that Costa was an unusual man. He had proposed marriage after only a few minutes, something Jules had anguished over for years. She liked Costa. She would call him back. He was perhaps a good friend.

"He is a con man." Marini drove at high speed through crowded Paris streets. "I wouldn't pay any heed to his invitation—I mean, I wouldn't go to his palace. You'd die there of hunger and boredom."

Out of a stinging wind Marini ushered his three companions through the tiny door of Lidojošā Varde (The Flying Frog), where Elizabetes iela crosses Valdemara in the center of Riga. This cozy establishment looked more expensive than Vērmanïtis, which was famous not only for its generous servings of Baltic cuisine but also for its reasonable prices. Vērmanïtis also profited from its proximity to the Reval Hotel Latvija, the Cathedral and the park, and the Daugava River. Lidojošā Varde was that other tourist desideratum, the found gem. Its centerpiece was a big wooden frog with wings.

"Whoever kisses the frog is granted three wishes," Marini told them. "But you have to speak out one wish in a loud voice."

They sat down around a table in an alcove near the only other diner, a man eating alone. Three laughing waiters fed the animals in front of a very welcome woodburning fireplace. "It is always quiet on Saturday morning," one of them said. "Evenings we are very busy."

Marini asked the speaker to close the door of their small dining room, so the animals would not escape again. Everyone was hungry, animals and people. It was cold on the streets of Riga. Moreover, Margaret had left Paris with her lunch uneaten. And *rousquilles fondantes* had not filled Jerome's stomach.

"We'll visit Jurmala, and try to get some good amber stones in Lielupe, Dzintari or Majori." Apparently Marini was feeling magnanimous. These places were famous beauty spots on the Gulf of Latvia west of Riga.

"Why not just go to the stalls behind Saint Peter's Church?" Jerome ventured. Street vendors had traded in amber there for more generations than anyone could remember.

Marini's eyebrows shot up. "We're not in your lovely France," he said. Jerome gaped.

Margaret suddenly jumped to her feet. "I want to kiss the frog!" she called in a singsong voice, tripping across the floor like an excited five-year-old.

Jerome tried to mimic her tone. "I want to find my love, I want to find my love, I want to find my love! I will kiss the frog for you!"

Margaret stood still and kissed the frog, repeating Jerome's words in a loud voice.

"Lieben belebt," she said as an epilogue of the scene. And for the others not knowing German: "I am alive as long as I am in love."

Bruno weighed in murmuring "Goethe". And after a short pause: "I hear there's a good Armenian restaurant on Miera Street. I would have *shashlik*." He wanted to go to Aragats. Marini said nothing but merely pointed in the right direction. Bruno left.

"Let him go," Marini said, turning a shoulder to Jerome and addressing Margaret. "He needs some space to sort all this out. He's attracted to you, you know, in spite of himself. He doesn't know what to do or how to hide his feelings. He hates these animals too. I think he's allergic. He will have enough Armenians."

Marini ordered a salmon prepared in the Norwegian way. "I understand why his wife got mentally ill. Soon we all will be sick of him. Germans are boring and full of routines. To be in Riga and eat Armenian food, well, only a German would do it. I'll teach you the power of loneliness," he abruptly continued. "You don't need a man. Loneliness means power and creativity."

"I don't feel lonely. I feel empty." She was not greedy. Her life was not complete.

"One is power."

"Two is for human beings."

"No. *Nê*. Love is weakness."

"In fairy tales, yes, it is not the princess who goes out looking for love. But when love finds her she is glad."

Margaret, however, had sought love. She had also disdained the basic rules of the quest, and now this came back to her with a searing pang that shook her frame. She had divorced twice; two men had divorced their wives for her. She had left each of them after a while, miserable and ashamed of what she had done. Was it her ego, her ambition, something that would not let her admit a lesser being into her life? Now with scintillating clarity she saw her punishment. She longed for redemption. A man loving and wanting Margaret as she was. Was he real?

"*Paldies*. Thank you." Marini had struck up a conversation with the man at the other table, who introduced himself as a cab driver. Marini invited him to join them. "Cheers! *Priekā!*"

Margaret's awareness blurred into the warm rosy glow of the fireplace as Marini and Jerome buried their heads in their rattling plates. The cab driver was speaking softly in a drowsy, melodious voice. A waiter edged into her reverie, asking if she was enjoying her pork cutlet wrapped in fried eggs. It was heavy and tasty, she was about to reply, like a good Latvian dish, when she heard the cab driver murmur: "What about Khrishnamurti?"

It was Margaret he addressed. His back was to Marini. Delicately he lifted spilled crumbs and laid them, one by one, on Margaret's plate. "Khrishnamurti says that if you have a nice family and love in your life, the world passes you by. You never discover what the world is. Now, it seems to me that you have first to find out what the world is, and after that you will find the one who is also looking for you."

Then he rose and stepped to the door. He opened it. He smiled. The three animals proceeded through the doorway in very slow motion, their tails raised as if passing a reviewing stand. Everyone watched in silence.

Then with a shout Marini was running, with Jerome at his heels. Just inside the main door they collided with Bruno, who turned and stamped after them. Margaret had not moved. And even though the cab driver had disappeared, she heard his voice whisper:

"You must experience the sea. Don't let it pass you by."

Noon on the Baltic Sea. A biting wind. Sharp pale light of late April. White and pink shells among algae and pieces of debris discarded by waves glowing in the finely sifted sand. A gently restless tide. An infinite unfolding range of amber nuances. Fragrance of pines.

High in the sky an unswerving constellation of birds journeyed north with unfathomable knowledge and faraway noise. Closer birds chirped in the evergreens, calling and building nests. Margaret stood still and the sun rose majestically above the pines. For a moment it rested atop the trees, consecrating the transparent and gracious air with an easing of the day's momentum.

Margaret's long shadow emerged, reaching over the murmuring tide as if trying to cover as much of the sea as possible. Stepping gingerly on the sand, as fine as dust, she trod on small, delicate seashells, more suited she thought to a pond than to this great and fabled sea.

She untied her purple silk scarf with flowers of many colors, folded it, and put it into her purse. Bending her knees slightly, her hands pulling at her black velvet skirt, she knelt and sipped the water. It was sweet, with a vaguely salty taste. She compared it with the intense salt of the ocean at Rockaway Beach in New York. She thought too of the deep blue of the Atlantic as it merges to violet, nothing like this pale blue of the Baltic.

She lifted her head. There in front of her stood a transparent wall, the one separating this world from the other. And it seemed that Glenn's solemn face was somehow behind that wall. It was a hallucination that vanished rapidly.

One move and she could go through. She rose and felt the shimmering energy, challenging her to do it. At the threshold grew a gigantic flower with blue petals at the edge, red petals next to the center, and a pistil of transparent amber. A gate was ajar. She was trying to move but succeeded only in touching with both hands the amberish middle. The huge flower embraced her. For an instant she was a seed in a cocoon. She did not go through. But a transparent trace of her hands remained in the middle of the pistil. She heard a gate close, and the shape of her hands trembled for a few more seconds. Then it all vanished.

On stormy days deep, relentless currents plunder the forests of submerged amber that outline the Baltic coast, and pounding waves catapult fragments of every size along its shores. Margaret saw furious strings of dark clouds streaming toward her. The Arctic whipped at her and threatened, a voice in her ears. Distorted clouds writhed like angry serpents in the sky, piled in ever-changing layers. The north wind drove the water toward the shore. Margaret ran from the beach, in terror that the violently withdrawing tide would suck her down to the seabed where the forests of amber awaited her.

"We have lost them again. Let's go!" Marini impatiently waved Margaret into the Lexus. He was not anxious, just ready to go. This unnerving intercontinental travel seemed to have no effect on him.

Margaret had felt as she ran up from the shore that the car had been stalking her and now they expected her to divulge what she had seen and heard. But she said nothing. Jerome had taken to sitting in front, close to his life manager. He needed to discuss strategies for his future. In the back seat, Bruno turned to Margaret and said: "I was afraid you might get lost on those deserted lands by the sea."

But soon trepidation jolted them all. The Lexus ES400 struggled with something like a storm, a flaw (Marini said) in the antigravitational force that propelled it.

"It happens while changing hemispheres, I cannot fix this problem." And addressing Jerome: "You'd better watch that locator. Brazil is huge. Any error there means hundreds of kilometers of wasted time."

On the way to Brazil it was dark and quiet. The Latvian lunch hung like a stone. Bruno's Armenian food was not mentioned. But in a few brief sentences that passed between the three men Margaret discovered that Marini's influence had been strengthened. Somehow, when she had not been aware of what was happening, Bruno and Jerome had each signed a piece of paper naming Marini as their "Life Manager." Already Jerome had set up an appointment with a movie director through email. He was supposed to start shooting a movie in Hollywood in two weeks' time. Marini's recommendation had been more effective then any portfolio or drama school or Broadway experience. When Bruno checked his email, he had discovered a contract for a book with a prestigious publisher in his field of expertise. He had also been awarded a major honor, as a result of which he had been offered a tenured position at Harvard Law School as director of a new international taxation program.

But Margaret could not have foreseen Bruno's next words, spoken very softly in the quiet darkness. "Tell me about Jules," he said.

Did he know she was thinking of Jules? Of course, the darkness and closeness encouraged Bruno to ask about him. Yes, Jules was an enigma for all of them. Was he not an enigma even for her?

Jules was a dealer, she was thinking. He knew how to sell his products and himself, and how to make her believe whatever he wanted. He was an accomplished faker of embarrassment, vulnerability, innocence, and love. He could make her feel guilty when she had nothing to feel guilty about. He could lure her. At this moment Margaret did not want to talk about Jules. She would rather have escaped him. She felt his skin against her breasts when she closed her eyes, his fingers intertwined with hers. His desire. The harmony of making love with Jules. Forcibly she contracted her eyelids to contain the bursting tears of frustration.

"Whereabouts was he born? On which hemisphere?" But this was not about Jules. Bruno was whispering about Marini, joking about Marini's changing of hemispheres remark. Margaret realized Bruno had changed tactics and was coming to the main subject from a side topic.

"The Southern one," Margaret said, withdrawing herself from Jules' imaginary embrace. "Around Congo."

"What do you think of him?"

"A savage meat-eating animal. A white man who mocks the values of European civilization. He hunts our kind and in this resides his main satisfaction. He offers riches, beauty, power, fame in exchange for the betrayal of the deepest beliefs that in various ways we all cherish. In my case, it is perhaps only the strong appearance of youth on my face lately that makes me happy. He knows he cannot give me love."

"I can give you love and pleasure." Bruno avoided Margaret's eyes. He spoke as if he didn't want her to hear.

And there it was, her attraction to Bruno. It had been there all along. But still it was Jules in her mind, not Bruno. She hurried on with the whispered conversation about Marini.

"He likes to go on safari in his Land Rover. He is a hunter. And at home he hunts souls. He has no mercy."

She remembered a story of Marini's. It was dawn, the air was still, the elephants silent. They wrapped their trunks around clumps of grass, uprooting them. Gazelles ran on the plain. Lions slept in the grass. Marini, jumped at by a leopard, confronted it and escaped. She envied his freedom, his power, and his riches. But that coldness around him cancelled everything.

"Have you ever seen the dark presence?" Bruno whispered urgently, as if he wanted to get a precious piece of information from her. It seemed to Margaret that the luxurious Lexus was overheated. Her face was flushed.

"Have you?" Margaret turned to him. She felt sweat on her brow.

"Is he a white man?" inquired Bruno.

"Yes."

"Looking about ten years older than we."

"I believe so."

"And blond with blue eyes. As tall as me."

"Perfect."

"He is a banker traveling all over the world with his dog."

"And a graduate of l'École Normale." And Margaret added: "He is a Cancer."

"The worst astrological sign for a man."

"That is not important. The dark presence is eternal."

"Why do we feel the urge to sign a contract with 'the life manager' if knowing all of this?" Bruno was questioning himself.

"Intelligence and genius are hugely impatient. Mefisto and Lucifer speed us to layers of destiny and rush us to a stage we would attain later anyway. We perceive this."

"Why are you encouraging this 'life manager' business?" Bruno's tenderness was very affecting.

Margaret spoke carefully. "Perhaps out of curiosity. I also care for the cat. And I get bored waiting for what will happen eventually anyway."

Then she kissed him on his lips, kissing Jules in her mind. She was sure Bruno knew this and accepted it.

It was still Saturday about 7 AM, but in a very different place.

It was the middle of the *campo cerrado*, in the middle of South America, where it is enough to scratch the soil to get to the white and pink and violet stones sustaining the continent. Margaret saw a bumpy grassland with jacarandas and *buritti* palms, three white cows grazing, and a few gigantic red-and-white termite nests. Marini stealthily drew the others' attention to a large bird stirring silently on a nearby branch. "Carcara hawk," he said. In the still air the sun was merciless.

Walking on a path of pink and white crystals, a bright line through the grass, they entered *Chapada dos veadeiros*, on a trail left behind by *garimpeiros*, thieves of crystals who cut big stones and polish them on the spot for sale to visitors. The *chapada* led to a big *garimpo*, a field of semiprecious stones. Jerome, carrying the locator, said the three animals were close by, near a cascade or a lake.

"I see it!" He called from the top of a rock. He pointed, then scrambled down. "We can purify ourselves, too," he said, grinning. "On Saturdays the water washes away all the spells put on us by witches." It was what they believed in Provence.

"Be careful," Marini warned. "There are *surucucu* and other dangerous animals here." He sounded genial. And indeed he was in a garrulous mood. As he took the lead through several further *chapadas*, he amused himself by telling smutty stories about the last emperor of Brazil and his famous mistresses. The names and titles of these ladies rippled off his tongue: La Condessa da Estrella, Luisa Amelia da Silva Maia, Princessa Francisca Baronessa da Vassonras, Alexandrina Teixera Leite.

There was no escape from the blistering sun.

When they came to the lake Jerome jumped in immediately, leaving on the nearby volcanic stones his elegant cream-colored sweater, the impeccable white shirt and Polo denims. It was a spectacular spot: flanked by volcanic red rocks, a magnificent waterfall cascaded into shimmering water that seemed to swallow it, curtaining a dark cave of indiscernible depth. Marini looked at a map he was carrying and said: "*Cachoeira do Garimpo*."

Bruno and Margaret found a pebbly area where the water lapped gently around their feet and they knelt together to splash their faces and take a few sips from the cold and refreshing source. An ancient ceremony, Margaret thought. She wasn't listening to Marini, whose mood had not changed despite the challenging climb of the *Chapada dos Veadeiros* and the still, intense heat. But Bruno, Margaret could see, had abandoned his cynicism. The dry, hot air and the proximity of wild animals were too much for him.

Then, from the middle of the lake, Jerome shouted: "I've got them!"

He was on Goppollone's back, cavorting in the waterfall. Madame Blavatsky, like a wet rag, slept on a stone in the hot sun. Wagner's barking echoed in the cave.

"My dearest creatures!" Marini opened his arms, his face and demeanor radiant with tenderness.

It was a happy reunion.

By silent agreement, everyone now felt hungry. With noon a few hours away, and no breakfast, they all wanted something to eat and a place to rest. Marini looked at the map and then across the lake. He pointed. "There," he said.

It took no more than ten minutes to walk to the village. It was only Bruno that did not carry an animal in his arms. He got too hot in his dark blue suit.

They came to the *pausada Casa das Flores*. In this kind place the red and yellow and pink flowers, which out there in the arid *campo* bargained with the cruel sun, were here clustered in cultivated profusion. A gentle breeze from nowhere brought them bougainvillea and palm and just-boiled fresh milk. For an instant Margaret was back in the brightly-colored midday austerity of a Transylvanian village.

On a wooden bed covered with hand-made blankets, Margaret fell into a dream, her weariness struggling with her fear that the *surucucu* serpent would slip under the door of her tiny room.

Outside of herself she heard her own voice reverberate as if in some vast space.

"What is time?"

Carried on a voice without qualities an answer came: "Years do not matter. Centuries do not matter. Millennia do not matter. Only tens of thousands of years matter, for they are the constituent parts of the units of Time. The unit by which Time is measured is one hundred thousand years. To remain within the memory of Time, you must, even as a small kernel, bring about something of such force that it will endure for the ten-thousand-year period in which your life falls."

In a shadow world with more darkness than light Margaret touched a unit of one hundred thousand years. She felt a flat surface, smooth and warm. Moving beneath it she thought she could feel flesh and bone, human life and other life. Small protruding nodules moved about, the size of half a pea. This was a finished unit. Her ten thousand years was still in the making.

She moved back.

"Time is my flesh. My flesh is Time." Again her own voice, far away.

Dimly she saw that what she had touched was merely one of many similar block-like protrusions extending from a huge form resembling a wheel. Between the blocks were narrow spaces of emptiness. The wheel seemed to rotate slowly counter-clockwise, but not around a fixed center. It was also engaged in a barely perceptible movement from right to left. It made no sound.

She understood clearly that a wheel of Time has more than a million years.

"Must I comprehend how Time is curved, as the wheel is?"

Silence.

She stepped farther back to see it better. Yes, not too far away was another revolving wheel moving from right to left in the same slow motion. Farther away were many others. It was not quite dark, but the shadows of those colossal wheels showed that light was coming from somewhere.

"Does this motion have a purpose"? Margaret asked.

The answer came immediately.

"Yes."

After a late lunch Bruno and Margaret agreed to explore the place. They left Marini and Jerome at a table set on the porch and followed a path that trailed among trees and flowers. A toucan, far away from its Amazonia, stalked along the edge of the swimming pool. The bird shook its huge beak at them and flew off. *Chuveirinho,* "little flowers" of amethyst resembling dandelions, and pulpy violet *candombá* strewed their trail, which they soon learned led to a bar where a band played the *pagode,* bringing the noise of the *ressaca* that washed the beaches in Rio to this thirsty land yearning for rain, not due for several months yet.

They sat and had sugar cane juice, *pao de açúcar,* with *queijo,* a delicacy made of local cheese, and strong *caipirinha de cachaça.* Bruno had left his jacket and red tie. With his white shirt and rolled-up sleeves he looked ten years younger. Margaret, in her white chemise, felt like the two of them were teenagers taking advantage of their parents' temporary absence while on holiday. But she was obsessed with her dream, and sidestepped Bruno's insistent need for serious conversation.

"Do you feel what happened to us as déja vu?" Strong *caipirinha* helped Bruno speak easily.

"Like what?" Margaret was not sure what he wanted to say.

"Something that you know existed before and you live it again in your own life," Bruno explained, unsure. "It is like a story you have known, and all of a sudden you play it with elements of your real life."

Margaret was too absorbed in her dream to concentrate on what Bruno was saying. As she hesitated, he spoke again.

"Don't you see that it is as if I am supposed to be your seducer, you are supposed to be seduced, Jerome is supposed to be my apprentice, while Marini is supposed to give me power, money, and success in exchange for something very volatile and ambiguous?" Again she struggled silently for an appropriate response, and after three seconds he said: "I feel I am framed up."

"It is unusual what has happened to us," Margaret said. Trying harder, she continued. "But I do not want to analyze anything. In fact I feel it is I that am supposed to seduce you, with Jerome my apprentice, while Marini pursues me. And Wagner is more than a dog, let's say a devil of some sort."

Bruno looked around as if Marini might be hiding under a table.

"Do you think that I can change the play?"

Margaret laughed.

At this point a middle-aged woman approached Margaret from the bar. "I can tell you about your life. Take your glass and come with me." She turned to Bruno. "You too."

Bruno of course disliked fortune tellers, but Margaret took his arm and compelled him to walk with her. The woman led them to a tent at the edge of the inn's interior garden. It was dark inside in contrast to the dazzling sun of the *cerrado*. Several decks of colorful cards, crystals, and other objects littered a table illuminated by a green-shaded lamp. The woman introduced herself as Eliza Braga, and gave them each a business card. She asked Margaret to choose among tarot, standard playing cards, or numerology. The consultation was free of charge.

"Numerology," decided Margaret.

Eliza Braga looked carefully at the numbers conjured from Margaret's first name, last name, date of birth, age, and year of last birthday. The numbers showed rigor and discipline, independence, initiative, and devotion to collective causes. These were her lifetime missions—*missao de vida*. But number 2, the one that gives life in coupling, marriage, and the like, was missing. Her soul listened to number 1, independence and initiative.

"You can be anything you want. You have energy. You can even become the president of your country. It seems also that you are alone."

"I have always liked odd numbers." She smiled at Bruno. "I did not know why. I have always felt a block of ice in my heart. No love was enough to melt it. Even the love of my son."

"Do you really believe in these?" Bruno's contempt for Eliza Braga and her accoutrements was palpable. He could not look in her eyes, or even around him at the collection of stupid objects. Eliza's eyes followed him carefully. Margaret, impulsive and curious as always, was amused by his discomfiture. This woman's eyes are his surucucu, she thought.

"You'd better believe." Eliza's voice was threatening. "*Capeta* is your friend, not mine. Go to la Vale da Lua to wash off the dark energies he is spilling over you!"

"What is *capeta*?"

Eliza did not answer. Bruno wrote the word in his notebook.

"Keep quiet." Margaret spoke in mock sternness. "And listen."

Eliza Braga told them that, despite the fact that she was considered a *bruxo*, a witch, she was an educated woman. But she really could read other people's minds. She knew who they were. She offered to look at Bruno's numbers, for free, but he refused.

Then the big crystals on the table filled with clouds and the lamp grew dim. The cards turned green. Was Eliza upset that they did not believe her? Lighting a candle, the fortune teller ordered Margaret and Bruno to stay seated. She wanted to tell them something very important, she said; perhaps the essence of her thoughts and life spent in *chapada*.

"It doesn't matter what you do with your life. How many proud accomplishments you can account for. On time's scale, almost none of this matters. Languages, countries, populations, civilizations come and go. We have had so many in the *cerrado* we cannot remember. The place is now all but a desert. In a hundred years nobody will remember your name or the energy you expended on so many things. What matters is your happiness and fulfillment. These are yours. Here and now is your eternity. In other words, the key to life is the masterpiece you are becoming. You are the great book you are struggling to write. It is the humanity and eternity within you that expresses you from one instant to the next. Your destiny."

"What is destiny?" Bruno interrupted.

"Mine could be this, telling you what I have just said. In this instance, I am complete."

Margaret was only half listening. She was begging that they would quickly return to New York and she would have Jules with her for the rest of her life. It was an involuntary wish. At the same time her mind wandered to stories she had heard about Nossa Senora Aparecida, the black Virgin Mary, and Don Bosco, the monk that had seen the modern capital Brasilia in a vision four hundred years ago, and Saint Fatima. They all had cathedrals in Brasilia. They could grant any wish. She will ask Marini to let them visit Brasilia, Margaret thought.

"Take care about what you are praying and wishing for," Eliza was saying. "If a loved one is dying, don't be foolish and prolong their suffering. Or a lost lover might come back to you, but you will not be pleased at all with his presence. Disappointment is worse than suffering and loss." And then in a dramatic voice she added: "*Eu vos exalto, ó Senhor, porque vós me livrastes! Graças a Deus! Glória a vós, Senhor!*"

Goppollone and Blavatsky entered the tent. Wagner was under the table, trying to get at Eliza's legs beneath the long dress with many flounces. Eliza jumped to her feet and seized a crystal from a shelf. There was fear on her face as she slowly levitated to the middle of the tent's cramped space. All three animals also rose into the air, as if trying to surround and corner her. She spoke urgently, and light and fog billowed from the crystal in her hand, dissolving the animals, leaving only Blavatsky's mew and Wagner's bark.

Marini and Jerome burst into the tent.

"What the hell is this?" Bruno shouted.

"We lost them again," Marini said.

"*Capeta!*" Eliza screamed and vanished. Jerome, looking under tables and carpets, had to accept Marini's conclusion. Blavatsky, Wagner and Goppollone were gone.

"What's *capeta*?" Bruno asked Marini.

"The name of the dark angel in Portuguese." Marini smashed a few big crystals to vent his anger. "Let's go."

Everybody stood ready to leave immediately.

"They have to be in la Vale de Lua."

This was a sacred lake, where local white witches used to send people and animals to expunge their dark energies.

"More nonsense." Marini made a face when Margaret mentioned this traditional belief mentioned by Eliza. "Dark energies are as good as the white ones. They cannot function without each other."

"That depends," said Jerome. "My grandfather told me the opposite. The Albigensian heresy was built on what you say. My family crushed that idea eight hundred years ago."

"And you will prove its survival." A humorless smile crossed Marini's face. "You are the smartest in your family."

On the way to la Vale de Lua they walked through a field of wild and fantastical stones. It was how we think of the moon's surface, except that the stones were polished by *garimpeiros*. Wind, rain, and sun had for millennia had their way with a reddish granite barrier along the lake. A cascade drove furiously through a tunnel of rocks and forced its way into the lake, eventually emptying into the immensity of the *cerrado*. It was impossibly hot. Clouds hung in the sky, disposed in degrees, on different levels like stairs, imposing unexpected dimensions over the landscape. Small *paneiras*, imperial *buritti* and wild *cana* hinted at the distant, occult presence of Amazonia.

There were the three animals, cavorting in the water, playfully ducking the cascade's jet and jumping on the slippery stones. They paid no heed to Marini's orders to get back to safety on the shore.

"May we discuss my dream?" Margaret was curious about what Marini would say. She remembered his resounding title of master in theosophy and metaphysics. In the sand she drew what she had seen in her dream.

"It is prophetic, no doubt about it. You are told to accept my offer in order to leave an important trace in your one hundred thousand years. You have the potential to become a bubble, like the half of that pea you touched."

Margaret suspected Marini did not really care about her dream.

"I did not ask for that," she said. "My question was about the essence of time. I did not feel the urge to be a bubble or an important person in the memory of the human race. I felt I was the time, or Time. I am the substance of Time. Time is my substance, my flesh. Time exists through me and because of me. The elementary matter of those gigantic blocks includes everybody, not just me. We are all tossed in there."

This seemed to annoy Marini. He only wished to endorse his own theory. He had the contract prepared in his pocket, she knew. Would she sign, as Bruno and Jerome had?

Meanwhile, Jerome had jumped into the lake. "*Purificación!*" he shouted. "Who has the courage?" Jerome's strong neck, great biceps and firm pectorals were shinning in the light sprayed with drops of water coming from the cascade.

"Not I," said Margaret.

But Bruno surprised her. He lifted her in his arms and, carrying her, gingerly picked a path through the stones. His pants were rolled up to his knees. He laid her down on a rock that divided the rushing waters.

"*Purificación!*" Jerome shouted again, getting completely undressed. He and Bruno both skirted the cascade, slowly approaching the three animals. Margaret, feeling she had no choice, stripped down to her black underwear and followed them.

"Playboy! Yo!" Jerome called back to Marini. "Come on in!"

Marini was not amused. The dark shadow of annoyance on his face gave him an intimidating, ominous look. He did not seem to feel the heat of the day. He might as well have been in New York on a cool night and not in the *cerrado* near the 23rd parallel. In his cashmere coat and mauve pullover he looked weirdly out of place. Bruno expressed a fear that he might abandon them.

"Get them back and let's go!" Marini ordered, standing on a glazed rock as perfect as the surface of an egg. All three of them made a grab, each at a different animal, but the cat and the dogs rose into the air and rocketed toward the north as if a vortex had scooped them up.

But the locator did its work. The three animals were traced to an exact spot in the Northern Hemisphere.

The restaurant at the top of Hotel Rossia was cold and deserted. It was still Saturday, but in the evening. At the Kremlin and along the banks of the Moscow River, weekends looked no different than any other day. The dizzy whirlpool domes of Vasilii Blazhennyi Cathedral in Red Square lent the Kremlin, the walled city in the middle of the city of Moscow, the appearance of a withdrawn, secluded soul. As the four travelers and the three animals waited for their dinner, the gigantic clock of the tower sounded eight times the hour of the evening.

This was the bastion of the Eastern world that no European power could conquer, Margaret was thinking. Yet Russia always wanted more from Europe, as if Asia was not enough. Peter the Great, she had learned, had bequeathed Russians the task of taking over the world. Westward they got no further than Berlin, but on the other side they covered the vast distance to Manchuria and China and Korea. And after the geographical battles, came the ideological war that extended Stalin's brand of communism to Africa and South-East Asia and Latin America.

"Napoleon and Hitler could not stop the enemy of Europe," Marini pontificated, as if reading her thoughts. He was eating borscht, a dish he had ordered separately before dinner. "Napoleon stayed for a while in the Kremlin, but he abandoned it, unable to understand it. The Russians burned Moscow to get rid of Napoleon. How incomprehensible! What kind of a nation would burn its capital? Think of that fool Tolstoy, with his huge hymn to that insanity! And Hitler—well, he underestimated totalitarianism despite the fact that he was a dictator. But if Napoleon or Hitler had conquered Russia, communism wouldn't exist."

"Are you saying that the victory of Kutuzov over Napoleon brought communism to Russia?" It was Jerome, trying as always to grasp Marini's meaning.

Bruno was agitated. "Don't poke your nose into affairs of the Russians," he warned both of them. "They are listening to us." And he brusquely checked the table, plates, chairs, and glasses for hidden microphones.

"Who's listening?" Jerome was lost.

"You don't know what goes on!" Bruno shouted.

"Paranoid!" Jerome pointed at Bruno's head.

There was a silence. Then Bruno commented that the Kremlin church domes did not look like onions at all, but more like clubs or maces bristling with the sharp stakes of Eastern barbarians conquering the West. "They are clothed in the color of blood." He reminded them that Lenin and his followers had transformed the Kremlin's churches into museums, and that they were still museums. No prayers, no mass, and no candles were to be seen or heard that Saturday before Easter in those Christian Orthodox churches. Was Margaret aware of it? Yes, she accepted Bruno's theory, adding her own comments. "Yes, I see blood everywhere here." Crows swooped and squawked around the domes. Was there a corpse there? Was it perhaps the rotting corpse of Stalinism?

Jerome said he did not like Stalin's skyscrapers sparkling through the hotel windows. They were the kind built during the nineteen-fifties all over Russia and the Soviet Empire. They displayed no elegance or refinement. They did not belong to any known school or artistic trend.

"It is the Soviet style," Margaret murmured.

The waiter came, the only waiter in the deserted restaurant, carrying vodka and caviar.

"Is Pushkin's house still on Arbat Street?" Margaret asked.

"It is." He was tall and blond, with oiled hair and a strong nose. The pimples that covered his face seemed to bury his small eyes. When he spoke, he wrapped the muscles of his face up around his eyes, deepening the impression of hidden eyeballs.

He answered many questions raised by Bruno and Jerome. Marini was concentrating on Wagner.

They had been lucky to find the animals near Lenin's tomb in Red Square. The animals had tried to get into the mausoleum but the security was too tight. Now, after so many troubles for both humans and animals, a snack in the restaurant was more than welcome. Milk for Blavatsky, bones for Goppollone and Wagner, caviar and vodka for the four travelers.

The waiter was soon breaking into the conversation with his own thoughts. "The communists had the ambition to change destiny—*sud'bu*," he told them. "To tailor the New Man—*novyj chelovek*. To force people to go through a pre-designed life using propaganda, censorship, the gulag, and reeducation camps. The Party did the thinking on behalf of everybody and took the initiatives for all. The Party wanted to replace destiny—*sud'bu*—and God—*Bog*—with its own *chelovek*." Introducing himself as Ivan, he made big crosses on his chest.

Marini looked bored. He seemed at ease in Red Square. Margaret, however, discerned in Ivan an unexpected opportunity to probe the secret of Russian communism. Some of her family had died in Russian gulags after World War II. Bruno said he remembered how German soldiers had been killed in cold blood in Soviet war camps. His father had been lucky; he came home. Bruno vividly described those years of his father's agony, how the prematurely aged man had been confined to bed, his lungs wrecked by the Donbas coal mines. A place to exterminate German prisoners, Bruno said. He recounted his father's last confession too. It was about happiness.

"It is unwise to interfere with other persons' destiny," Ivan said sadly. "*Sud'bu*." He brought more caviar and vodka, this time with whole meal bread that smelled and tasted wonderful, Margaret thought. The best bread in the world.

The restaurant was getting colder and colder. April in Moscow is not warm. As night fell behind the bright lights of Red Square, the Kremlin displayed its flat duotone red and green. The Moscow River loitered in its own frosty and bizarre light. Ivan brought blankets for Margaret, Bruno and Jerome. His conversation had matured into a gentle monologue.

"It seems we are protoplasmic organisms with no other sense than reproduction. Or the sense is the journey itself?" Jerome spoke for himself lost in Ivan's comments.

"If a person goes through a crisis it is because God has put him there in the complexity of life's events. This person will discover a particular truth during the trial and his soul will be lifted to another level of understanding. By forcefully taking a person out of that complexity of events, there are two dire consequences. First, the person will not come to understand the truth he was supposed to look for. The revelation does not occur. And secondly, he will soon enter a similar pattern causing him even more pain. And those who interfere with God's will, must pay dearly. There are agents of destiny," Ivan continued, taking a seat between Bruno and Jerome. "They appear from nowhere and disappear once their task is done. They help you, and they push you through life. They are points of energy in your existence, nodes, knots, and cruxes that jump into your existence and carry you to another level. They can help you achieve happiness."

Marini was pacing back and forth in front of the huge windows, his long brown camel coat waving like the flags on the Kremlin.

"And what is happiness?" Jerome asked. He was holding Goppollone, his favorite.

Ivan suddenly looked blank. He mumbled, but nothing came out clearly.

"It is success, money, recognition, fame. And seeing the world and experiencing it." Marini seemed to speak through his teeth as he walked back and forth in front of the windows. He was like an actor projecting the voice of the Kremlin that filled the stage behind him.

"I remember my father's definition of happiness," Bruno said. His voice was trembling. "He said that happiness is to be able to walk the streets you love on a sunny summer day; to enter a cafe and enjoy a cup of coffee, and after that go back out into the gorgeous cocoon of the day. To meet your friends, and talk, and share those small yet important things in life."

His father's favorite place was München's Marienplatz, where he liked hot red wine with cinnamon at the Burkhof. At the nearby Hofbrauhaus on Platzl 9, which had been there since the sixteenth century, he drank beer in huge two-liter mugs. When Bruno was a child, once in a while he tagged along and met his father's friends. There were many sayings posted inside the Hofbrauhaus; one said it is better to be thirsty than to be homesick. *Durst ist schlimmer als Heimveh.*

This was shortly before his father's death, after years of being confined to bed in terrible suffering. As Bruno sat by his father's deathbed they had remembered those convivial scenes together. How tasty the sausage platters, the roast pork, the Grossfass beer and the Münchner Kindl! Twice, Bruno now remembered, he had been allowed to sip weissbier. There was never any talk about the war or the Siberian prison camp or about the years as a lieutenant in the German army engaged in conquering the world. Only a recurring monologue, wistful and soft as a spring breeze, about the lovely Anna Café on Váci utca 5 in the center of Budapest, on the Pesti side of the Danube. There he liked to drink Puszta cocktail made of Barak Palinka, Apricot Brandy, Tokaji Szamorodni, and Mecsek, with a few drops of Zwack Unicum, a liquor made of herbs, that he added himself. Near Váci utca was Erzsébet Bridge where he stood sometimes thinking of his family and home far up the waters flowing from his Germany.

The last time at the Hofbrauhaus, his father stiff and helpless after a time when he had seemed to be getting better, Bruno had tried to talk about old times. But the old man's mind was somewhere else. "They were almost his last words," Bruno said. "He pointed to a small alcove and said something about destruction coming from somewhere close by. It was the room where Hitler had delivered his first speech and turned the national party into a hate and war machine."

Nobody spoke.

"That's absurd." Marini finally burst out. "This is a vision of a sick old man. It's touching, I suppose, and I can respect that, but I cannot agree. It is minimalism, surrender, the last resistance, the last resort to a frail ideal of happiness. It has no meaning for a young, healthy and ambitious man or woman."

At the time his father had told him this, Bruno said, he himself had had the same attitude as Marini. But now he was ready to argue. Margaret, however, restrained him. It was neither the place nor the time for contention, she said. Their first and foremost goal was to leave this spot as soon as possible.

"Are you a philosopher?" Jerome asked the waiter, trying to deflect the tension. Jerome's hair was still neatly combed to the back. The perfume he wore, a Caron or a Chanel or an Opium brand, infused in his elegant creamy sweater, seemed to become more pervasive.

Ivan was a high school teacher from a far away village, somewhere in Uzbekistan. He was a Russian, not an Uzbek, Ivan told them, puckering his face and forehead about the eyes. This gave his look an air of being upset and tormented. He left his family hoping for a new start in Moscow. His dreams were yet to be fulfilled. He had plans to get out of Russia.

Marini checked the pets one by one. After this review, he took his glass of vodka along with him on a tour of the empty restaurant. It seemed he had memories related to that place, memories he did not want to share with anybody. The cityscape of Moscow was defined by the color of red. Skyscrapers looked like iron stakes waiting for the next victim. Marini fired a few sarcasms at Ivan, but nobody paid any attention.

"There are also partners of destiny. Or Destiny's partners," Ivan went on showing no patience for interruptions. His golden teeth couldn't belong to a poor Russian. The restaurant did not welcome large crowds, yet Ivan seemed to have no money problems.

"They are the ones you share your existence with, learning from them. Going together through life's experiences, its moments of happiness and drama. One discovers in this togetherness a new sense of life. One has a revelation through powerful and meaningful events. Destiny's partners could be one's mother or father, a friend, one's husband or wife, one's children and relatives."

"I hear that if you design a mandala on your own, your destiny changes by one hundred and eighty degrees," Jerome said, running his fingers through his hair. Goppollone humped his chest while trying to warm himself up.

"That's another jurisdiction," Marini sneered loudly at the empty restaurant. An echo expanded the inflexions of his sentence. "You, blockhead, don't mix Ivan's religion with Buddhism." And went on berating the foolish comparison.

"Are you saying that help is not allowed in this life?" Margaret seemed at a loss. She wrapped the blanket tighter around her shoulders to warm up a little in the cold of Moscow, so awful after the sultriness of Brazil. She also acknowledged that she secretly envied Marini's freedom of being anywhere and any time and knowing all and getting people together.

"He made me feel dizzy," Margaret complained to Bruno about Ivan who continued his monologue.

"One must help a drowning person, a child crying for food, a sick friend. But do you really think you can influence someone to make a life decision, break a relationship for example, based on your preconceived ideas, and on your advice, with your good intentions merely through the power of love? We see states liberated through a *coup d'état* unable to find the right direction even after decades. Instead they fall back into similar political patterns like those they were in before, and only because the change came from outside. It is the same with human beings."

"I have come to the same conclusion," Margaret nodded, shivering under the blanket. Vodka and caviar did not warm her up as they were supposed to.

"Dan divorced his former wife because of you," Marini said to her, coming close to the table. "He had not learned his lesson. Your life with him was miserable. You left him. And he found another woman like his former wife. He went back into the same tension-filled situation. His path became longer than it was supposed to be. He became clinically mad. Manic-depressive. There was nothing for him to do. He would eventually get over this by himself or die without doing the homework of this life." And sipping from his glass of vodka he added: "And you go to hell anyway."

"This is inspiring. I will meditate on it."

"Don't get too much wisdom out of it." Marini's face looked like his life had spanned several thousand years already. "The wise one is no longer creative. Art comes from looking for answers to unsettled feelings. Wisdom will confine you to the level of contemplation. It's a higher level where the mind leaves the story behind. The wise like sentences only, or fragments of sentences. Like verses. Look at the prophets. They were unproductive in fiction, criticism, essays, poetry, art in general."

She knew he was right.

"Do not forget the lovely free will," Marini chuckled in derision. "Ivan, it seems that you haven't chosen very well. There is no Heaven for you either, my friend."

Ivan came swiftly over by Margaret's side, bringing hot water for the tea.

"There is a falsity of the free will," Ivan said quietly. "At least in my case. I hope I'll get into Heaven—*raj*—not Hell—*ad*. God must determine that. Since I have lived all my life in a Communist country, and nothing much changed in Russia after 1991, I have always been forced to choose between one pig and another pig. Obviously, I have always chosen a pig. I never knew that I could choose between a lion and a pig, for I never came across a lion."

"That's interesting." Bruno found Ivan's English too good for a waiter and for that place. He asked Ivan for hot water. He was shivering, like Margaret and Jerome, with the blanket wrapped as a mantle around his dark blue suit jacket.

"In other words, are you telling us that you are above sinning? That sinning is not your portion? Or what?" Bruno asked.

"Why should I feel guilty—*vinovatym*? Or be a sinner—*greshnikom*?" Ivan snapped his fingers. Bruno and Marini hated it, and Ivan somehow was aware of their displeasure. He diverted his nervousness to scratching a pimple on his face. "Life is all about making choices. Avoiding it leads to death. In my desperate moments I talk to God."

Ivan half kneeled, half hung on his chair as if in front of an imaginary icon. He was making crosses, rocking his body and speaking in Russian. He was asking God for forgiveness—*proshchenie*.

Margaret did not find him ridiculous, although Bruno and Jerome were ready to make fun of him. She touched his arm to ask a question, but Ivan did not react.

"God is therefore guilty for sending me pigs only, and for giving me a destiny of a lioness surrounded by pigs?" Margaret asked him with glint in her eyes.

Her remark touched Bruno and Jerome. Marini alone was silently following her thoughts. Night was taking over Moscow. It was so cold and empty that all of them had the vision of a Siberian landscape.

"You are alone but you are not lonely. For you know that I exist," Bruno told her after a pause, a bit stiffened by the presence of the cat. He shifted the cat to his chest and reached out to touch Margaret's hand. Wagner settled on his leg. Bruno did not sneeze. It seemed that his bout with allergy was gone.

In a Rudolph Valentino sort of declamatory stance, Jerome continued Bruno's sentence:

"Loneliness is losing your sense of belonging to someone else. And we do belong to one another!" He had to stop waving his hands as Goppollone was reaching out to lick his fingers.

"To hell with it! You are not in Hollywood, or Gollywood." Bruno was really embarrassed. He punched Jerome in the head. Jerome cringed, but went on undeterred. "We are in Moscow, in the Kremlin, doing a super production entitled *Yvain in Russia*."

And turning to Ivan, Jerome asked something that he was not supposed to, given the time and the place. "How about your countrymen who have sold their souls to the Red Devil?" At the back of his mind was an interesting conversation he had recently witnessed—one of his professors pointing out the huge advantages such a person enjoyed as part of the *nomenklatura*.

"You are mad," shouted Bruno. The grizzly beard engulfing his jaw, his jowls and his lips, and the wild hair covering his ears and tumbling over his forehead moved vehemently. However, Jerome did not give up and he was out of Bruno's reach this time. He wanted an answer that would satisfy Marini.

"That was a good one," the latter chuckled, looking for Wagner.

"I often think of this," Ivan answered. He had anticipated the question. "Evil is something negative in one's existence. An existence with something lacking in it." And after a short break he added: "An existence without consistency."

Jerome did not understand what he was saying, so far away from his question about material advantages and less work, but he was forced to keep quiet by Ivan's monologue, like a torrent that could not be diverted.

"There are souls that God wishes to be worthless," Ivan continued. "It is their punishment. Nobody knows for what. The Evil One picks them up, promising and giving them what they have always longed for. So idiots become writers, the stupid powerful managers in charge of other people's lives, and madmen leaders. This is my explanation of history's lapses and of the distorted minds that flourish within it."

Marini looked at Ivan with a sort of contempt. Was Ivan totally stupid? Or was he smart? Or neither? Jerome tried to get at the gist of his sentences. Something was amiss in Ivan's answer. Bruno and Margaret were anxious to leave the question there, as well as its answer, and to get out of that place quickly.

Marini took Wagner in his arms and oiled his warts. They had been so successful in getting all the animals together! Blavatsky purred softly on Bruno's lap. Margaret took Blavatsky from Bruno. She kissed and hugged the cat, murmuring words unknown to the others, like *mushatâ, eshtzâ mushatâ ca unâ steauâ.* She wanted to slide the golden collar around the cat's neck, but Blavatsky rejected it. Jerome hugged Goppollone against his chest, curiously exploring the animal's parts. Half dog and half cat.

"Gorgeous, you are as beautiful as a star." Margaret translated her strange words. "My grandmother used to tell me this. I miss her," she added. "This is her language, a Romanian dialect called Macedo-Romanian. Her tribe lived for centuries in the Pindus Mountains of Greece without mixing with any populations around. Part of them came back to Romania at the beginning of the twentieth century. My grandmother now lives in Sibiu, in Transylvania, but actually my family from her side is still in southern Romania, in Baia, Tulcea, and Constantza in the province of Dobrudja."

Blavatsky seemed to like those exotic words. Margaret parked the cat on her lap. Blavatsky purred and meowed as Margaret played with her paws and tail, scraping her belly and her chin. But every attempt to slide the collar around her neck was unsuccessful.

"Is that in Romania?" Bruno tried to locate the last two places. Margaret nodded showing where they were on an imaginary map. The Danube tied the two of them together, as it flowed from Germany's Black Forest down to the Black Sea.

"You miss your tribe, dear," Marini diagnosed, grinning like a cat.

It was time to go home. The Lexus, more luxurious and glowing than ever, waited in front of the hotel ready to start the journey back to New York. Gently, Bruno and Jerome attempted to curtail Ivan's stories. Marini paid the bill, leaving on the table a substantial tip.

Carrying the cat and the two dogs in their arms they made for the elevator. But they had to halt. An armed patrol had silently surrounded them. Soldiers, with colossal Siberian dogs sniffing all over the place, asked for their papers.

"Your passports."

"Here they are." Marini calmly took out from his cashmere jacket four passports bearing Russian visas. Jerome wanted to ask how he managed to obtain them, but he found that he was unable to open his mouth. Margaret and Bruno did not understand. It was scary. Ivan had disappeared.

The Siberian dogs came close to Blavatsky in Margaret's arms. The cat hissed, and scratched a dog that attempted to get close to her neck.

Marini asked the soldiers to restrain the dogs.

"Do you have papers—*dokumenty*—for the animals?" one of the soldiers asked.

"What papers?" Marini made the mistake of asking and instantly they all knew they were in trouble.

"Take them all—*Vziat' ikh vsekh*," the Captain ordered his crew.

"Why?" Jerome said innocently. "Have I missed anything?"

"We've been watching you. You've failed to comply with the rules. Spies—*shpiony*. Intruders—*nezvanyie gosti*." The Captain's voice intimidated Bruno. His father's recollections from Siberia came back to him. He did not want to go to that place.

"Why is everybody here watching everybody else? What is this? A country of guardians?" Jerome asked. His mouth got stuck again.

"We are here to protect you," the Captain said.

"They want to arrest us," translated Marini. And as an order: "Discipline your fears!"

The cat slipped out of the circle. Wagner and Goppollone followed her. The Siberians, out of their leashes and muzzles, ran after them barking down the escape stair case. The soldiers went after them. Sirens started whistling and a terrible voice coming from a loudspeaker repeated obsessively "*Vnymanyie!*"—Attention!" The group managed to get into the elevator. The animals' disappearance had been a good diversion. Seconds later Margaret, Jerome, and Bruno were running from the hotel, following Marini. They heard the roaring engine. They burst into the car grabbing all doors. Marini locked them in. He touched the steering wheel and the Lexus shot up the road. The car, like an animal confused by strange surroundings, tried to pick its way through the darkness. The air was foggy and had a chill to it.

"Why do they still keep the hammer and sickle on the façade of the Bolshoi Theater?" This time it was Margaret's turn to make a foolish remark.

"Locate the path," Marini shouted while Jerome was blankly looking at the locator. Lights and curves invaded the screen in a stormy fashion. After a while the curves pointed in a clear direction.

"They're heading south." Jerome was amazed to hear his voice. He was able to talk again. He opened his mouth wide. The jaws felt flexible. He promised to himself to keep silent. It was hard to stick to his promise. But it was the beginning of a sort of awakening he would experience during the hours that ensued.

In the oldest part of the city of Sibiu, called the "Red City" after the color of its shingle roofs, churches were celebrating Saturday Vespers. It was eight past ten in the evening. The sweet scent of blossoming shrubs lingered everywhere. It was warm and peaceful. Small houses with narrow windows dating from as far back as the twelfth century mingled with those of many later centuries in a blend of ineffable mystery. The Turkish army that had failed to conquer the Red Fortress in the eighteenth century had called Sibiu a demonic city.

This aspect was fueled also by Dracula's castle, another nearby place the Turks had never conquered. The shadow of the vampire—or the vampire himself—defended Dracula's castle. It was said that Sibiu was steeped in the magic practiced by its magicians and elves. Dwellers in the city alleged their continuing existence at the dawn of the twenty-first century. The natives would see them and talk to them. The elves of Sibiu had always conducted a sort of war with the magicians who practiced black magic.

According to legend, one could not talk to elves and tell about it. That would lead to the loss of one's voice. And indeed there lived in Sibiu many people who had lost the faculty of speech. But now Margaret, astonished to find herself in her grandmother's town, confessed that she had met an elf during her childhood. He had given her a golden marble. She had hidden it in her grandmother's house. She knew she could find it again. But she stopped trying to remember, fearful of the ancient curse on those who disclosed their encounters with elves.

In pursuit of the three animals through the oldest part of town, Jerome and Marini followed *Movila* (Knoll Street), descended on *Felinarului* (Lantern Street), went left on May 9th Street and stopped for a few seconds in front of Herman's villa. They continued on *Brutarilor* (Bakers' Street), the *Noua Stradă* and *Olarilor* (Potters' Street), slowly progressing from the twelfth century neighborhood into the eighteenth century. On *Pielarilor* (Tanners') and *Vopsitorilor* (Dyers') Streets, Jerome wondered what it was like to live in houses built six or eight centuries ago.

The group ran into a courtyard on 18 *Faurului* (Ironsmiths') Street, and then continued on *Turnului* (Tower Street), *Podul Minciunilor* (The Bridge of Lies), *Piata Mica* (Little Plaza), and *Piata Aurarilor* (Goldsmiths' Plaza). Following the indicator, they spent some time in front of the inscription from the year 1567 on the Fingerling Stairs, and went back and forth through the maze of tiny streets of the guilds of the Middle Ages. At last they entered an old house and there they found the cat and the two dogs in the living room eating from plates carefully set under a piano.

"This is unbelievable," Margaret cried. She ran up to an armchair close to the windows and hugged a person buried in its folds.

"Grandma!"

The old lady took Margaret's head in her hands, slowly kissing her forehead and cheeks, one by one.

"*Feata ly mamy! Mushuteatza ly mamy*! My girl, my beautiful one!" She spoke calmly, misty tears moistening her blue and tired eyes. "I knew you'd come home." And training on the group a queen-like gaze: "Which is your husband?"

"I am not married, Grandma."

The old lady rose slowly from the armchair, leaving a book on the coffee table. Smoothing her dress, she advanced a few steps toward the group. She examined all of them in silence.

"I'd like to marry her but she doesn't want me," Bruno said half jokingly, half seriously. He bowed to the old lady kissing her hand in the old-fashioned European way.

"You would make a good husband," she conceded, hugging him and doing so with Jerome too.

"This is my grandma Zoë." Margaret took her in her arms, kissing her and hugging her with a childish enthusiasm. Without any doubt, Margaret would have loved to have Jules there. It was her secret wish, to bring Jules to meet her grandmother, to tell her that she had found her man. They had discussed the trip, but Jules had always postponed it.

"*M'pary ghyny că te zburâmu odată*. I am happy that we can finally talk," the old lady said as if they were continuing a conversation. "Your cousins are waiting for you. We have to plan a family reunion, but I do not know how to gather all our relatives, more than forty of them." She was anxiously thinking how to plan for the party.

"*Shedzi âmpady*! Have a seat," Zoë invited Marini, Bruno and Jerome to sit around the mahogany table with its big vases of dahlias and zinnias and platters of red eggs, pies, cakes, honey gold apples, and red Bartlett pears. Wagner quietly approached Marini, sorrow and guilt showing in his eyes. He licked Marini's shoes and hands the moment Marini knelt to administer the anti-warts medication.

"Good boy," Marini said, massaging Wagner's tail.

"Do you remember Domnul Mushat?" The old lady asked Margaret, pointing to the other armchair in the living room.

Margaret translated for the benefit of her friends. "*Domnul* is 'Mister' in Romanian and comes from *domn* meaning 'king' in the Middle Ages. *Mushat* stands for 'gorgeous' in the old Macedo-Romanian dialect."

Nobody had noticed that there was another person in the room. Domnul Mushat was tiny, like Puck. The brown color of the armchair blended into his clothes and his complexion. Margaret took his tiny hands in hers and stared at his peppercorn eyes.

"Do you remember that golden ball you gave me as a charm so that wonderful things would happen in my life? It worked!" She spoke with joy. What she said was not quite the case, but she wanted to cheer her old friend. She kissed the old gentleman on both cheeks. He was so wrinkled that his age was impossible to guess.

"Is this the imp you've been talking about?" Jerome came closer to shake hands with the old gentleman.

"He is our neighbor," Margaret added at the same pitch of enthusiasm.

"The carpenters haven't finished fixing the roof. They have worked on it for ten years," Zoë resumed her conversation with Mushat. "It is his problem too. Old buildings and new materials don't go together. The old walls reject the new roofs."

"*Ti supârai*? Did you get upset?" Margaret longed to ask her grandmother in the old Macedo-Romanian dialect. She clipped back her hair with a quick motion.

Grandma shook her head with an ambiguous motion.

While Bruno moved his chair closer to Domnul Mushat, Margaret helped Zoë to bring from the kitchen spinach pies and house-baked bread, silver baskets with eggs dyed red, *brânză*, *plăcinte*, *cozonaci*, *prune* and *gutui*—different kinds of pies, pound cakes, plums, and quinces. It was almost Easter. In a few hours, at midnight, Jesus would rise once again from the dead.

Zoë reminded Margaret of the powerful presence of her late mother Hriseis. Her Greek name means the "one that brings gold to the family." Hriseis had been entirely of her tribe: stubborn, faithful, energetic, and courageous. Zoë's favorite child. Hriseis' life had been dedicated to her family, to her native tongue, and to her friends. She had been able to communicate with the other world through visions, like every woman of her tribe. The Virgin Mary had come to her twice, granting first her daughter and then a vision of the afterlife when she had the boy. She had talked to God and her prayers had sometimes been listened to. Angels would guide her through vivid premonitions. She knew about the future, but could do little to avoid disasters. Breaking the ancient rule against her will, she had married at Zoë's behest a man outside the tribe. It was a painful life with a man so different from her race! He was a charming and powerful husband that liked laughing, joking, partying, losing money, playing cards, singing, even flirting with other women. And her children had also been a disappointment, showing no unconditional love or sacrifice for family. The women of Hriseis' tribe had always been more powerful than the men. Mothers protected their boys. An Aromanian girl could find her way alone. In ancient times, in order to help boys survive in a tribe with more boys than girls, boys were engaged from the first day of their life to a girl from the same tribe. Brides were older. At fourteen, boys were officially married to girls with strong mothers. If the boy was older (perhaps the first bride did not want him or she had died before marriage), a search committee would be appointed to examine his family's past for indications of weakness, moral values, goals, and respectful behavior. If the boy proved too weak during the first years of marriage, an older brother or father was called in to fulfill manhood's obligations. Children were to be secured, for they passed on the language and the well-being of the tribe itself. Hriseis could not do anything of the sort with her children. She died in sorrow for she had failed in her lifetime's task. And Margaret felt the same guilt of having failed in her task too.

Domnul Mushat showed Bruno a golden coin from the time of Alexander the Great. It was his finest treasure. Clearly he was fond of talking about history, and Alexander the Great (he said) was a good example of how much destiny can accomplish in a very short time. Alexander died when he was 33 years old, having conquered the entire known world. Several times Domnul Mushat pronounced "Alexander the Macedonian." Alexander was one of their kin. Their ultimate myth.

"Destiny is the path that naturally and gradually becomes visible. It is the door that opens in front of you as you proceed down the path. Tricks are no good." The imp smiled, but the smile looked like a frightful grimace. With some concern he was looking on as Marini concentrated on Wagner.

Bruno respectfully allowed the tiny man to expound his thoughts.

"What's the truth then?" Bruno asked, playing with the golden coin on the obverse of which Alexander the Great was represented as the world's emperor.

"The truth is whatever comes to you on this path and what you find by entering the open door. Truth comes in small pieces. It is you who have to put the pieces together. You might go on many paths and enter many open doors in your lifetime. The greater the distance in time from past paths and opened doors the better your understanding."

Short of breath, the elf stopped and then continued.

"Truth comes in morsels, through dreams and lightning revelations. The striking connections take you by surprise in your vulnerable moments, or during your relaxed ones, let's say. Truth is your lifetime accomplishment."

Margaret heard the last words while hugging her grandmother. They were sitting in the same armchair in a fond embrace. Was she supposed to believe Jules' murmurings in their nights of love? Words such as: "You are a wonder of this world; a marvel of this world; I want you so deeply, my lovely darling." Were they the salesman's strategy to get her and keep her while offering nothing?

"Are there vampires here?" Bruno was questioning Mushat with some embarrassment. Midnight was close.

"There is a lot of negativity in Transylvania, but it is under control." Mushat said seriously. "It is an ongoing battle. It will take many more centuries before a balance is struck. Now it is better than it was, anyway." He hinted at past events that Transylvania had gone through, paying a terrible toll. He spoke of the communist dictatorship that had spread demons and appalling evil spirits. Many souls had worked against their own people. Was it their destiny? "Perhaps," said Mushat. They opened the wrong door. "Magic is the forward escape, the fullest experience of reality," he explained with gravity.

A mouse crawled slowly out of Domnul Mushat's vest. He picked it up with his finger tips, placed it on the palm of his hand, and introduced it to Bruno.

"His name is *Făt-Frumos*—Prince Charming—and he is my best friend." And he went on, adding to Bruno's confusion: "Prince Charming has just reported a victory. He had Dokya on his side, a famous white sorceress that lives around here. My friend Dokya has just killed a witch."

To Bruno's way of thinking, these stories had to be ascribed to senility. But he did not contradict the old man. And Margaret was glad that he did not do so. She knew all those stories. It was obvious that Mushat liked Bruno very much and disliked Marini. The same was true of Zoë.

"Nonsense," shouted Marini, looking at his watch.

He was rude, and insensitive to Margaret's joy. It was time to leave this place where Marini felt uncomfortable. Margaret promised Zoë she would come back as soon as possible. Jerome wanted to come back too to spend more time there. The cat got on Zoë's lap and allowed Margaret to slide the golden collar over her head. Such a relief! It was about time. Blavatsky's heart might have stopped in a few minutes without it.

"Bring Bruno, too," Zoë and Mushat put in, speaking at the same instant.

"He is getting married soon," Margaret said. She was getting tired of all these strategies to fix her up with Bruno.

Mushat shook his head ambivalently. Prince Charming slowly got down from Mushat's knees and headed across the living room floor towards Blavatsky, who was busy lapping her milk. It took him some time to be observed by the cat. For a while, they played little friendly games together. Prince Charming slapped the cat on the nose and ran under Mushat's chair. The cat followed him. The mouse climbed up a curtain and so did the cat, jumping on a counter with pies and from there onto the table and from the table under it again. Wagner and Goppollone joined Blavatsky, but clearly more in earnest to get the mouse.

Marini attempted to restrain Wagner but without success. Soon, it was obvious that he was no match for the determined dog. Barking, Wagner and Goppollone almost seized the mouse. Blavatsky had Prince Charming between her paws for a moment. But the mouse escaped and slipped into a hole in the wooden floor. One by one, getting as small as the mouse, Blavatsky, Wagner, and Goppollone followed him into the hole. And then Marini also followed them before Margaret's, Bruno's, and Jerome's disbelieving eyes. Mushat giggled in his armchair. Marini reappeared soon, quickly regaining his normal size. He went straight to Mushat and said something in a language nobody understood.

"*La Dracu!*" Zoë whispered.

"*Woland*," Mushat acknowledged.

"*Au diable*," Jerome shouted.

"Devil's tricks," Bruno growled through clenched teeth.

"Do you like magic?" Mushat sniggered, paying no attention to a furious Marini. Marini's dark uplifted eyes stared at Mushat as he tried to steady himself.

Marini threw a sort of dark light towards him. But Mushat was gone before it reached him, as if he had never been there. Zoë looked annoyed. She did not like fights in her house.

"There are miles upon miles of tunnels under this old city," Marini shouted in anger. "I want my Wagner back."

Jerome glanced at the locator. Stormy images going in bizarre circles. Zoë fell asleep. Margaret covered her with a blanket and lowered the blinds. She would come soon to see her and spend more time. She would bring Bruno there. It was her grandmother's wish. What about Jules? Margaret realized she had mixed their names up. She had meant to say Jules, not Bruno.

"Will you take me with you?" Bruno wanted to make sure he had been invited. Margaret gave no answer, quietly closing the front door behind them.

"They went east." Jerome pointed to the diagram scintillating on the locator.

With another erratic leap through time and space the car was screeching and swinging and twisting. Their livid faces showed the toll this trip was taking on them. Only Marini's composure did not change. As he concentrated on driving, continuously operating the switches on the dashboard, he allowed no emotion to show on his face.

Jerome could not keep his eyes open anymore. At one point, Bruno's snoring awoke him for a moment. At the back of the car, Bruno held Margaret tight to prevent her from sliding off the leather seat and get hurt. She lay exhausted, her eyes drifting upward, her hair all around her head like translucent linen. She could not sleep. She could not understand why her mind worked so well in a speedy car. Her thoughts were coming fast. Ideas rushed at her. Once in a while the car stopped abruptly and then set out again in the same way. The same thing was happening with her mind.

A streak of light split the darkness somewhere on the horizon. They were a few hours ahead now. It was Easter Sunday, around 5 AM in Aurangabad. The shining morning seemed to say that India had been waiting for them.

Time moves slowly in Aurangabad—something they all became acutely aware of as they drove down the paved way leading to the Ajanta caves. Around every bend, down every road, there were dazzling settings, as if they were in a movie super-production.

In the Maharastra region, trees on both sides of the road displayed red and white painted circles around their trunks. Cows from the Cujat region, with camel-like humps, and herds of white cows with horns dyed orange were scattered over the landscape. The gigantic trees' faded leaves bore witness to a spring drought. The dusty grasses and cacti looked like agonized chandeliers, and almond trees with red leaves, banyan trees and red, orange, and yellow bougainvillea vividly embellished the sides of the road. The Ajanta Valley was a gigantic precipice in the form of a horseshoe; a perfect hiding place, Margaret thought.

"A bodhisattva is a reincarnation of the Buddha," nodded the guide squeezed between Bruno and Margaret in the back seat. "The lotus—*padma*—is a representation of the numberless dimensions of the human being. And *Devi* means goddess. May I call you Margaretadevi?"

Margaret was flattered. Bruno saw in Shubish yet another man going after her. He had actually set out on this journey with the idea of becoming responsible for protecting Margaret. But "devi" was something that perhaps no woman could resist. And Margaretadevi, going through the valley, felt that Maharastra's landscapes resembled very closely her native Dobrudja.

"I would like to know if we can have something to eat at the caves. Is there a restaurant there?" Bruno grumbled.

They all got tired of the curves and loops and circles of Shubish's style of talking. But they had to have a guide with them. The animals were hidden in the caves and only a guide would know all those hiding places. But it was difficult to communicate with Shubish, although he was an educated man with degrees in history and German literature. He composed all answers so slowly and so convolutedly that no one could follow his circumlocutions.

Shubish shook his head. Margaret felt dizzy again. Later she would say she felt dizzy all the time while in Aurangabad.

"I only want to prepare you for the caves." Shubish rotated his head over and over in a sort of spiral movement.

"The Buddha keeps in *panin*—his hand—*padma*—the lotus, and the shell—*shankh*—another symbol of life and the Universe." And keeping his hands close to his chest he said fast: "*Bodhisattva padma-pani.*"

"Does a restaurant exist there?" Bruno shouted in exasperation. His beard and the locks on his forehead were moist with perspiration. He still wore his dark blue jacket and red tie, as if the Moscow cold lingered in his bones.

"It does," Shubish said enigmatically and went on with his lecture. Was he afraid that they would not tip him if he omitted all these introductions?

"What's a mandala?" Jerome jumped in with a question. After a nap, he looked full of energy.

Shubish was wearing a black suit, black tie and pale blue shirt. He wanted to look very professional for these tourists coming from so many countries. The secret service had approached him with a special request to keep a close eye on this group. It looked suspicious: a group of friends from New York holding different passports and citizenship.

"A mandala represents the human being, the solar system, the galaxy, the universe."

Ajanta's panoramic gorge appeared in front of the car. No mortals have seen Eden, but some here could think they had come close. Shubish stopped talking. The site of the ancient caves was cloaked in glorious shades of green and the fragrances of a thousand varieties of flowers. A waterfall cascading down the cliff fed the natural pool Saptakunda. The volcanic elements of Aurangabad had softened into lush forests, gardens in perpetual blossom, and valleys blanketed with small fields of fruits and vegetables. The caves in the valley were protected by an impenetrable wall along the mountains.

Descending into the valley, eternity seemed colorful and infinity dilated. In the caves, the famous paintings adorning the walls and ceilings depicted stories of the life of the Buddha and his bodhisattvas.

It was so hot outside the caves and so cool inside that they found it hard to go in and out of them time and again. Shubish persuaded Margaret to climb on a stretcher carried on the shoulders by six men along the path between the caves. But this was worse, for she suffered from vertigo on the edge of the ridge.

"Could we rest for a while?" Jerome pointed to a small resting place among the rocks with seats hewn in stone.

It seemed to be cooler there. Marini did not enter the little niche. He did not seem to mind the scorching sun. He left them there and went ahead. Margaret and Bruno followed Jerome. Shubish continued his lecture with movements of both head and body. The light and heat outside the caves soon became unbearable.

"Are there cobras around?" Jerome smiled. "Is this true?"

"Yes. They rest now in the valley," acknowledged Shubish in the middle of his head motion.

And indeed there were cobras in the middle of the ravine, slithering toward the entrances to the caves.

"Do you see what I see?" Margaret asked Bruno, shuddering.

She drew close to him as if asking for protection. Then she chose the stretcher after all. It seemed safer. But the jerking movement of those six men carrying her on their shoulders made her dizzy. Bruno grasped a corner of the stretcher to stabilize it. He acted as if those men would bite her, or even throw the stretcher into the valley to their relatives waiting for food. Was there a fear in his mind of a conspiracy between the real cobras and the human ones?

Jerome was distressed too by the incident. Shubish should have warned them against such dangers. That was what a real guide would do. He had touched many stones, inserted his fingers into narrow holes for purchase in climbing, entered many small niches alone, and now he realized he had been easy prey for serpents hungrily awaiting victims. He had been lucky indeed. Filled with visitors, the caves were feeding grounds for the cobras.

"In India," Shubish noted, "around one hundred thousand people are bitten annually and nobody cares."

"Shubish moves his head like a cobra." Margaret drew closer to Bruno, trembling as if she had a fever. From his corner, carrying the stretcher on his shoulders, Bruno looked at her in consternation. Shubish was a human being acting like a cobra.

Suddenly it felt bizarre on the stretcher. Margaret saw the carriers swaying their bodies, heads, legs, and arms like cobras, ready to bite, ready to hide.

Marini had left the rest of them far behind. He had the locator, and Jerome felt free to enjoy these moments of irresponsibility. His job with the locator had become a burden. The whole trip had become for him a waste of time. His contract in Hollywood was waiting for him, but he was stuck here with his life manager and his friends. Who could tell how long it would take to get the pets into the car and back to New York?

Then, looking at Margaret wrapped in a silk shoulder sash bought in a hotel shop, Jerome saw a queen any Maharajah would love to have in his harem. He himself would have loved to have her.

"*Maha Rami,* my great queen," whispered Jerome to Margaret on the stretcher. She had begun to read the book she kept in her purse. It was her habit to read whenever the opportunity arose.

"*Bodhisattva pustak padhte huye.* A bodhisattva holding a book in her hand." Jerome read the sentence he wrote in his notebook. Then he put his hand on the stretcher as servants do to protect their queen. He was her devoted servant out of love. A *chevalier* from the twelfth century. A crusader discovering a queen and protecting her.

But he was still annoyed by the heat. "Is it always so hot in Aurangabad?" He hated his long-sleeved shirt, long pants, and shoes. He dreamed of T-shirts and sandals.

"The only variations are from hot to hotter to hottest." Shubish merely moved his lips to utter the line.

"What does one do when bitten by a cobra?" Jerome's curiosity pressured Shubish to disclose more secrets about the place.

"The cobra bites fast and runs off," Shubish answered calmly. "The only way to survive is to chase the cobra, get hold of it and take a bite from it, chew it, and swallow."

Shubish was gently swaying his head in a coil-like fashion. Margaret knew now why she got dizzy in Aurangabad. Everybody moved their heads in the same way. Even the cars on the road moved in the same fashion. Everything observed the coiling rhythm. In this world she was supposed to do the same. It was about survival.

"The inhabitants of today's India are the ones who have survived, having chewed the cobra's meat," murmured Margaret. It was an enlightened revelation.

Their logic was cobra-like. Sinuous and undulating. The shortest route from A to B was not straight but twisted. It went first through D and E, then C, then F and G and eventually B. Many points such as D and E were not obligatory stages; they might be part of a non-present reality. It was a perpetual swinging among different worlds.

"Their logic is sequential, but not continuous. Everything is sinuous, and so different," Margaret noted down on a piece of paper. And she started to illustrate what she had written. The result was a star-like image similar to the swastika, the ancient symbol seen all over India. It had revealed to her its hidden message.

"Margaretadevi," Shubish said, bowing. "You should see the sculpture of the great reclining Buddha. I know you have been here before."

Near the cave's entrance, the head of the great Buddha captures the outside light while the rest of his body reposes in darkness. The twenty-foot granite body is surrounded by family, friends, and monks from his life on earth. They all beg him to stay. He simply smiles. By his death he has achieved salvation from the cycle of rebirth—the *Mahaparinirvana*.

Margaret remembered her mother's death. She had breathed her last, but her body was still warm. Her mother's blood was ebbing gently back from those fingers that had fed, fondled, and caressed her. Holding her mother's body Margaret had felt peace and calm. Her mother had left this life serenely, intimating happiness and contentment. She did not want to come back. She was too tired. And she wished for her daughter to stop crying. That was her mother's last lesson.

Touching the Buddha, Margaret touched her mother in that last peace and glory. Life had no definitive end. Death was only a momentary transition and separation.

Margaret wanted to inquire about eternity and life and the balance between them. But she desisted. She realized that she wanted no more answers to her spiritual quest. Her curiosity about the unknown was foolish. The answers would come to her anyway. Why rush? Everything she longed for would eventually be revealed and fulfilled. Her mother's message: "What we have is our eternity. Don't waste your time. Do anything you want to. Now. And here. On this side." It was not *carpe diem*, nor *dolce farniente*. It was about hard work. It was about accomplishment, seeing, feeling, and doing your job, the one you have chosen.

Suddenly, Goppollone and Blavatsky ran out of the cave and behind the Buddha. Wagner also dashed out into the open. Then they all vanished.

Marini consulted the locator. "They are still very close," he fretted. "Ellora." He took off, running. They followed him all the way back to the car as fast as they could, down the same coiling path along the top of the ridge.

It did not take long to drive from Ajanta to Ellora. Jerome took Bruno's seat in the back of the car, close to Shubish.

"Are you a Buddhist or a Hindu?" Jerome interrupted Shubish's stories about the Jain, Hindu, and Buddhist caves.

"I am a Hindu and I believe in lords Ganesha and Shiva and Krishna."

"How do you say 'I love you' in Hindi?"

"If this is what a man says to a woman, then it is *Main Aaapse Pyar Karti Hu.*"

"How do you say that you love her a lot?"

Bruno was listening attentively.

"My boy is getting hot," Marini chuckled. "He's rehearsing for Hollywood."

"*Mai Aaapse Bahnut Pyar Karta Hu. Karta* means lady."

Jerome repeated it several times. Bruno did the same. It was not clear if they were serious or only joking. Margaret covered her face with the purple scarf and turned away from the sun's glare and the dust, pretending to watch something on the road. She longed to say those words to Jules. He was with her even at that moment. She carried him like a poison she had voluntarily accepted. Again she felt the pain she could not escape. Not even Bruno's and Jerome's sweet flattery were of any avail. She wondered if perhaps Marini could help her.

Wandering in the maze of sculpted galleries, filled with granite Buddhas, Bodhisattvas, Shivas, Ganeshas, and many other gods, the group got close to the cat and the two dogs and lost them several times. They finally trapped Wagner, Blavatsky and Goppollone in a cave wherein sat a Buddha carved from a gigantic monolith. They slowed their steps peering into the cave, wondering whether some other watchers might be hiding there.

Shubish disclosed the secret of that cave where every sound is echoed seven times. A *stupa* was built on the Buddha's head. On top of that *stupa* was a *harmika*. The entire assemblage stood for a sort of passage between the earth and the gods. The breeze coming from an uncertain direction enhanced that feeling.

Lying in a semicircle in front of the sculpture, the cat and the dogs offered no resistance. It was as if they wanted to be caught.

Margaret approached Marini. "What do you want me to do to get Jules back?" she whispered. She got close to him, paying no attention to the Buddha. She had covered her head with the purple scarf, like any Hindu woman.

Marini was applying the anti-warts medication to Wagner's body close to the gigantic legs of the seated Buddha. He showed no surprise at Margaret's question.

"Get my laptop from the back of the car and start writing that statement we talked about. We'll get some rest at the Ambassador Hotel in Aurangabad. I still have some business to attend to here."

He handed Margaret a contract from his pocket. She reached up and smoothed her hair. Then she signed the document against the stone the Buddha rested his legs upon. Marini folded the signed paper into his cashmere coat without looking at it and went on treating Wagner.

Then Shubish uttered a Hindi sentence. He wanted to demonstrate how sounds reverberate in the cave. He did not choose a Buddhist prayer or song, but a story related to his gods. It was about little Shiva being a liar and a thief. He liked to steal butter. It was what Shiva always told his mother when he was caught: "*Maiyya mori main nahi makhan khayo*—Mother, I have not eaten the butter!"

An intense web of vibrations filled the cave. With their eyes closed they all absorbed the signals, enhancing each other on so many levels of reverberations and becoming more and more persuasive. The last sound seemed a distant but clear call to something hard to define.

"Sing," Bruno urged Margaret. It was an order that came back to her many times amplified with such a power that it seemed she had no other choice but to obey.

She took a deep breath and concentrated on her vocal chords. The contraction of the diaphragm opened the roof of her mouth, so the larynx was ready to receive the rush of air coming up from her lungs. The breath struck her vocal chords in keeping with the score printed in her brain. The sounds, perfectly modulating the score's architecture, burst through her glottis.

Norma, the High Priestess of the Druid Temple, was invoking the moon, praying for peace and love. Bellini's *bel canto* sustained its soft modulations as the casta diva's sounds reverberated through a series of echoes. Margaret's voice effortlessly encompassed several octaves of sweet and profound incantation.

She sang as if floating on air from one level of the musical scales to another by means of amplified echoes. Her voice put great stress on every word addressed to "*Casta diva, che inargenti queste sacre antiche piante.* Pure Goddess, who silver these sacred ancient plants." Sounds sent on high came back, touched the ground and returned with greater power. It was perhaps at that moment that Margaret realized who she was. Her voice disclosed to her something of her own essence hitherto unknown to her, giving her a sense of regaining and rediscovering dimensions she would otherwise not be aware of.

Shubish twisted his body. One could read ecstasy on his face. Jerome and Bruno had similar expressions. A few Hindu visitors at the entrance swayed their necks, their heads, and their bodies like Shubish. Eyes closed, they were transported. Awakening cobras possessed them and transported them to a higher plane. They undulated to the waves of the music, a forest of swaying bodies.

Margaret stopped singing as the echo went on intoning Norma's prayer to the Celtic gods. "She is weak and thirsty," murmured Shubish. "Gods are revealing themselves and truth not only through light, but through sounds as well. Your eyes and voice are not of this world." He looked like he was trying to foresee something. And reflecting on that mixture of *bel canto* prayer addressed to a Celtic goddess and sung in front of the Buddha by a Christian to a mostly Hindu and Muslim audience (there was quite a crowd of Hindu and Muslim visitors respectfully waiting at the entrance of the cave), Shubish made an unexpected remark. Marini, keeping Wagner close to him, grinned while listening to it.

"In God's kingdom there are many mansions," Shubish told Margaret. "And every mansion is a religion." Was this a variation on a line from the Gospels? This is what Bruno believed; Margaret could see how the remark echoed in his mind. Running his fingers through the grizzly beard engulfing his jowls, he seemed to promise himself to spend some more time thinking about it.

Dressed in her black velvet suit and silk creamy blouse, her head covered in purple, Margaret stood on the granite floor in front of the Buddha. She wanted to feel the grace of the moment. Blavatsky, in her arms, licked her face. Goppollone was taking similar care of her legs. Gradually she regained her composure and, leaning upon Jerome, exited the cave followed by Bruno, Shubish, and Marini. The cat and the two dogs did not seem to feel any urge to run away.

"Stay away from this stupidity of gods. They are of no good whatsoever and their revelations are meaningless." Marini was bored by the whole thing and this made him more cynical. Shubish was an insignificant item on his agenda. And that was a warning to Shubish that his comments on the synergy or complementarity of religions was not understood. Or was it only ignored?

The Ambassador Hotel in Aurangabad is a splendid place of marble floors and glass walls, with a spectacular array of old works of art.

But the whole group was so worn out from emotions, adventures, and jet lag that nobody cared to stop and admire.

Margaret was confined to her room. Bruno, who stayed with her, watched from an armchair. Blavatsky lay near her in bed, close to her chest. Goppollone protected Bruno's legs as if he wanted to prevent him from running away. Jerome was downstairs looking for food.

A mandala hung on the wall. The circles or wheels of the mandala reminded Margaret of her dream in the Chapada and of the strange imagery at the Baltic Sea. She remembered also Parvulesco's prophecy for her. Was that what she had experienced?

The mandala painted on a papyrus-like fabric had betrayed the three-dimensionality of her vision. But was that real or only in her mind? Following her eyes, Bruno saw the mandala differently. There was a principle hidden there. The mandala's principle, developed by Buddhist monks in Tibet, seemed to come from the perfect symmetry of the lotus, so different from the cobra-like logic. Two worlds existed simultaneously but without any connection between them whatsoever.

She started writing the statement for Marini on her laptop in bed. Meantime, on a corner of the bed, Shubish was computing the numerology of Margaret's date of birth. He said Margaret's life was ruled by Saturn.

"The fact that you are in your kingdom, India, without being the ruler, must be annoying. Remember that Saturn is the only planet that works good deeds for those it patronizes. Saturn is a planet that can make or break a person's life. You have experienced both sides of it. It is time to rest and allow all that you have experienced to sink in. *Om shanti shanti shanti.*"

"We'll have to fix up Shubish with Eliza from the *Chapadas.*" Jerome was back, making fun of Shubish. The restaurant downstairs was closed, but food would be coming to the room soon. "They can open an Internet business and get rich. Numerology from Hindu and Brazilian perspectives! What a great idea! I feel I am better qualified for this than Marini. Shubish, would you hire me as your life manager?"

Bruno didn't pay any attention any of them. Margaret was awake, but she kept her eyes closed in order to calm down. They were all sleep-deprived from jumping back and forth in time. Sleep means forgetting and being disconnected from real life. The tension of insomnia brings lucidity. They had learned to rest with their eyes open. But now even their eyes were tired.

Marini, back in the room, shared news about a new transaction. There was a collection of jewelry for sale in the lobby. He had bought a golden set with diamonds, known as Kanthi Almas Kanval Wa Parab, gold toe rings set with diamonds, and a turban ornament named Sarpech Larli Wa Kanval Almas made of gold set with spinels and diamonds. They had belonged to the Nizams, maharajas of India.

"Are you trying to buy her?" It was obvious to Bruno that Margaret could not afford anything like this. But Marini carelessly left the necklace next to the cat and concentrated on Wagner.

Shubish wrote down his numerology findings for Margaret. Jerome's comments had cut off his transcendental connection. Bruno kept Goppollone quiet on his lap, apparently experiencing a sweet feeling of togetherness and transformation. He seemed different. They all seemed different.

They had to leave for New York very soon. It was hard to imagine life without each other. Except Marini. He was not their friend. Only their life manager.

It was almost five o'clock in the afternoon in Aurangabad. Margaret had written a large portion of the statement for Marini and her wish had come true. Jules had called her on the cellular. He had arrived in New York from his business trip and was waiting for her in her flat. He still had her keys.

"You write in order to overcome mortality and transcend the limits," Shubish murmured. "If life is endless, why tell stories?"

"The immortal mind! Such boring stuff!" Jerome really seemed annoyed. He did not want to trade his humanity.

Margaret was far from having an answer to Shubish's question. She put away Jules and the anticipation of knowing him in her flat and bed. She was feeling something related to her encounter with those reverberations in the cave. They were coming back to her. They exposed a discrepancy between the serenity of the Buddha and what he had left behind in India. He had not finished his job. His lesson was cold and ascetic.

"Your work is a failure, look around, it is a big failure. Nothing has been accomplished. Your people still struggle to survive. You left them waist-deep in shit."

The voices in her mind became more persuasive. The mandala on the wall gave her incentive to continue.

"You must come back to finish your job. It is shameful to confine yourself to serenity. Your kingdom is a sham. A big deception. Come back to help your people."

Two golden lamps framed a mirror in front of her. At that very moment, in Varanasi at the Gate of the Dead, a few corpses were burning slowly in a Hindu ceremony, sending the smell of burning human flesh over the Ganges. At Haridwar and Rishikesh corpses wrapped in white were tossed into the Ganges. In Jaipur, on Amer Road, the most beautiful silk on earth was woven by hand at the Dusshera Kothi at the Small Scale Cottage Industries. In Delhi people were living their lives on the streets, acquiring in time the color of the streets as in a chameleonic transformation. In Bombay, crowds implored Mahalakshmi, the goddess of fortune and happiness, to change their lives while Shiva ignored them from his eternity carved in Elephanta's stones. All over India, women kissed gigantic lingams at the altars of Shiva reposing in circular wet basins. Monks in red from Tibet asked for guidance in front of the gigantic stupa in Sarnath, near the Dalai Lama's palace.

The golden lamps framing the mirrors acquired a luminescent reflection. From within the golden plates, as if engraved there, Margaret saw the Buddha looking at her. It was he on the golden plates of the lamps, the golden Buddha, coming to her. It was like Glenn's face as she had seen it on the Baltic Sea.

She closed her eyes and opened them again. The Buddha was still there, looking at her more intently than before. Glenn had disappeared. She jumped out of bed. There was nothing engraved on the lamps. Had he listened to her? Had he answered?

"You are a Goddess, or a spirit, not a woman." Shubish was swaying his head in the cobra-like motion. "A direct and inspired contemplator of spiritual spheres. You live at the prophetic level of revelation." And after a pause he said: "Darshan."

Shubish's respect came close to veneration as he listened to her recounting that imagery. Bruno seemed dubious now that Shubish wanted to get Margaret in bed. But what was it all about then?

"What is darshan?" Margaret motioned as if a cobra had taught her to sway in the air.

"A darshan, in simple terms, is a display or a vision granted." Shubish was at ease. He loved what he was about to say. "Generally we use this term when one is vouchsafed a vision of the Lord, or when the pilgrim who has been to a temple has benefited in grace from viewing, perceiving and enjoying the presence of the Lord presiding there. In fact, even a mere sighting of the Lord in all his grandeur and regalia, as he is generally bedecked and draped, is considered a good darshan, for it is a spectacular sight which most people do not get to see every day."

"You are terrible. You must be a monster." Now it was Marini's turn to proffer a cynical comment on her vision. "This is the translation of what he has just said from the point of view of the earthly world. No wonder your Buddha was silent. Who dare talk in front of you?"

"Sounds good." Jerome entered the conversation with no clue of what they were talking about. "You've got it!" He looked comfortable on the Persian shag rug.

"What do you know about her?" Bruno disliked Marini's cynicism. "She is like me. You have to know me first in order to talk about her." Bruno took her side while caressing Goppollone. The dog was the cat's closest friend. Somehow Blavatsky and Goppollone were a team playing against Wagner, deceiving him. This was an observation Bruno wanted to understand more deeply.

"I am not your twin sister." Margaret gave Bruno the cold shoulder. He had gotten too close to her. She was not sure whether she wanted to encourage that closeness. Bruno added something which she could not hear clearly. And leaving him to his mood, she turned on Marini: "I am not a monster! You are a monster! Don't you try to throw me off balance!" The little afternoon demons coming to her as sweet dreams of Jules were gone. But for once she appeared to accept that womanhood and spirit were at cross purposes. Womanhood as giving is a hot force ready to sacrifice itself for the loved one. Spirit as selfish contemplation and creativity is distant and cold.

The women of her generation were the first to emerge in the public eye. They had to compete with men and imitate them in order to succeed. Many of them had enjoyed success like men. And many of them did not find a true relationship. Having a child did not fulfill a woman's life after all. As much as a cat or a dog. Blavatsky purred on her chest. She planned to ask Glenn, the owner of the cat, to give it to her. At least for a while. Marini's comment actually had thrown her off balance.

"I've wasted my life in so many ways. I feel that everything I have done is useless." This was her only conclusion. Jerome, at the side of the bed, was massaging her toes. They all silently agreed that Margaret had had a breakdown. In reality, the almost one hundred Fahrenheit degrees in Aurangabad, the journey on so many continents, and their traveling over so many time zones had made them all fragile.

"Am I wasting my life?" Margaret kept repeating the question. Had she gotten the love and recognition she had expected? Her work. Her struggle. Her failures. And Jules. She was sure he had someone else in his life. He had betrayed her for another woman.

"I wouldn't care for that," Shubish was saying. "I will do what I like to do no matter what the result might be. And even if I were to lose everything, I wouldn't care."

"Would you tell me why you love Jules?" Jerome's impolite question was spoken nervously, but it was something everybody wanted to know yet nobody dared to ask. Margaret was not about to tell them how wonderful she felt when she and Jules made love together. She limited her response to something equally important, namely the fact that he understood her.

"He is the only man that can follow what I say. I speak with him as if speaking to myself. There is a complete connection between us and a spiritual intimacy."

"This is a man's trick when he wants to get a woman to go to bed with him and does not want to offer her anything," Marini put in from the armchair from which he had been listening to the conversation. "He is quietly listening to her. He doesn't care a cent for what she says. He approves anything she says. And she thinks he understands her. He only wants her in bed." And addressing Bruno and Jerome: "Gentlemen, could you confirm that?"

Jerome and Bruno shook their heads in disapproval, without enthusiasm.

"As for betrayal and that kind of woman's fury when a man goes to bed with another woman, well, I will tell you the truth." Marini lowered his voice to a whisper as if to be heard only by those men to whom he was ostensibly entrusting a secret. He wanted to show Margaret that he was a real monster and he liked that.

"There's no difference between a dog pissing by the side of a road and a man having sex with a woman."

"That's pure cynicism." Bruno was outraged. "There is also love."

"Marini, you are so bad!" It was Jerome's turn to feel embarrassed.

"The biological and psychological mechanisms in the male's brain are the ones I have described." Marini invalidated their comments. "Forget about betrayal when referring to your man going to bed with another woman. If he loves you and you love him, well, and you want a life together, you have to accept that. It is mental and biological."

"That is promiscuity," Margaret replied. "You are a promiscuous man, Marini. And cynical."

"I'm only telling the truth." Marini defended himself. "Don't confuse nature's rules with cultural rules and standards built by civilization." And to Jerome: "Why don't you design a mandala of your own to add more substance to your destiny?"

It seemed that Marini was in good spirits, laughing at everybody. He had not forgotten Jerome's remarks about the mandala. It was his way of ridiculing Jerome for his silliness and laziness. "You have to draw first those one million lines and intricacies, and after that to color every little microscopic spot with the right hue. It may take you one or one and a half years," Marini added, barely keeping himself from laughing.

"I am not stupid." Jerome frowned and shook his head. "I have enough work. Changing means more work. Who knows what and how much? I am better off like this." Sitting on the rug he ignored Marini's amusement. The mandala hanging on the wall was a huge intricacy of lines, colors, and symbols that did not match his intentions about how to spend the next few months.

Marini was having a good time. He laughed, greatly amused by Margaret's rage and Jerome's discomfiture. Shubish, swaying and lengthening his neck, wanted to comfort Margaret by disclosing a little of himself.

"It does not matter that having lost so much I may lose some more," he said, coiling his arms with his eyes almost closed. He seemed to fall into a trance. "Everything I have done has made me happy. So it must be with you. I am looking now for an alliance with a Hindu Brahmin educated girl. My parents are involved in this search."

But Margaret was thinking: now Jules has come back. She saw him differently after Marini's comments. She stirred, but her limbs did not move. It was almost true that she had preferred her former life: no husband, no obligations, other similar things. Being free to do what she liked the most. Was she guilty of Jules' betrayal? What if she had been the one pushing him to it?

"What do you mean by an alliance?" Bruno was suspicious of Shubish's evasive words, although he was thankful to Shubish for changing the course of that stupid conversation.

Shubish was lengthening his neck as if the cobra within him wanted to bite something. "It is about marriage." Obviously, the euphemism expressed his manners more precisely.

"How old are you?" Jerome was curious to hear more about Shubish's alliance. He reclined on the rugs covering the floor. It was cooler there. He thought of his parents in Toulouse who were involved in something similar for him, too. Shubish appeared to be in his late twenties.

"I am forty-five." Shubish swayed his head, keeping his eyelids lowered as if asleep. Then he turned to Bruno. "I can make your annual prediction." This abrupt change was Shubish's way of deflecting Bruno's focus from him. "You are an Aries, like Margaret. Right?" Bruno acknowledged this, unsure what Shubish was aiming at. "Ganesha says it is your destiny to enjoy this year the pleasures of life. You will take an interest in all surroundings as we Hindus do. You'll have *artha*—prosperity—and *dharma*—the sense to lead a good life. Faith, imagination, love, and the spirit of adventure have imbued your existence. You need to understand and work more on *moksha*—the detachment from worldly things and attainment of the state of completeness. Ganesha is with you."

Bruno did not seem interested in Shubish's review of his future for the year. He looked at Margaret, who was wrapping her body in the bedsheets. What Shubish told him applied to her life too. But now she was concentrating on the document she had prepared in her head, ready to be put down in writing. Traveling at high speed had made her mind conceive things at lightning speed. It was now harder, more time consuming, to put all those pages from her head into written form. The laptop had slipped between her legs like a pillow. Her brassiere had slipped and showed her breasts. Her skin had a translucent luminosity, like her hair that had spread onto the pillow. She caressed Blavatsky. She struggled to get some rest. She would have loved to go to sleep. She longed for her nights of deep heavy sleep, like a coma.

And Bruno longed to be held in her arms, close to her warmth, touching her hair. He wished to feel her legs. And her torso. To touch her womb. Pretending to take Blavatsky from her so she would feel more comfortable, he laid himself down on the bed and put his head onto the pillow supporting her back. The cat did not want to leave. Bruno didn't either. But he had to, because Goppollone was asking for his attention.

Suddenly, cornering Shubish, Marini affected a courtroom manner. He became a double of himself, but with a very different personality. He threw hard, rapid-fire questions that demanded yes or no answers.

"Are you content with your life?"

No answer.

"You have no memory of your wife's death?"

"No." Shubish swayed his neck.

"You have no idea who set her on fire in your own kitchen?" Marini got intrusively close to his victim.

"No." Evidently, Shubish couldn't get more than one word out.

"Was your mother there with her at the time of the accident?"

"No."

"You have no memory of that?"

"No."

"Your mother was holding your wife Mara tight. Do you remember that?" With his arms Marini demonstrated the degree of tightness.

With a gesture Shubish rejected what Marini had said and closed his eyes.

"Is it true that you inherited your wife's dowry?"

"I haven't thought of that."

"Is it true that by divorcing her you should have had to give back the dowry?"

Swallowing hard, fighting anguish, Shubish glanced back. Marini was coming after him. Bruno, Margaret and Jerome seemed helpless. It was as if they looked inside Marini and found a mist of cruelty. There was nothing else. No pity, no nothing. And if Marini was right, Shubish was as cruel as he.

It was still Sunday in Aurangabad, about six in the evening. Marini seized Wagner's muzzle. Margaret held Blavatsky wrapped up in her silk scarf. Bruno kept Goppollone tight to his chest. Jerome took care of distributing tips to a long row of hotel employees, lined up in an orderly fashion from the front desk to the car. They left India and Shubish, arriving sooner than expected in an astonishingly beautiful New York dawn.

It was only eight in the morning Eastern Time. It was still Sunday, as India is more than ten hours ahead of New York. The car stopped abruptly in front of Margaret's building on East 36th Street, near the Pierpont Morgan Library. Men, dogs, and the cat escorted her in silence to the entrance.

"I shall leave soon for my cold and rainy Germany." Bruno stood waiting to hear a word from Margaret but she said nothing.

"May I see the contract?" Bruno turned to Marini. His beard engulfed his jaws, looking more civilized than ever.

Marini handed him the contract and Bruno tore it up. He deposited all its pieces in the inside pocket of the dark blue jacket of his suit. Was he afraid that Marini would put all those pieces of the agreement together and bring him to court for breaching it?

"I appreciate your efforts, Mister Marini. We are still friends." His tone clearly conveyed the opposite. "My institute needs me. And my family needs me even more." Bruno smiled and added: "I am actually tired from too much work. I even turned down Harvard's offer. I'll take it easy from now on."

"You bet!" Jerome looked very contented with Bruno's judgment.

Marini did not react. And Jerome, scratching his head, asked for his contract too. He read the contract, rolling it between his fingers. Then he tore it up and scattered the bits of paper all over the sidewalk. His golden hair, combed straight back, allowed a few out-of-place curls to decorate his temples.

"I accept my father's offer. Here people work too much. Life in Toulouse is not bad after all. Nice wines, nice girls, afternoon naps, and good food. You are invited to taste them all in my Provence castle." Somewhat red-faced, Jerome looked at Margaret and Bruno. Obviously, Marini was not invited.

Margaret knew Jules was in her apartment waiting for her. It was she that had to fulfill the contract.

"I'll be back soon," Marini waved his cashmere coat sleeves. He did not seem upset with Bruno's and Jerome's breaches of contract. Obviously they had made a mistake. They would soon call him to fix it. This was what they all read on his face.

Blavatsky refused to go back to the Lexus. The dogs would not go without her.

"I'll be back in less than an hour to pick them up," Marini said looking at his watch. In the meantime Margaret had to go over the last paragraphs of her script. Marini did not care that Jules was in her flat and that she also had to rest after the journey. He wanted things done and finished. As soon as possible. This was part of their contract.

Margaret did not like to see Jerome and Bruno leave. But she could not invite them in either. In turn they each hugged her and then, refusing Marini's offer of a ride, both of them jumped into a cab. The Lexus roared off at a speed Margaret could not endure any more.

Jules was sleeping in her bed. He had come back to her. He was in love with her. And she was supposed to consider her quest ended. Her destiny had gotten the ultimate accolade.

She took out a few plates, poured some milk and put out food for her new animal friends in the kitchen. She had become attached to them. Blavatsky was particularly close to her heart, despite her unpredictable moves. How would her life be without them? Would Glenn give her Blavatsky for a while?

Those pages written for Marini in Aurangabad had been waiting for their closure. She had to accept that she had entered the limitation of love. Her quest was over. But she did not accept that entirely. She slipped out of the suit and silk shirt (that she had worn for almost an eternity), the string of pearls, the purple silk scarf, stockings and shoes. She put on a T-shirt and shorts. She liked the feel of her bare feet on the floor.

She knew Jules was there because of Marini. He did not come back urged by his own free will. The contract she had signed had a power over him. Would she be able to cope with that? Stories from her beloved Sibiu came back to her mind. Many girls had gotten the men they loved with the help of black magic. They got married to those boys they loved. But with the passage of time, they suffered terrible punishments. They had to pay with their entire lives for the spells they had surrendered to.

It could happen to her too. Could she cope with not having him in her life? She had already learned that. What she needed that very moment was to have some time on her own. To sort out what had happened to her during those thirty-odd hours of New York time. She experienced more than that, a sort of expansion corresponding to months and years in her life. So she decided that it was better to let Jules go.

She looked at the bed. Jules' athletic legs and powerful torso belonged to a man of the prairie. The man of her life. They might still be happy together. But Marini did not guarantee that. And she remembered Eliza's words in the *chapada*: disappointment will be what you get when you ask the universe to bring back the one that has deceived you.

Could she bind herself to a being that had so deeply disappointed her love? Obviously, there was more in her life than her obsession with Jules.

Outside, trees were in blossom. Doves and seagulls crisscrossed in the sky. The bright light of the New York morning stole through the windows. The pulse of her arteries reminded her that a day of real tasks lay before her.

The prospect was filled with an exciting exploration of a new idea for a book revision and with her poetry reading on CD-ROM. In the evening she would talk on the phone with Stefan and listen to Terry's songs on his latest CD. Both eager to read her work in progress. Thoughts crossing her mind led to other thoughts she had never considered.

"What is true love all about?" Margaret asked herself, trying to be sure she was still in love with Jules. Blavatsky purred around her legs, demanding attention and love. Holding the cat, Margaret tried to find the best answers.

It was about feeling the presence of that other person every minute of life no matter what. It was about falling in love again and again with him despite betrayal, disappointment, and frustration. It was even more. Love despite hate. She loved Jules. And it was all right he did not love her.

And yes, her own universe could not limit her love for Jules. The greater universe was the only thing that could limit her.

So what was her life about in the end? The sense of it? Margaret thought of the mandala in Aurangabad. Life and death were unfolded there. She didn't want to vanish on the seashore of the Baltic, either. Her expectations were different. How far beyond had she to look?

Happiness and fulfillment were both a sort of needlework with unexpected colors and crossed threads under the fabric. One had to look under the embroidery in order to see the real design. Wrong and right moves revealed themselves as having been necessary in order to push life to another level of meaning. Every new level of life meant a metamorphosis. She could not know how many levels of metamorphosis there were. Most people get stuck at the first one. Others die pushing toward the second. Some survive, and fewer and fewer proceed through the elaborate distillation of the infinite texture of those "pipes" of Destiny. And looking at all of this, she accepted her contentment with her life as it was. The life she had. And the life she could foresee for tomorrow.

Marini frowned, coming unnoticed as always. He wanted her piece of paper. He sat down in the armchair, waiting to get the job done.

"It is time for the conclusion." As agreed, it was supposed to be a celebration of the dual powers of the universe. The ultimate hymn to egotism, sex, rapacity, greed, power, fame, money, anything else that might be considered evil. Even eating carbohydrates or red meat.

Margaret was just finishing typing the last sentences of her essay on the satanic characters in the novellas of the Middle Ages and Renaissance. She felt she had to keep her word despite the fact that she did not need what Marini had gotten for her. She went on typing the last paragraph. Marini uttered a few words aloud, helping her out with some appropriate sentences.

"You can take Jules back," Margaret said, refraining from clicking the print button.

"Nonsense," Marini smiled. "The man in your life? Are you giving him up? Choose anything else then; I can manipulate the entire world."

He was emphatic; powerful. He was afraid she might break their contract. And he lured her with something she loved as much as Jules. "I can give you the chance to see the whole world. Places you haven't even thought of."

This was what she had enjoyed in her journey with Marini. Discovering the unknown. But her answer showed a difference in her approach to his offer.

"The earth is beautiful," she said remembering those places. "The earth is the same all over: beautiful. Now I know the secret. Marini, I have had enough of it."

She was content with the place where she was. And she did not give Marini the chance to contradict her, to argue that she was wrong.

"Can you give me infinity?" She had eternity, part of the texture of time, one piece tossed like anybody else among the endless wheels of time and space. She wanted his answer quickly. She could hardly wait to take a shower after such a long journey.

Marini looked alarmed. Here was the paradox he could never resolve during his entire existence.

"You cannot manipulate infinity, can you?" Margaret asked again with a cunning look in her eyes.

Marini pretended to be focusing on Wagner, who rested under his chair. "No, I cannot," he acknowledged after a while.

"Here is something much easier, then," offered Margaret by way of a suggestion, in a playful tone. She had braided her hair and put it up. She came over to Marini, and forced him to remain seated on his chair. She put her hands on his shoulders and looked into his eyes. Marini could not intimidate her any more.

"I need money for someone who wants to set up an electronic legal center in a third world country. The president of that country rules as if his people were still living in antediluvian times. Something has to be done there that the government greatly dislikes: disclosure. That is much less than infinity. But is it within your range of capability?"

"How about Jules?" Marini wanted her to refocus her thoughts on her boyfriend. "He has come back to make love to you. Isn't that what you care about most in your life?"

The printer was printing out the paper.

"I want a blank check." Margaret continued. "To fill it out with the right amount at the appropriate moment. You trust me, don't you?"

Marini pulled out a checkbook from his jacket, opened it, and signed the next check, leaving the spaces for date and amount blank. On the bottom left corner, however, he specified: "For the construction of Marini Legal Center."

Margaret slipped it into her bra. Then, with a soft red pen gingerly tendered by Marini, she signed her full name below the text of the compact. There was coldness in her heart. Jules had been traded off for the right to information of a people in a country just emerging from ruthless suppression. Her name had been placed under words she did not believe in. And she saw again those gigantic wheels of the Universe, from the dream she had while in the *chapadas*, moving slowly from her right to her left. And the next sequence was the golden girdle she had become a part of.

"Does Jules know that your date is off?" Marini's lips curled sarcastically. He intended to grab the paper, but a noise distracted his attention.

It seemed that while Blavatsky and Goppollone were playing in the kitchen, Wagner had jumped on the gas stove where the teapot was boiling. He started whining. His tail had caught fire. He leapt through the passage separating the living room from the kitchen, yelping and taking refuge near the computer. Then he furiously barked at the printer, and finally ended on the desk, madly wagging his flaming tail.

Soon the desk was ablaze. Blavatsky and Goppollone tried to corner Wagner, who was racing like a live torch about the living room. In his fury he had smashed both the printer and the computer. The carpet near the desk caught fire. Marini tried to salvage the paper, but it had turned to ashes. Wagner took refuge on Marini's feet. Blavatsky jumped on Marini's chest with frightened meows. The orange dots on the cat's forehead grew intensely bright. Goppollone got onto Marini's shoulder with terrible barks and noises. It was not clear if Blavatsky and Goppollone attacked Marini or Wagner or both. Wagner bounded up at the cat. Marini's cashmere got caught in the flames.

Jules showed a confused face at the bedroom door. Margaret was fighting the fire, throwing water on Marini's burning jacket and trousers. Marini was trying to get the animals off him, while simultaneously busy with the computer. He would have been happy to transfer the document onto a disk and deal with the signature later on. But the water had an unexpected effect. Marini's face, hands, and neck were losing color. The discoloration was occurring so fast that soon only his burning clothes seemed to be moving.

"What the hell is this?" Jules shouted. "Call the police!" Jules opened the windows and the doors. He drew up the curtains and the blinds. A harsh light flared into the living room, followed by a cherry blossom fragrance. Soon the fire died down. The pets were gone. Marini's clothes were ashes. There was no Marini. Margaret made sure the blank check for the "Marini Legal Center" was still in her bra.

On his way to Margaret, Jules touched by accident the CD player. Suddenly music filled the room. It was a favorite song of Margaret's. She had told him many times she would like to dance with him to it. It was a romantic tango tune. Jules hugged her. He kept murmuring how deeply he had missed her. He looked weird in his pajamas; like a con man, she thought, that had for too long played with her emotions.

"The sweetness of your lovely body makes me fall in love with you again and again." He expressed a desire to make love to her right there on the floor. His athletic legs and torso encompassed her, and she could do nothing. He had been waiting for the entire night, alone in her bed. The time had come. He took her hands. Their fingers intertwined as they used to when they made love. The beauty of lovemaking involved talking in a special kind of language, with terms of endearment, and little cries, and kisses. She could hardly forget the tenderness of his skin and its warmth, which would make her desire him again and again.

"I think love is an obsession. Full of desire and of sex. Of wonderful sex," whispered Margaret, closing her eyes so as to feel his body more fully. It was like a deep crevasse she would love to let herself forever fall down into. Was it Marini's spell that worked on Jules despite Marini's disappearance?

"Well, what's wrong with it?" Jules grabbed her closer. "Silly little thing, I adore you." He had filled all vases in the living room with her favorite purple, pink, and white mountain laurel.

She tried to grasp what she really felt. "Love is about moving through time and sharing life's adventures together. It is about building bonds on the basis of common memories, experiences, and feelings. I do not know if you feel that way. In fact, we have not shared anything in our lives, but the bed." And after a while, gasping for breath: "Jules, you are not a part of my real life."

"That is why I am here. Because I truly am a part of your life." Jules contradicted her while kissing her neck. He was again discovering the sweetness of her being as it lay hidden in the delicate shell between her skin and her profuse hair.

"You had told me the opposite," Margaret reminded him. "You were not sure I was the woman you would spend your life with."

"So what? Are you absolutely positive about that?"

She was not. But neither was she sure whether it was Jules or Marini who had spoken to her right then. The journey had made her realize that she did not necessarily have to live in frustration any more, that happiness is an inner matter unrelated to anything else. That she no longer had to suffer. Jules hurt her. She will no longer accept any limitation.

Yet it was not easy to resist Jules. She needed a diversion to get Jules out of her apartment. To sort things out. To see if the new Jules was real. So, how about that planned Easter lunch at Glenn's restaurant? Was the invitation still standing? She dialed Bruno's number. He might have been at the airport or in the plane flying to Germany. Luckily, he was still in his studio on Mercer. She reminded him about having Easter lunch at the Grand Ticcino, as planned on Friday evening. Marini and Wagner have vanished. Something funny has just happened. She would explain. Jerome too would be welcome. The cat and Goppollone have left already for the trattoria. They would celebrate. Jules might join them too. It was part of the plan to go back to Glenn. Almighty Glenn, keeper and custodian of the mystery.

"That was stupid," Jules challenged what she had just said to Bruno. "We have no problems!" A sort of shell of light shone strangely on her face, deepening its brightness around her coy lips, eyes, and forehead. The shell had pinkish and bluish colors superimposed on each other. For Jules, the shell was merely a flower of light.

Margaret replied: "We have no life together and therefore we have no problems. Life and love mean a lot of problems."

Jules looked dizzy. Yes, something had unsteadied him. Margaret said: "We have now a problem!" Jules agreed. What made him feel dizzy? Was it the light on her face? Her moves? The sound? Casting her eyes over Jules, Margaret improvised something that sounded like an incantation. She was swaying her neck in a way that would have made Shubish proud of her.

"Is there another man in your life?" Jules wondered aloud, clutching her hair in its cobra-like weaving. He held her again close to his body and kissed her on her lips. Although he had listened to her conversation with Bruno, he did not take it seriously. He knew Margaret. She loved him. She was unable to resist him.

But she did.

There's Margaret, silently disengaging herself from his embrace. Returning to him that ambiguity she had had from him so many times in the past. Concentrated on the truth from inside.

Paradox was right there, within and without. Loneliness, the artist's power.

The animal within was scared. Loneliness felt destructive and sterile. Yet her deal with Marini was still out there.

She had traded Jules for the blank check in her bra.

And after all, Jules was also fifty.

Time of decomposing? And fear?

Jules never read her work.

Looking around, she felt that rock of ice in her chest ever more sharply. Enfolding her heart. And the viscera close to it.

A matter of putrefaction, soon to be swallowed in the matter of time.

Bruno's father's definition of happiness: to take a walk on a lovely summer noon, drinking coffee and enjoying the beauty of the place. She loved to walk around Washington Square Park, just across from the School of Law. It was her favorite haunt, a place where she enjoyed her coffee during her lunch break. The July light at noon was dense and juicy. Trees and flowers absorbed it with grace and joy. The jazz band in the kiosk gave an edge to those pleasant noon hours. The artesian well murmured its sing-song, offering brilliant showers to thirsty passers-by and plants. Squirrels and pigeons played in the grass while groups of girls and boys imparted an energy you could feel in your bones. And so did Garibaldi's statue, and the Triumphal Arch sustained by forceful eagles, and the kids' playground and the dogs' running field. Under a tree, a painter was sketching the portrait of a young blond girl wearing a dark flimsy blouse. A guitar player from the Caribbean was tuning his instrument. In the north side of the park a filmmaker's crew adjusted the lights for an evening shooting. Visitors kept asking where was what. A woman slept under a tree while her husband read a newspaper. Ice cream and cold drinks vendors plied their trade under huge umbrellas. The place was a nexus of being. Yes, Margaret was happy there sipping her iced coffee. July was not too far off. And May was as good as July or any other month of the year to experience happiness. One can encompass eternity in a lifetime. As well as infinity in a tiny spot. Reality or deceit? Truth or imagination? Could happiness be not a goal but a road?

It all depends on a unique feeling and state of mind that belongs only to one's own experience.

It was Glenn that had allowed her to see it whole. Throwing her into this adventure: a ceremonial hunt of animals leading to the unknown. The hunter lured by the chased prey. Bringing Bruno and Jerome. Her new Jules. And Marini. Seeing magic as an obligation to the spiritual significance of the world. Or a glimpse from a surreptitious world? Glenn Almighty—Blavatsky's and Goppollone's master—the mystery incarnate. She was ready to face his grandeur again. Soon she will be there, in the dim cellar, where everything starts and ends. And she could not help wishing for that passing moment with Jules to linger. Moving slowly in elegant rhythms, swaying her body. Contemplating the brightness of the living room.

Margaret dissolved into bright sharp light. Then she was leaning in laughter to dance as she had learned in her youth. She turned on her right foot keeping her composure with a straight torso. Making the cross movement, with equal steps and balancing her body, she moved, switching from one leg to the other, while her ankles drew closer to each other. After a while, she coiled up her arms around Jules, holding his gaze. Glenn's benevolent smile was everywhere, bringing to the womb of the room the colors of the Baltic Sea, and the glistening of the golden girdles from Warsaw's garden, and the sounds from Ellora's cave. The gigantic wheels moving in her dream in the chapadas reposed for a fraction of duration in the glow of that brilliance. The words of "A Person Like Me," the song playing on the CD, filled the living room: "I declare/Yes, I care/But what am I supposed to do?/I'm so afraid of losing you/You see, love don't come easy/To a person like me…"

Epilogue: One More Love Story

It was asking for English. Like a child crying for his mother. No way to express it in other words and grammar. It was impossible to say "No."

"Dammit!"

I wanted to go on with my endlessly postponed novel: *Amânat în America/Deferred in America*. What I wrote was a totally different story. Actually, six stories.

Something perhaps screwed up in my brain had gotten my two languages mixed up, the one set aside for writing and the one employed for earning a living—the language of my job.

"Phew!" Having to write about this unexpected adventure at the end of it.

The right words are hard to find. To hell with subtlety!

Better avoid description and psychological exploration!

The theorist of fiction took the lead once again. My thousand-page opus on the History of the Novel from *Ramayana* to *Don Quixote*, published in Romanian, reminds me of shortcuts and tricks. Prose fiction writers have used them successfully for the past five thousand years. I will do it one more time on these final pages of the book.

The narrator's voice cringed.

Action.

Adventure.

The twisted surprise ending.

Exploiting the recipe for the everlasting novel: a love story with divine or sudden psychological revelations, developed as an adventure in a violent time or amid violent events (wars, revolutions, dictatorships, a.s.o.); the adventure unfolds in an exotic space or in a meaningful one (tribal, archaic, aristocratic, etc); and a deeply embedded drama is revealed at the end by the exposure of a hidden secret.

The ancient Greeks knew this formula. I'll have to use it to overcome, to defy, my shyness with the language.

I actually have learned the recipe not only from the ancient Greeks but also from the fiction writers who had taken it over in time: the Romans of the first century B.C. and of the first A.D., the Arabs of the eighth century, and the Byzantines of the ninth and the twelfth. I have also fresh in my mind the novels written by Japanese princesses in the tenth century.

"No" to philosophy! Ideas fade easily in time.

More emotion.

And the color of the moment.

The vibration that gives to the whole its unique sound in the universe.

The enigmatic vibration.

The laptop engages in another Thesaurus search. How to say it with the maximum sound effect? Dictionaries lie all around, keeping to themselves the mystery of language.

It is grotesquely cynical.

I do not think Thomas Mann would have gone to this extreme of insanity. He did not need to, actually.

An American colleague looked at me commiserating: did you really read all those thick volumes? Poor thing!

Thomas Mann wrote in German: a language spoken by all cultured individuals in Europe at the beginning of the twentieth century. The Holy-Roman Empire of the Middle Ages and the Hapsburg

Empire of the eighteenth and nineteenth centuries made German a "must know" language in the civilized world. Actually, great writers' works from one cultural empire were translated into all other languages of coexistent or successive cultural empires. A matter of courtesy and a matter of finding predecessors.

Tolstoy and Dostoyevsky wrote in Russian. The Russian empire's elite language was French: the language of a cultural empire lasting from the twelfth century to this very day. And so Tolstoy's and Dostoyevsky's works got easily to Paris.

Joyce wrote in the language of the British Empire.

Cervantes wrote in the language of the Hispanic Empire.

Dante in Italian, the literary language of the Renaissance.

My native land did not have the chance of becoming an empire. Or a cultural one. A great handicap for Romanian writers. I can only hope they'll have a better fate in the next three thousand years.

"To live in New York and to write in Romanian!" I'm rolling this sentence over and over again in my mind. "Like living in Paris and writing in Burmese," runs the cynical remark of a friend who does not write in English, but aspires to.

Emil Cioran and Eugéne Ionesco. The burning examples. The deadly comparison. They've made it. My countrymen who moved to France and wrote in French. They've left their mark on French literature.

Nabokov and Conrad. More fire to my emotions. These Slavs wrote in English and got directly into British and respectively into American literature.

I am writing at a small square table for four in the living room. I have an entire weekend for writing. Otherwise I have to limit myself from 6 a.m. to 8 a.m., when I get ready to go to my job.

The soup is boiling on the range in the kitchen. Saturday morning's cooking and savory smells. On an empty stomach. I cannot eat while I write.

I cannot eat anyway. A root canal went wrong. I've been on antibiotics for more than ten days. I have to limit myself to liquids. The tooth canal is open: a direct connection to my flesh where anaerobic bacteria throb in the anomalous bifurcation of the root. "Your roots are unique," said my dentist, complimenting my body's anatomy. "No resemblance to ordinary people." Uniqueness means more pain. More peroxide to rinse the inside of the canal with a syringe.

On my right a few oil paintings hang on the wall. A very small one shows the back of a tall, youngish looking woman dressed in a long blue skirt and wearing a white hat. She looks at the sea. On the seashore's stone slabs, close to her, is a half-cat, half-dog creature, looking straight ahead too. I bought it from the artist, a close friend. Pure coincidence: by that time I was writing about Goppolone, the whitish creature, half-cat, half-dog, in *The Life Manager*. The Faust-like kind of love: Margaret, Bruno, and Jerome engaged in the pursuit of those strange animals (a cat, a dog, and a half-dog, half-cat) that lured them into the knowing of their own selves.

Four crystal mirrors on the same wall reflect the world outside. I've always liked better what I see in mirrors than through the windowpanes.

The blue knee-length long-sleeved cotton nightgown bought in Paris matches the blue-and-white striped cotton slacks and white socks. They keep me warm while lost in my imagination: that other world of pleasure in which my brain, once immersed, is secreting endorphins. The act of literary creation. Blue slippers abandoned on the carpet help me get into the kitchen to refill the coffee mug. It is my third. And only 9:45 a.m.

I pass in front of the mirrors. A tall woman still young-looking with her hair in a knot held by pins, wearing glasses, beams out a childish smile. The creature dressed in blue is waving at me.

Caesar liked blue. He said it was the color of serious men. Cicero and Caesar, two men I admire. I don't remember if Cicerone Tiramollini, the character from *On the Road to Formio* obsessed with

Marcus Tullius Cicero (like the other main character, Helen), liked blue. Helen believed that Cicero had blue eyes. That is why she married Hamilton. Obsessed with Cicero, she twice escaped the same kind of death. She was lucky. Anyway, the Italian senator Cicerone Tirmollini's love fell into the same category: a political man's kind of love. All around him were murdered by those who killed him too.

Near the laptop, on my left, there is a bouquet of fresh flowers: pink roses, yellowish lilies, white calla lilies and freesia. Their smell is numbing, yet it keeps me going. Like the Novocain that makes me so happy at my dentist's. I think of the stupor created by the smell of flowers in *Doña Juana*. I imagined that they were brought to Huatulco from Bogotá. They had the odor of sperm. It was Guillermo who passed on to Mary the strong desire for sex overpowered by that flower's odor. Donjuanity passing from one to the other in a ritual as old as the human race.

I have tried over the latter years spent in New York (beginning with January 1991) to get at the writer's Sphinx. (Gosh! I am thirteen years old in the English language. If I were Jewish I could have my Bat Mitzvah by now. Born again at a mature age!) The Sphinx's answer to my crucial question (what language should I write my poetry and fiction in?) was supposed to solve my dilemma. American writers in New York are hard to make friends with. It is hard to meet them and talk with them about the secrets of writing. What language to opt for, though? What do you think?

Katherine came to meet me by the side of Washington Square Park on a shining summer day. She was the publisher of a literary magazine on the Internet. She had rejected one of my manuscripts. But she was curious. She answered to my e-mail. A cozy restaurant on Cornelia Street was the scene of her advice.

Katherine's husband used to be an editor with a famous publisher in New York. He had brought home Nabokov's manuscripts in English. It was Nabokov's English, she told me. Nothing to blame in that. His manuscripts were always seen by an editor. Nabokov had of course the final say. He fought to get acceptance for his choices, yet he had to give in often enough, as well. "If you'd seen those manuscripts you would stop having doubts. English should be the language of your writings from now on. You will also find a congenial editor."

I explained that writing in English felt like putting my makeup on with a wooden hand.

"Your language is good," Katherine said. And she stressed again: "At this juncture you do need an editor."

My English was six years old at the time. The way I spoke it was for Katherine the proof that I could make it.

Then I met Lois Gould in the Village at a dinner for female writers hosted by a teacher of playwriting. I had three lunches with Lois in the following year.

First of all, she wanted me to join a sort of a writers' home in the Village, a place where I could rent an office and come to write.

Where to write was not my problem. I had a place to write. But Lois said that this would be my place to connect with people. I visited that place with Lois and did not like it. It looked depressing. Writing demands privacy. It was like in a *kolkhoz*. "Are they established writers?" They were not.

I disappointed Lois. I did not rent my place there. But at least I had gotten one answer from her.

"I cannot see myself writing in French," said Lois at our last lunch. She knew French. She was fond of Irish people and French literature. She was a European in many respects.

"You have to write in Romanian. We will find someone to translate your works into English. A writer can write only in his mother tongue."

Lois wanted to introduce me to her agent from Chicago. She died of cancer before having the chance to do it.

I did what she said. I asked a translator in Bucharest to do the job for *Platonia*, one of my novels published in Romania. Looking at the first ten translated pages, I had a shock. The language of the translation had no relation whatsoever with the living American literary idiom. And I had no way to find a translator in America. No way of being able to pay for a job like this.

Ambivalent thoughts keep assaulting me. I have to write about the third experiment. It was actually something unexpected. I am outside of binary logic.

Poems were my first writings in English. While learning English, many words got me drunk with their meanings and perfumes and sounds. They lined up in poetic sequences, eventually.

When my poetry written in Romanian was translated into English, I gathered all the poems together. I gave them to an American born literary critic and novelist, wanting to know which poems were the best.

To my astonishment, more than fifty percent of my poetry in English was considered "wonderful." And only five percent of the translated ones were listed.

I asked Annie Gottlieb why she felt that way.

"It's true that while I liked many individual lines in the translated poems, I liked the whole poems written in English better," she said. "Maybe it's because the ones in Romanian naturally partake of modernist and romance-language poetic conventions. The ones in English you have almost had to invent from scratch. That makes them adventurous."

Annie gave me the third way of looking of things.

I am in the middle of a big mess.

I look at my recipe for the everlasting novel. I know how to cook soup and novels. I have good recipes. Could it be possible to build a novel right now as I did in the past in Romanian? I obviously need more strength from English. Mother English. Getting along in my literary brain with Mother Romanian. I need a joint blessing. It is their love that I am hoping for. Love. Writing for love. And about it.

The turkey soup is boiling on the stove. I am happy I am alone. I can do what I like the most. The frosty sky of winter is reflecting into the crystal mirrors and two Murano lamps. *L'hiver, seson de l'art sereine, l'hiver lucide.* Mallarmé.

It is Saturday, January 24th, 2004. The day when Romania became Romania: the Danubian Principalities united in a single country. 1859.

I do not answer the phone. But I have to. It is my son calling from the Medical School of the University of Grenada. He does not quite understand my literary struggle, but he respects it. He cannot grasp why I traded earthly goodies for writing. He does not understand my loneliness. I talked with him in the past about ancient gods that punished intelligent, gifted women. In fact, it is Elsa from *The Loneliness of Magnificent Women* who was supposed to give him an answer. My son did not read the manuscript of this novella. I hope he will read it as printed in the book.

It is past noon. My glasses are all over. I have about seven pairs of glasses. I go back to the novellas' table of contents. From there to *On the Road to Formio*. It was the first one that refused to be in Romanian. It started with the canopy of pines at the Tyrrhenian Sea. Why? It was 'the canopy of pines' that I first heard in my inner ear in English.

I don't know what to do. I am in the middle of a big mess.

The Bonfire of the Vanities is near the laptop on the four-seat crowded table in my living room. What a lucky man, Tom Wolfe! This Tom Wolfe is a lucky man indeed, as are John Updike, Saul Bellow, Philip Roth and many others. They were born in that world language to which everybody wishes to be admitted, recognized and considered. It's a must simply in order to exist. What a luxury taken for granted! What would they do, were they in my shoes? Perhaps they would have come to little more than nothing.

I have to defer my native tongue in order to communicate with the humanity I live in. I fled Romania afraid of my life and my son's.

It was in the dangerous time after the 1989 Revolution. It was about survival. Now it is about being heard. Things from the past affecting my present. The essence of my life. My every living second. My voice as a unique vibration.

"How you doing?"

"Fine."

"You ever been here before?"

"No."

"In another life?"

"No."

"Hey, you need another brain."

The soup is boiling. My time is boiling like Sparrowulf's eggs in the morning. I'm referring to Shrike in the novella of the above title. The lonely psychotic man trying to stay away from the world found love at the bottom of the sea.

An ambulance screams on the street. Death does not care that it is weekend.

Saturday: a day of emigrant writers' meetings in New York's literary ghettos. I am invited to attend one. Their English sounds weird. Patterns of strange cultures disfiguring English syntax. Grammatical sparseness and next to no meaning. What did you want to say?

A circus-like atmosphere.

I belong nowhere.

I belong to myself.

I cannot find my world.

And love, after all.

My sincere and deep love for writing becomes an adventure in another language that is taking place in the exotic city of New York, in a stormy time, the time of my life, and revealing at the end a well-kept secret. The secret of these pages could be that the author and the main character, as well as the narrator, are truly the same person.

The striving for literature. Is it this message imprinted on my neurons' synapses as is the message of changing hemispheres on migratory birds' brains?

The love of telling stories. The way of expressing my mortality. Why sell stories to the immortals? That is actually a line from *The Life Manager*.

Why not try to forget it? To bury myself in the next project?

My next novel is on the back burner of my mind.

My secondary mind is my uterus.

My breasts, getting smaller and smaller, seem to turn into testicles. And I into the writer.

0-595-31861-4

Printed in the United States
19215LVS00004B/145-165